THE MARKED EARTH

THE CURSED KEY TRILOGY BOOK THREE

MIRANDA BROCK
REBECCA HAMILTON

COPYRIGHT

CHAPTER 1

A YELL PIERCED the air as I stabbed the lioness, my blade sinking into the tawny fur and soft flesh.

I blinked, and the animal was no longer there. Instead, a woman was in her place. Her face was pinched in agony, her mouth open in a wordless scream. Somewhere in the distance, a little boy screamed for his mother.

A cruel sneer curved my lips, and I sank the blade farther between her bones.

I jerked awake. My heart jackhammered as I stared up at the ivory ceiling. I rubbed my fingers against my palms, certain I would find sticky blood staining my hands. They were clean. I let out a slow breath. It had been a month since Kael and I had returned from Africa, and I still dreamed of killing the lion shifters.

No matter how many times Kael had told me what I had done was necessary, the thought of being a murderer would always taint my soul.

I sat up, and goosebumps rose on my bare arms. A shiver scattered through me. Why was it so cold?

I shifted off the bed, and more bumps rose on my legs up to the hem of my shorts. The bedroom window curtains were closed, and I twitched them open. My eyes grew wide in surprise.

It was snowing.

Growing up in the north, it wasn't as if I hadn't seen snow, but in South Carolina, the sight outside the frosted window was unusual. True, South Carolina did occasionally see their share of a wintry mix, but I bet they had never seen anything like this.

A fierce wind rattled the bare branches of ice-heavy trees, causing them to crack and snap in a sound reminiscent of gunfire. It was a wonder it hadn't woken me up sooner. Snow drifts hugged the sides of the houses, and the streets were blanketed in white. There had to be at least a foot or two of snow outside. Just yesterday, it had been near seventy degrees.

Another chill ran through me, but it had nothing to do with the temperature.

Something wasn't right.

I closed the curtain and pulled a throw blanket from a beige chair near the window. Hugging it tightly around my shoulders, I headed toward the kitchen to brew myself a cup of coffee.

The house was the kind of antiquated and cozy that reminded me of a grandparent's home. The wallpaper was a bit old-fashioned, and as I made my way down the short hall, I found myself thankful for the deep green carpet on my bare feet.

This was just a borrowed home while I lived, or rather was held, in South Carolina. It had been provided to me by the Paranormal Intelligence and Tracking Organization, or PITO. I was being "protected" as Mason Anderson, the head honcho, had put it. In truth, I was being held captive in the style of a Cape Cod home with shag carpet and food delivered to my door.

Having already prepared my morning brew the night before, I simply had to push the button and wait. I leaned against the counter as the percolator gurgled beside me. The yellowed linoleum floor was cool, and I shifted back and forth on my feet, wishing I'd taken the time to grab some socks. Thankfully, I didn't have a long wait, and soon, I was settling in on the couch with a steaming cup of black coffee.

I turned on the T.V. and hit the number for the local news channel. The man on the screen was going on about the weather, saying the abrupt and unusual storm weather was affecting the tri-state area.

I took a sip of coffee, and cursed when it burned my tongue. With a sigh, I wiggled deeper into the back of the couch and wrapped my hands around the mug, letting the warmth leach into my fingers while I waited for it to cool to a consumable temperature.

A horrible wind whistled outside the window, and I watched as snow whipped by. PITO always had guards watching my house, though I rarely saw them. It was annoying, and an invasion of my privacy as far as I was concerned, but at the moment, I couldn't help but feel sorry for whoever was stuck out there in this nasty weather.

I glanced at the phone beside me on the spindly-legged side table and picked it up. I quickly tapped out the number for Renathe. The fae man was unusual, and our friendship even stranger, but I liked him.

As the phone rang, I watched the snow, and I couldn't help but wonder if he had perhaps gotten drunk and got a little too carried away. He could, after all, create and control the elements of winter.

The ringing switched to his voicemail, and I hung up.

Should I call Kael? He may know something I didn't. I glanced at the clock. It was past eight, so he would likely be at headquarters by now. If he knew anything, though, he probably would have already let me know. Likely the weather was nothing more than an anomaly. At least, that's what I told myself, but the unease churning inside me didn't quite believe that theory.

I put the phone down and turned back to the news. I hardly ever watched anything else these days, not since I had learned my friend and colleague, Sarah, had been murdered in her hotel in India. The artifact she and the rest of the team had been transporting had been stolen as well.

The one behind the murder and the theft was undoubtedly Vehrin, the dark mage who was bent on the dominance and destruction of this world. We hadn't yet learned why he wanted the artifact, but it couldn't be for anything good.

The sooner Vehrin was bound, the better, though I was still unclear how exactly we were supposed to do so. He couldn't be killed outright, not without risking his malevolent power transferring to the one who destroyed him.

I kept waiting to hear of other artifacts stolen, but so far, we'd heard nothing. Kael worked tirelessly with PITO, giving me reports when he could, and I, well, I did a lot of waiting.

A deep sense of restlessness was beginning to take hold of me. Even if I wasn't the bearer of two magical keys and a powerful sorceress reborn, in my normal life, I rarely took a vacation. Sitting around in this quiet house was beginning to drive me crazy. I needed to do research, explore, go to a library, or *something*.

Kael understood; he was feeling much the same. We both had a restless energy, a need, to be out doing something. Vehrin wasn't going to stop, and sitting around while we waited on his fellow agents to discover something useful was only going to put us farther behind.

Still, he said we had to be patient. Both of us were under the watchful eye of Mason and Kael's other superiors. We couldn't just leave without raising suspicion. Besides, we had yet to work out the *problem* between us.

We were mated.

The bond hadn't been on purpose. True, I had strong feelings for him, so when I had touched his wound with my own bloody palm, the bond had snapped into place. The fact we had been lovers in a past life had only made the mating bond that much easier.

I took a deep drink of my coffee and untangled my legs from under the blanket. As I'd gotten into the habit of doing lately, I shoved the thought of Kael being my mate to the back of my mind. I had other things to worry about at the moment, like what I was going to do today.

The agitated side of me wanted out of this house. I contemplated going to the gym at PITO headquarters to workout with Aidan, something I did a few times per week, but as the house creaked with another blast of icy wind, I decided against it.

Instead, I headed toward the bathroom for a hot shower. The warm water and thick steam went a long way toward calming my nerves and warming my chilled skin. I stepped out onto the fluffy mat and pulled a towel around myself.

A small smile touched my lips as I beckoned at the ever-present magic in my veins. I let a trickle out, and the energy seemed to rise from my pores. As it did, my skin warmed more efficiently than if I'd taken a blow dryer to it. I capped the magic off, satisfied by the toasty sensation it had left behind. Even my hair, though still damp, was no longer dripping. I opened the bathroom door to find a figure in my bedroom.

I jumped and let out a short scream. It took me a moment to realize it was just Renathe sitting on my bed, lazily flipping through the book I'd left on the nightstand the evening before. He looked up and grinned.

I quickly tightened the towel back around my body.

"Ren, what the hell? You just break into my house?"

He set down the book—and lost my place in the pages, I noted with irritation. His vibrant teal eyes sparkled as he studied me. "That's a good look for you, Olivia," he said.

Ren's purring voice rippled over me. If I wasn't already tied to someone else, and didn't know what a deviant the fae was, I might enjoy hearing more of his soft words. Instead, I scowled.

"Better not let Kael catch you saying that," I said.

His grin deepened. "Are you going to keep the mating bond, then?"

"Mind your own business." I crossed to the dresser in search of warm clothes, though my options were limited.

Was I going to keep the mating bond with Kael? I tried not to dwell on the question too often. Being mated was like being married, right? I didn't think I wanted to be married, not for a long while, if ever. But if I didn't, would that mean losing Kael?

With an armful of clothes, I turned back to the irritating intruder. "What are you doing here, anyway? Shouldn't you be home by now? You have a business to run."

Ren was the owner of the nightclub, Pinnacle, back in my hometown of New Haven, Connecticut. He knew about the danger of the dark mage and had become an invaluable ally in our fight against him. Still, I wasn't certain what he was doing just sitting around with us.

He rose from the bed and walked over to me. "I was on my way to the PITO headquarters and thought you may like to accompany me? Mr. Anderson has some things he would like to discuss with me. I hate meetings, but having a beautiful woman to keep me company may make it more bearable." He winked. The fae had such a playful charm about him that I couldn't help but smile.

"Fine." I chewed my lip, and my gaze swept to the blizzard outside my window. "You didn't start that, did you?"

A deep frown pulled at Ren's lips. "Of course not. Fae can manipulate earthly elements and weather, but we must follow strict guidelines. We cannot just conjure up a blizzard or whip up a hurricane for kicks, you know."

I nodded. "I'll go with you, but you need to get out so I can get dressed. There's coffee downstairs if you want a cup."

Ren left, and I hurriedly dressed in jeans and a cozy sweater. I'd even managed to scrounge up a pair of fuzzy socks. Then, I went downstairs to grab my boots from where they sat next to the living room door.

"Here." Ren walked from the kitchen and handed me a small thermos of coffee.

I smiled. "Thanks." I pulled on my jacket, unfortunately the heaviest outer layer I had here, and then swung my trusty bag onto my shoulder. "At least this is appropriate, now." I pushed back my sleeve to reveal the bracelet with the crystal snowflake charm Ren had given me. I also still wore the green and gold woven bracelet that had the ability to turn into a sword at my command.

Life had become very strange for me. Magic and swords. Fae, witches, and shifters. Dark mages and cursed keys. And here I thought being an archaeologist would bring all the adventure I ever needed.

Ren opened the front door, and I gasped as a blast of icy wind tugged at my hair. A moment later, the brisk breeze died down. Even the snow had stopped swirling, but only for several feet out. The fae at my side gave me another wink and gestured toward the sleek, silver car parked at the end of the snow-covered sidewalk.

I slid into the car. He'd left it running with the leather seat warmers on. Ren settled in and pulled out onto the road. I couldn't help but notice the snow seemed to billow outward from the pavement in front of us. The man was more effective than a snow plow.

Most cars were still parked at their homes or along the curbs outside of business. Only a few people had ventured out.

"You know, you could just drive around and clear the roads for people."

7

Ren let out a laugh. "For one thing, humans would notice that. I'm doing just enough to get us to where we need to go. And for another, the city certainly wouldn't be able to pay me enough for my services."

I rolled my eyes. "You *could* just do it out of the goodness of your heart."

"I never just do things out of the goodness of my heart."

That was certainly true. Every promise or action a fae made had a catch. I'd already had to pay Renathe in my dad's vintage car and two dates.

"So, what does Mason want with you, anyway?" I asked as we pulled into the parking garage at PITO headquarters.

Ren gave me a level look, an edge of somberness touching his features. "Oh, I think you already know."

And I did. Just like the earthquake that had nearly taken the lives of both me and Kael in Africa, this wintry phenomenon could only be caused by one thing.

Vehrin.

CHAPTER 2

REN DIDN'T BOTHER BLOCKING the cold as we hurried into the building. I clenched my hands around the strap of my bag and pulled my shoulders in with a shiver. A blast of warm air brushed my face when the doors closed behind us, and I sighed.

When Kael and I had arrived back from Africa, the lobby had been tastefully decorated in gold, red, and green for the holiday season. Christmas and New Year's had passed without much fanfare on mine and Kael's part, though he had managed to make us a small Christmas day meal that Ren had conveniently decided to crash.

Ren and I crossed the shining floor toward the main desk. The woman sitting behind it gave both me and Renathe a disapproving stare. Most shifters didn't like the fae, and as for me, well, I guessed most here still saw me as an intruder in their agency. Not to mention the fact they were having to spend resources they likely could have used elsewhere just to assure I was 'protected.' Besides, I was well on my way to becoming a powerful mage myself, something they weren't too thrilled about.

"We're here to see Mr. Anderson," Ren said. He gave the

woman a polite, friendly smile. She softened up a bit. It would have been difficult not to under his beautiful, unearthly grin.

"You can go on up. He's expecting *you*," the woman said. Her eyes locked on me with a frown.

For a moment, I wondered if she was going to tell me I couldn't accompany Ren, but she didn't say anything else. I reached out and grabbed a few leftover chocolate kisses in a bowl near the edge of the desk.

I gave her a cheerful smile. "Thanks."

Her suspicious glare followed me to the elevator. I didn't care. There was only one shifter in this building whose opinions held any worth to me.

"Olivia!"

Make that two.

I turned to see Aidan, the massive bear shifter, trotting toward us. His forehead was shining with sweat. Did he ever do anything except work out? The man practically lived at the gym. I'd never seen him in anything except athletic wear.

"Hi," I said. "What's up?"

The elevator doors slid open, and the three of us stepped in. Ren hit the button for the top floor, twelve stories up.

Aidan leaned against the wall of the elevator. "Nothing much. Heading up to see the boss."

"Us, too." I didn't bother telling him I hadn't actually been summoned. "Nice weather we're having."

"Yeah." Aidan's voice was slow, and his gaze slid to Renathe, who was staring coldly back at the bear shifter.

What was his problem? He had a tendency to make jabs at Kael when the three of us were together, but nothing that would be considered mean. Ren was just too mischievous for his own good. The look he was giving Aidan was downright hard, sharp, and icy as the wind outside. Aidan returned the expression. Did this have something to do with their prejudices, or did it run deeper?

The elevator slowed to a stop on the fifth floor. I shuffled closer to Ren to allow whoever would be getting on some space. The doors slid open to reveal a broad-shouldered man with dark hair and golden-brown eyes. A citrus and rain scent wafted toward me as he stepped in.

Kael.

"Hey," he said. He gave me a smile, but it was merely a cordial, friendly, every day kind of smile. It wasn't the sort of smile you gave someone you cared deeply about, the kind of smile from someone you'd fought with, and bled with, and depended on.

I would have been disappointed, if it wasn't for the rush of warmth that flooded through the bond between us. On the outside, he was stoic. Inside, it was as if he had stepped into the elevator and found the sun shining on his face.

It was difficult not to scoot closer to him, and give him the kind of smile I was keeping trapped behind my lips. When had I last seen him? It felt like a week, though it had only been a couple of days.

"Kael." Aidan gave his fellow agent a nod, which Kael returned.

A sense of awkwardness fell on me as the elevator ascended. The three men around me seemed to be having some sort of a stare off. Aidan had seemed to be the person Kael was closest to in PITO, but there had been tension between them since our return. Somehow, he seemed to know about the mating bond between Kael and I.

Kael's boss didn't seem to know anything about it. When we were in his presence, we kept our distance. Kael had explained to me the alphas of any species could see a spark between mated pairs if they were right beside each other or touching. Aidan was a beta, so Kael assumed he likely sensed something, even if he couldn't say for certain.

Why hadn't Kael told Mason about the bond? Was it because he would get in trouble, since it would be frowned upon with me being a human? Maybe Kael was waiting to see if I would reject the bond, and he didn't want to let people know, just in case.

I chased away the sudden guilt with annoyance. It wasn't completely on my shoulders. Kael hadn't even told me how he felt about the bond. Admittedly, I didn't see him much these days. He seemed to always be working. When we were together, neither of us brought it up. Instead, we just had this elephant we carried around with us from room to room, an elephant that was seeming even larger than usual in the cramped elevator.

"What's with the bag?"

I turned to Aidan. "Huh?"

He nodded to my messenger bag hanging on my shoulder. "Your bag. You always have that same one with you."

"Girls carry purses, you know."

He grinned. He knew it acted as more than a purse. I had a spare set of clothes, weapons, and even a few tools in it. My bag had been filthy when we had arrived back in the States. I'd spent a long time washing the blood stains and grime out of the thick fabric. It was a tether to the life I loved, a life of history and adventure. I never went anywhere without it.

The elevator stopped, and our small group stepped into the hall. We walked down the stretch to Mason Anderson's office. Aidan knocked, and a voice inside told us to come in. Once inside, Kael put as much distance between us as the room would allow, and Ren's lips curled up like the Grinch before he stole Christmas.

The head of PITO was an intimidating man. He was a wolf shifter and seemed to be formed from harsh mountain air and cold earth. He had always been fair to me, if a bit overbearing, but our past few meetings had been…strained. Each time I saw him, he watched me, as if expecting me to attack or flee. If I had to stay trapped in this city much longer, the latter may come true.

Mason was watching the news. They were still discussing

the weather and were speaking of the car accidents and power outages it was causing. He turned away from the screen, and his eyes narrowed slightly as he found me among the men.

"Olivia. I wasn't aware you were summoned. There must have been a mistake." His tone wasn't harsh, but I caught the undercurrent of annoyance.

"No mistake," I said. "I chose to come. I wasn't aware I'm not allowed." I probably shouldn't be snippy with the man at the head of this agency, but I couldn't help it. His control cloaked in safety and concern was really getting on my nerves.

For a moment, he stared. Then, he said, "Well, you're here now." He looked at Ren. "This weather is causing problems. This has to be stopped."

Ren strode toward him. His back was straight and his gait was smooth and fluid. He almost looked deadly, like a serpent slithering into the wolf's den. It made me wonder who would win in a fight.

"I certainly hope you do not think my kind has something to do with this." Renathe's words were light and sharp as an arrow.

"Do they not?"

Without invitation, Ren sank into a chair across from Mason's desk. "You know it is not. Only a fool would believe a fae to be behind this."

"Sometimes young fae get out of hand." To my surprise, it was Aidan who spoke. He really *didn't* like Ren. Was that the reason he'd been glaring at my fae friend, because he thought his kind had something to do with the wintry disaster outside the window?

"It's Vehrin," I said.

The other four men in the room turned to stare at me.

"I agree with Olivia," Kael said. "With the effects of this blizzard being so strong and out of place, he must be near. There is no other explanation."

At the thought of the dark mage being nearby, I reached

up and grabbed the keys around my neck. One of them almost seemed to hum under my touch. It was the one my soul was bound to. Whoever held the ancient, golden key would be able to control me, and my power along with it.

I'd already gotten to taste how terrible it could be, thanks to Vehrin. I refused to go through that kind of helplessness again.

Mason must have read my sudden rigidness and pinched brows as fear, rather than determination.

"I assure you, Olivia. You will be kept safe," he said.

Safe. I didn't want to be kept *safe*, like some delicate bird in a pretty, latched cage.

I dropped my hands from the keys. "I need the freedom to fight him."

"Absolutely not. The last couple of times you were nearly killed. We cannot risk it," Mason insisted.

I mulled over his last sentiment. I could have sworn he had been about to say they couldn't risk the keys. Not they couldn't risk *me*, more like they couldn't risk my power ending up in the wrong hands.

"Sir, I must say I agree with her." Kael stepped closer to Mason, though still kept his distance from me.

Mason rounded on Kael, his voice stern with authority. "Do not disagree with me. You are already on probation, Kael. Do you want to lose your position here?"

I stared at Kael as he fell silent, a muscle working in his jaw. I hadn't known he was on probation. Was that why he had been working so many hours, so he wouldn't lose his job?

Not one to give up easily, I argued, "Vehrin is *my* enemy. I appreciate your help and protection, but I'm going to have to face him at some point. My power is growing. I can handle it." A sense of caution trickled to me through the bond with Kael.

The wolf shifter studied me for a moment longer. "You are dismissed."

Seething, I turned to leave with the others.

"Not you." Mason pointed at Renathe.

My friend glanced at me as if he wasn't quite willing to leave me alone with the shifters, even if Kael were with me. He nodded, however, and turned to the head of PITO.

"I've already contacted my brethren. They are prepared to step in and..." Ren's voice faded as I closed the door behind me.

Aidan stood with us in the hallway, then followed us as we made our way to the elevator. I wished he had stayed with Mason and Ren. I really wanted a moment alone with Kael to talk.

"Have you had breakfast?" Kael asked.

"No." I realized I didn't have any means to go and get some. "Ren drove me here."

"We can go down to the cafeteria. It's on the third floor." Kael reluctantly turned to his fellow shifter. "How about you?"

Aidan's gaze lingered on us for a moment before he shook his head. "Nah. I already ate. Catch you two later." He waved and headed past the elevators.

We didn't have to wait long before the elevator doors opened. Thankfully, it was empty. As soon as the doors closed behind us, Kael stepped close to me, leaving hardly a foot of space between us.

"Livvie." I had grown very fond of the way his nickname for me rolled off his tongue. "Are you okay?"

"Yeah, I'm fine." I tilted my head back to peer up at him. "Are *you* okay?"

A heavy sigh lifted his shoulders. "When it started snowing earlier, I thought it was weird, but once the storm really got going..." He paused, his gaze running over me as if he were memorizing my face. "I sent Renathe to pick you up. If this is Vehrin's doing, I don't want you to be alone."

"You sound as bad as Mason."

Kael smiled. "I only meant I'm going to be around a lot more. I hope you don't mind my company."

I stepped closer to Kael. Whatever uncertainty I had about being mated to him, I was absolutely certain about one thing: the attraction I felt for Kael ran deeper and stronger than anything I'd ever felt about another person. I didn't even care anymore if a part of it was influenced by our mutual, ancient past. Whatever we had together was here now, and I was going to enjoy it, and enjoy *him*.

Kael's lips were suddenly crushing mine as he lifted me closer so only my toes touched the floor. The bond between us blazed to a point I was certain we would both turn to ash if we kept this going. I didn't care. Let us burn.

I moaned as his tongue swept into my mouth and he made a deep noise in his throat. My back suddenly hit the wall of the elevator, and with the sturdy pressure supporting me from behind, I wrapped my legs around him.

A quiet voice in my mind told me we shouldn't be getting carried away like this, especially in an elevator at his place of employment. The louder voice in my head told the practical one to shove it.

The elevator lurched to a stop and Kael released me so quickly I nearly fell. I would have been insulted if I didn't see the crowd of people walking about as the doors slid open. The pair of us walked out, both breathing a bit hard, and headed toward the cafeteria.

My emotions were a tangled mess. What, exactly, was my end game here? I had to make a decision. Obviously, we had chemistry, and he was the closest friend I had, but was that enough? Did I want to be mated to him? Something deep inside told me he was mine, had always been mine, and always would be, but I just wasn't certain what to believe.

We had just entered the cafeteria, the large room loud with the amount of chatter, when Kael's cell rang. He answered it, and just as I was continuing toward a counter that looked like it held French toast, my partner reached out and grabbed my arm. I stopped, and he released me.

"Yes. Right, I understand." Kael glanced at me with worry. "I'll take responsibility for her." Was I in some sort of trouble? Perhaps Mason was reprimanding Kael for the way I'd spoken to him.

Kael ended the call and shoved the phone back into his pocket. "Olivia, your house has been attacked."

"What?" My voice came out as a shriek. In the background, the buzz of voices quieted. Why would anyone attack my house? I hadn't been in Connecticut in months. Then, I realized I was thinking of my *home* in New Haven. Kael meant the house *here*, in Charleston. "What do you mean, attacked?"

"It appears someone broke in and set off some sort of explosives, or something. It's also been set on fire. I'm sorry, Livvie, there's nothing left."

I had just been there in that house. If Ren hadn't picked me up, I would have been blown up. Magic flared in my hand, some instinctual need to protect myself humming through me. Then, I looked past Kael and realized all the shifters were staring at me. Most watched me with disapproval, but some held malice in their gazes.

It didn't occur to me until that moment, as the heated stares of the shifters bore into me, that Kael hadn't mentioned *who* had attacked my home.

Had it been Vehrin, demons, or someone else entirely?

CHAPTER 3

EACH STARE WAS like a pinprick stinging my skin. I knew the majority of the shifters didn't like my presence here, but would that dislike run deep enough for one or more of them to wish me harm? Would any of them dare go behind Mason's back?

Kael, despite his wishes to keep our relationship a secret, let out a low, guttural growl toward the onlookers. A few raised eyebrows. Most of the others went back to talking or eating.

"Mason wants me to escort you back upstairs," Kael said. He gave me a regretful look. "Promise I'll get you something to eat afterward."

My stomach grumbled in protest, especially after the scents wafting from the cafeteria, but I followed Kael as he headed back down the hallway.

We were alone in the elevator again. All I could think about as we rose to the top floor was the fact I had practically been crawling up Kael just a few minutes before. What had gotten into me? My cheeks burned a little at the thought, but I had to admit I'd do it again.

Amusement flitted down the bond between Kael and I. I looked up to find him smirking.

"Quit reading my mind," I snapped.

"I can only read your mind in jaguar form. It's your emotions I'm reading now, and I can't help that. Maybe you should quit thinking about me."

I stared at him with narrowed eyes, uncertain if I wanted to kiss those quirking lips, or smack them.

I crossed my arms. "You're not as irresistible as you think you are."

Kael chuckled. "Says the woman who attacked me in the elevator."

"Uh, excuse me? Who really attacked who here?" I jabbed his chest with a finger. "You started it."

He sighed as the elevator stopped. "If only I had time to finish it."

My stomach fluttered in a delightful way at his words.

The hallway was empty as we stepped out of the elevator and back to the boss's office. Through the window opposite us, I could see the blizzard still blowing in full force.

Kael didn't bother knocking as we stepped up to Mason's office. The only people inside were Mason and Ren. The fae stepped over to me with a slight frown.

"I heard the news. I'm sorry about your house, Olivia. If you need a place to stay, you are more than welcome to accompany me back to my hotel room." He smiled. "I'm staying in the penthouse. I assure you there is plenty of room."

"I don't think so," Kael said, stepping closer. He seemed to have forgotten the need to keep his distance, and I tried to nonchalantly put some space between us before Mason took notice.

Kael flicked his gaze toward me and took a deep breath. He moved away a couple steps.

"What happened, exactly?" Ren asked.

My partner didn't answer the fae. Instead, he turned to his superior. "The attack on the house had to have been by the mage. We all know he's after her, and since he has the key that can override her own, we need to get her out of here before he gets too close. She needs to be outside the city, at least, but out of state would be better."

Despite the fact Vehrin was after me, and had possibly blown up my house, the thought of finally being allowed to leave filled me with relief.

"It would be best if Olivia stayed close," Mason said. "Until we know the whereabouts of the mage, it is safer for her if she stays under the eye of PITO."

I deflated inwardly. Ren looked irritated beside me. He knew I was tired of the babysitting. And what good had it done me? If I'd been in the PITO-appointed house this morning, I'd be dead.

A soft, soothing sort of sensation came from Kael. No doubt he was trying to calm my increasingly irritated nerves.

Mason, either unaware of my annoyance or not caring, continued. "We'll have to find somewhere else for you to stay. Perhaps we could find you a place in headquarters."

The very thought was horrifying. I'd be under constant surveillance. Besides, what if someone here had attacked my house, and not Vehrin? I'd only be easier to get to, and much closer to danger.

"What about the cabin?" Kael said. "I can stay with her. It's secluded. Vehrin knows you will keep her here, under tight security. He won't expect us to whisk her out of city limits. Maybe the mage will get cocky and venture close to headquarters. You can take him down, and Olivia will be safe."

I was curious about this cabin and watched with hope as Mason mulled over Kael's suggestion.

"All right," Mason said, if a bit reluctant. "I can send a team with you."

Kael shook his head. "That would only draw attention. One agent leaving won't be much for Vehrin to want to look into, but a team? He may send some of his followers to check it out."

The wolf shifter sighed sharply. "Very well." His sharp gaze bore into Kael. "You are not to leave the cabin until you receive word it is clear and safe to do so. Do you understand?"

"Yes, sir."

"There should be enough supplies for the both of you for at least two weeks. If locating and taking down the mage takes longer, I'll send more."

A couple weeks? Surely he didn't think he would be able to take down the dark, powerful mage in that amount of time? I had doubts they would be able to do so at all. I didn't voice my opinion, though. It seemed I was being moved from one prison to another, but at least I would be with Kael.

"We'll head out right away. Vehrin's own storm will be enough to provide us cover as we leave."

Mason nodded. He went to sit at his desk. "Renathe, you are free to go, too. If I need anything, I'll be in contact."

Ren didn't look at all pleased by the notion. If he had been staring at me with such cold intensity, I would have shrank back.

"I am not yours to summon, Mr. Anderson. I am here for a reason. Keep that in mind." The fae pivoted on his heel and strode out the door. I followed, with Kael shadowing me several feet behind.

We went down a couple floors to Kael's small office. He gathered up a few odds and ends, then stuffed them in a backpack. When we reached the bottom floor, Ren was waiting near the doors. He stepped over to Kael.

"Keep an eye out. I can sense something at work here, and it isn't entirely Vehrin's doing."

I grabbed his arm. "What do you mean?"

Ren's eyebrows pinched together. "I'm not entirely sure, but there is something, a malice of sorts, swirling in the air."

The faces of the shifters in the cafeteria flashed in my mind. Maybe they saw me as more of a witch than a human, even though I wasn't a witch. Kael hadn't liked witches when I first met him, or fae. He still barely tolerated Renathe.

"I'll take care of her," Kael said. "You know I will."

He had stepped closer, and I dropped my hand from Ren's arm.

The fae nodded. "Yes, I know." He looked at me, his brilliant eyes holding mine. "Stay safe, Olivia. You mean something to this world, even if they do not know it."

I watched him leave. "Sometimes I don't know if he sticks around because he's my friend, because he sees me as important, or if he's morbidly curious."

Kael jerked his head toward a door which led to the employee parking garage. "Probably all three. And other things..."

I mentally prepared myself for the blast of cold air as we went through the door, but it still took my breath away. I followed close behind Kael in an attempt to use his body as a windbreaker.

We hurried to his Jeep. It was black with big, knobby tires. At least he drove something that would get us through the snow and ice to wherever this cabin was located. A shame we didn't have Ren with us to act as a snowplow.

We made it through the streets easily enough. The city had made an attempt to remove the snow, and a portion of it had been swept to the sides, though the wind was blowing some of it right back to the slick pavement.

I assumed this cabin was some sort of safe house PITO used. I imagined it to be small, dark, and cold. Hopefully it would have electricity and running water.

It took us an hour to get outside of city limits, with Kael checking the rearview mirror every minute or so. As we wound up into a snow blanketed forest and finally came to a stop, I was pleasantly surprised.

The cabin was small, likely only one or two bedrooms, but it had a peaked roof with a loft, wide windows, and an inviting front porch. It looked fairly new, and I was relieved to see the electric lines running to it.

We hurried from the vehicle, more in a rush to get out of the elements than fear of being spotted. There was a keypad beside the door and Kael punched in a series of numbers. After a quiet click, he pushed the door open.

"Thermostat's over there," he said as we stepped into the living room. He pointed to a right-hand wall. "I'll get a fire going."

I turned up the temperature in the cold cabin as Kael set about starting a fire in the fireplace. The cabin was rustic, but charming and cozy. It wouldn't be such a bad place to hide away for a bit, even if I didn't approve of the hiding part.

"How often do people come here?" I asked. The cabin was clean, with no musty, stale scent of disuse.

Kael stood and wiped his hands on his jeans. The kindling in the fireplace crackled and popped as small flames licked the wood. "Someone comes by once a week to clean and keep things stocked." He studied me for a moment. "You hungry?"

"Sure. What've you got?" I shadowed him to the kitchen, though I regretted leaving the warmth of the fireplace. I could have used my magic to warm myself, but until we knew the mage's whereabouts, I didn't want to risk him sensing me unless it was an emergency.

After a quick search of the cupboards, Kael made us a breakfast of pancakes. I ate every bite, and with warm and full bellies, the pair of us settled back into the living room. The fire was blazing now. I pulled a fleece throw onto my lap and folded myself into Kael as snow fell beyond the frosty window panes.

"I lost all of my clothes," I said. Along with all my other

necessities. I didn't have much in the way of personal items, save for what I carried in my bag, and I was thankful I'd brought it with me.

Kael put his arm around me and rubbed my shoulder. "I'll get you some more clothes. Don't worry, Livvie. I'll take care of you."

His words melted me, and I realized how nice it was to have someone I could completely count on.

"Do you really think it was Vehrin who attacked my house?"

"I don't know. The guards weren't there since you'd left, but aside from possibly demons after the relics, who else would it have been?"

I chewed on the inside of my cheek for a moment. "What about...shifters?"

Kael twisted to peer at me. "Shifters?"

"Yeah, you know, from PITO?"

He shook his head. "They wouldn't do that. Why would they?"

"You've seen the way most of them act around me and look at me. What am I supposed to think?"

Kael didn't respond, and the cabin fell silent, the quiet only interrupted by the wind and rattling branches outside. But when the quiet became too much, I pressed on.

"Kael...would they harm me if they knew I was mated to you? Maybe someone found out and got angry."

"No." He didn't sound entirely convinced.

I pulled in a deep breath. One of the many reasons I hadn't even thought about making a decision yet was because I didn't know how us being together would affect his position at PITO.

"I don't want you to have to choose between your own kind and me. It isn't fair."

Kael's fingers tickled the side of my neck as he shifted

closer to me. "It wouldn't be a hard decision. I would choose you, without question."

I hadn't wanted to bring it up, not with Vehrin waiting in the wings somewhere and our lives in danger, but I had to know.

"What do you think about the mating bond? Do you want to keep it?" I lifted my gaze to his. "I need to know how you feel about it, and me."

With warm fingers, Kael took my hands. He looked at me with a gaze so intense, if I hadn't already been tethered to him, his stare would have done the trick. "Livvie——"

There was a sudden knock at the door.

I rolled my eyes and sighed heavily. "I bet you anything that's Ren. The man can't seem to keep his nose out of things." I was certain he broke into intense, emotional moments between me and Kael on purpose.

Kael rose from the couch and stalked to the door, muttering under his breath. He flung the door open, and through the blast of icy wind, I heard him make a sound of surprise.

Then, a gunshot rang out.

CHAPTER 4

As I BOLTED from the couch in the cabin to my feet, the green and gold bracelet hugging my wrist twisted and fell away. The intertwined strands shifted and hardened into sharp steel, and then my sword was in my hand. I charged toward the door, fear and fury burning with each breath.

Kael stumbled back and revealed our attacker.

Aidan.

The bear shifter looked down at the gun in his hand and cursed. He started to cock it again, but it appeared to be jammed. I grabbed Kael's shoulder and jerked him back out of harm's way. The second he stumbled back, another shot rang out. Kael grunted beside me.

The need to protect him flooded my mind. I swung my sword at Aidan, and he jumped back. His lips curled up in a snarl. It twisted his normally cheerful features into something wrong.

What was he doing? This wasn't him. Why would he do this?

"Livvie!" Kael pulled me back and kicked the door shut. Throwing his shoulder into it, he slid the lock into place.

"That won't stop us, Kael," Aidan said.

Us? Were there more agents with him?

I pivoted Kael around to look at him. A pair of dark splotches were spreading across his shirt. One in the shoulder, likely the first bullet, and the other in the side. It was a miracle Aidan hadn't managed to get him in the heart.

A loud thud thumped on the other side of the door. I grabbed Kael's hand and tugged him. "Come on."

I wasn't sure where I was leading us. Was there a back door? If there was, would Aidan have sent someone to it by now?

"This way," Kael murmured. He led me down a short hall toward a doorway. We were only a few feet away when the door creaked, then burst open.

Two men filled the doorway, both of their faces pinched with malice as they stared at me. Kael and I retreated, but I quickly found we had nowhere to go. I heard splitting wood and knew Aidan had managed to bust the front door open.

Kael and I hovered between the kitchen and the living room. I held my sword up as Aidan stepped toward us.

"Why?" Kael growled.

Aidan didn't have his pistol aimed toward us. He didn't need to. With the two men who had come in the back door, and the other agent behind the bear shifter, we were outnumbered.

"You have mated with someone who is barely more than a witch, a fae-friend, and a curse on this world. You are throwing away everything for her. All of your potential, all of your worth, you're tossing it away for her. You are an agent of PITO. That used to mean something to you."

Kael brushed my shoulder with his, and his feet shuffled. He was going to lose his strength if he kept bleeding out.

"There are more important things at work here," Kael ground out. "If we don't stop the mage—"

"The mage?" Aidan interrupted. "He wouldn't even be here if it wasn't for her. She's the one who took the key and placed it in his hands in the first place." He moved forward a step. "She's a problem that needs to be controlled. Unfortunately, with you being mated to her, you're not going to let us do what needs to be done."

Once again, Aidan lifted the pistol. In a heartbeat, my sword disappeared to wrap back around my wrist, and I raised my hand. Magic seared through my veins and crackled around my hand. Energy shot forward, straight into Aidan's chest. He fell back, and I knew he was dead before he hit the floor.

Though he'd left me little choice if I wanted myself and Kael both to survive, my heart still panged to lose someone I had believed was a friend. How had I been so wrong about him?

A snarling filled the room, and before I could take another breath, two wolves and a tiger rushed toward us. I planted my feet and threw my hands forward. The tiger jumped past Aidan and smacked straight into a wall of shimmering magic. He hit the floor, but was quickly recovering.

The wolves pummeled into Kael, and all three of them barreled over me. I hit the floor and pulled in my magic. I didn't want to accidentally hurt Kael. Growls and snapping jaws filled my ears as I struggled to get out from the frenzy. Kael cried out, then cursed.

I managed to disentangle myself just in time to have the tiger shifter reach toward me with sharp claws. I twisted, and the claws rent through the wooden floor. With gritted teeth, I reached across my chest and smashed a glowing hand into his neck.

The smell of burning fur filled my nostrils as the tiger jerked back with a terrible, guttural sound. Fuchsia flames crawled over his body as his legs kicked and tore at the floor. After few more violent twitches, he stopped.

Kael, despite his injuries, had managed to kill one of the wolves with nothing but his bare hands. It was lying dead beside him, his head twisted in an odd direction and pale, yellow eyes vacant. I sat up and hit the other wolf, who had his jaws clamped around Kael's arm.

The wolf released him with a yelp, but my attack wasn't as strong as I would have liked. He retreated a few steps and eyed me warily. Then he lifted his nose to the air and howled.

Somewhere outside, a chorus of howls answered him.

I got to my feet and tugged on Kael, grimacing as I helped him stand. "Come on."

With my gaze locked on the wolf, I walked backward toward the door. My bag was laying against the wall, and I bent over to scoop it up. I held my palm toward the shifter, letting him know I'd blast him if he came closer. I didn't know how many other shifters were coming, but we had to get out of there. Now.

Besides, now that I'd used my magic, Vehrin may very well be on his way.

As we exited through the front door, cold air kissed my cheeks. I hurried to Kael's Jeep.

I reached into Kael's pocket and grabbed his keys. "Get in."

"You're not driving my Jeep."

I yanked open the passenger side door and practically shoved him inside. The fact he fell in so easily told me just how much of a toll his wounds were really taking on him.

As the urgent howls reached me, I quickly rounded the car and glanced over my shoulder to see at least four wolves racing through the snow. I hurried in, just managing to shut the door right as a wolf reached the car.

Kael muttered something as I cranked the key and threw the Jeep into reverse. I was fairly certain I hit something, though whether it was a snow bank or a wolf shifter, I didn't know. It would take our pursuers at least a couple minutes to round everyone up and get in their car, so I hoped we'd be able to lose them.

"Where do we go?" I asked. "Should we go back to headquarters?"

Kael braced a hand on the dash as I slid around a corner. "Not headquarters. If Aidan has any allies, they'll head us off before we get there. I'm not sure headquarters is even safe anymore. I know a place."

I drove toward the small motel he told me about on the edge of town, though it took longer than I would have liked to traverse through the slick roads. I parked in the back.

"I'll check us in. Wait here." I threw Kael a stern glance before exiting the car.

I got us a room for one night, collected my jaguar shifter, and helped him into the room. I shut and locked the door, closed the curtains, and pointed toward the bathroom.

"Let's have a look at you."

Kael half-stumbled to the bathroom and sat on the edge of the tub. I shucked off my jacket and pushed up my sleeves.

"Off with the shirt," I said.

A smile quirked at Kael's lips. "Yes, ma'am."

I glowered. "This isn't funny. You're hurt." I could sense his pain through our bond.

"I'll heal, you know." Kael peeled off his shirt anyway.

Blood ran from the wound in his shoulder to mix with where the second bullet had grazed his side. The hem of his jeans were stained with rust-colored splotches, and his chest heaved with deep breaths.

"Damn, Kael." How was the man even capable of sitting up?

"If that's your reaction to seeing me shirtless, I'll be sure to go without one more often."

"How much blood have you lost?" I asked, glaring.

He shrugged his shoulders, then winced. "I wasn't exactly measuring."

I grabbed a hand towel and ran it under some warm water. As carefully as I could, I wiped away the blood at his shoulder, but each time, more blood ran from the wound. I worried at my bottom lip. What if I couldn't get the bleeding to stop?

Kael covered my hand with his and held it pressed to his wound. His golden gaze captured mine. "I'll heal, Livvie. Don't worry. Just, hold this here for a while."

I let out a slow breath. "Okay." I sat beside him for ten minutes. Neither of us spoke. Perhaps we were both trying to catch up to what had just happened.

Finally, I lifted the soaked towel. The wound was still there, but the bleeding had stopped. At least the one along his ribcage was shallow.

Kael's phone vibrated in his jacket pocket. I wrapped my hands around his wrist as he bent to retrieve it.

"It's probably Mason," he said.

"Mason can wait until you're cleaned up and resting," I said.

He straightened with a deep sigh. "You're bossy."

"And you're stubborn."

Kael chuckled, but fell silent as I stood.

"Think you can take a shower?" I asked.

"I'm sure I can manage." He tilted his face to look at me. "Any chance you want to help with that, too?"

My mouth went dry at the thought of joining him in the shower. I slammed back the emotions before he could get a read on them. "Just get cleaned up."

"Keep an eye out," he said.

He didn't take a long shower, but by the time he came out of the bathroom, his wound had mostly closed. It was still puffy and red, but thankfully it didn't seem to be causing him too much discomfort. The shot had been straight through, and a quick check showed the exit wound healing, as well. I showered next and changed into my spare set of clothes in my bag afterward.

Kael was on the phone with Mason when I emerged.

"...and tried to kill me...no, she's fine. We left the cabin, he had others there with him...Yeah." Kael gave Mason the address of the motel. "...we will. Okay, bye." He ended the call, then found me watching. "He said to wait here. He's coming with a team to escort us back to headquarters."

"Fantastic," I grumbled.

Kael gave me an apologetic smile and held out his hand. I joined him on the bed and the pair of us eased back into the too-small pillows.

"Are you all right?" I asked.

"I'm fine, Livvie. Stop worrying."

He most certainly *wasn't* fine. His closest friend at PITO, a man I thought was my friend, too, had tried to kill us.

"I can't believe Aidan would do that." I shifted onto my side to peer at Kael. "Do you think Vehrin got to him?"

Kael pursed his lips. "I don't think so. Aidan held PITO above all else. He wouldn't have joined a dark mage." He shook his head and adjusted the pillow behind his shoulders. "It just doesn't make any sense."

"What doesn't?"

"Surely, given your importance in all of this, Mason had given the order that you are to be protected. Aidan is so honor-bound to PITO he wouldn't have disobeyed. Not unless..." Kael sat up.

His sudden alertness set me on edge. "Kael? What is it? Unless what?"

A groove had etched between Kael's eyebrows as he peered at me. "Unless *Mason* had given the order."

My breath caught.

"Get your things," Kael said. He slid off the bed and grabbed his jacket from where I'd set it on the back of a chair. "We need to leave. Now."

I snatched my cell where I'd laid it on the bedside table and had started shoving my arms into my olive-colored jacket when the sound of tires crunching outside on the snow reached me, quickly followed by slamming car doors.

Kael's worried eyes swept to mine.

We were too late.

CHAPTER 5

ONCE AGAIN, we were trapped. This situation was worse, really. We didn't even have a back door. The only place to escape was right in front of us.

Kael's breath was warm in my ear as he bent down to whisper to me. "Play along until we're outside."

Play along? What if they tried to harm him? If he thought I was going to just sit back and watch, he was poorly mistaken.

There was a knock at the door. Kael gave me a stern "stick-to-the-plan" look before he opened it. Mason stood on the other side, with two men at his back. I recognized one, though I didn't know his name. He was a wolf shifter, and was one of the people who had been glaring at me in the cafeteria.

For a man whose agents had tried to kill one of his others, and harm the woman under his protection, Mason seemed rather put together. Yanking off his black leather gloves, he gestured for the agents shadowing him to wait outside. He shut the door behind him, blocking out the cold.

His gaze flicked between Kael and myself. "What happened?"

I let Kael tell the story. Mason listened, but kept giving short nods which gave me the impression he was impatient for my partner to get on with it, like he already knew the outcome.

"...then I told her to take us here. I figured if we were around civilians, anyone who may have been with Aidan would be hesitant to start any trouble."

Kael's tone was calm, but I caught the undertone of warning in his explanation. Smart. He had just reminded Mason we weren't exactly alone in the motel, not like we were in a cabin in the middle of nowhere.

Mason moved closer to me, causing Kael to step closer to my side. Clearly, he no longer cared if his boss knew about the mating bond. Mason, it seemed, either didn't notice, or already knew.

The agent fixed Kael with a level stare. "We need to get her back to headquarters, where it's safe. You will stay here. Perhaps if there are others who wish to do her harm, they will believe she is still at the motel. I will send you backup in case anyone shows up." Mason reached out and grabbed my arm. "Come along, Olivia."

Before I could even protest, or introduce the man's face to my fist, Kael reached out and shoved him.

Kael snarled. "Get your hands off her."

"Sir?" One of the agents outside must have heard the commotion, and had cracked the door open.

Mason waved him off, and the door clicked shut. He glowered at Kael. "I'm going to have to ask you to stand down, Kael."

Kael crossed his arms. "And I'm going to have to ask you to leave. She doesn't need your protection anymore. She isn't yours to order around, and she most certainly isn't going anywhere without me."

"You will do what I command, Agent Rivera, or you will lose your position at PITO."

With a slow and deliberate movement, Kael pulled me farther from Mason and closer to his side. It was answer enough to Mason, it seemed. His lips had curled back in a snarl so vicious, I could almost see his wolf shining through.

"Let's stop playing games. Why did you send Aidan to kill us?"

My eyebrows rose. So much for playing along until we were outside. Perhaps, with Kael being ordered to stay put, he hadn't wanted to risk them taking me if I'd agreed to leave with them.

Mason didn't bother with any sort of façade. "Not *us*, Kael. *You*. Killing Olivia would have done no good. Her power could have leached who knows where." His gaze bore into mine. "Her power is too much to leave untethered. She needs to be kept under lock and key unless the occasion calls for her to be used against Vehrin."

Mason's words sent anger through me like white-hot lightning. My nostrils flared. "I'm supposed to just be leashed and muzzled, unless Vehrin gets too close? I'm not an attack dog."

"No," Mason said. "Of course not. Dogs obey their masters. You are too much of a wild card. That's why you need a controlling hand."

As soon as the word "controlling" rolled off his tongue, I knew what his true motives were.

"You want my key. You want to control me and use my power."

"What?" Kael snapped. He tried to edge me farther behind him, but I elbowed him in the ribs. "If you think I'm going to allow that, you're insane."

Mason put his hands in his pockets. "Precisely why I need you out of the way, Kael. I had Olivia's house attacked, knowing you would want her taken to a safe place. The cabin would have been the most logical place. I sent Aidan and the others there. Once you were dead, I hoped Olivia would go back to headquarters, with her main protector out of the picture. I think even you know that would be for the best, even as you resist the idea. We're protecting something bigger, here. Sacrifice is necessary."

Magic slithered beneath my skin, and I spoke through clenched teeth. "What makes you think I need protecting?"

The agent kept his attention pinned on Kael. "I knew you would protect your mate"—his mouth twisted at the word—"above all else, even at the cost of your position and the best interest of PITO."

He stepped back, closer to the door, as if ready to let the other agents in. Did they have guns? Would they really take Kael down in a public place?

"A mating bond is one to be respected above all other obligations," Kael said.

Mason nodded. "A mating bond between *shifters*, yes. Tying yourself to this woman is an abomination. Shifters are of the earth. We were born here, our genes written into this planet's story from the beginning. Witches, fae, and mages are of unnatural elements, twisted into something that shouldn't be here." His stare swept to me, the hatred he had masked so well unveiled. "Who's to say that ancient power within her won't poison her mind, influence her to go to Vehrin's side?" His hand wrapped around the doorknob. "It's not a risk I'm willing to take."

"Wait." I took a step forward and reached into the front of my shirt. I drew out the pair of keys—one gold, and the other pale white, like ancient bone. "If I give you the key tied to my soul, will you promise to let Kael live?"

Kael grabbed my shoulder. "Livvie, no!"

I shook him off. "If you do, I promise to cooperate."

"Olivia." Kael's tone was sharp, commanding. "No. He'll never let you go."

I wished he was able to read my mind while in his human form, because inside I was yelling at him to shut up.

"Listen to your mate, Kael." Mason studied me for a moment, then gave a short nod. "Yes, I would let him live."

37

"We would be allowed to stay together?" I asked.

"You would be confined strictly to headquarters, and guarded at all times, but yes, you may stay together. Until you are needed, that is."

Kael seethed behind me. I could almost feel the anger rolling off him, but he remained silent. Perhaps he had caught on to what I was doing.

I paused in a show of considering, then nodded. "All right. I'll go with you."

Mason held out his hand. "The keys."

I tucked the keys into my shirt. "I'll hand them over at headquarters," I said. "Once I'm safely there. I would feel too exposed if I handed over the relics to you now."

The agent narrowed his eyes and watched me. I feared he wasn't going to go for it, but then he gave a short nod.

"Fine. At headquarters." Mason pointed a finger at Kael. "Don't you dare try anything. You may be a good agent, but your loyalty is no longer with our organization, and I would have no qualms about taking you down."

Kael's teeth ground together audibly, though he said nothing. I zipped up my jacket and mentally prepared myself for the cold outside.

"Let's go," I said.

Mason led the way. He spoke quickly to the agents he'd left standing outside the door. Kael gave me a look that told me to be ready. I hoped the pair of us wouldn't get shot or torn apart by shifters when we made our escape.

Energy purred beneath my skin as I readied myself to tap into my power.

The wind was icy, and fiercer than it had been when we'd arrived at the motel not long ago. Snow zipped through the air and covered the road. My cheeks were numb almost instantly. Beside me, Kael slowed to a halt.

His nostrils flared as he breathed in the sharp air. "Something isn't right."

One of the agents flanking us gave him an annoyed look as he flipped up his collar. Obviously, the weather was wrong, but I knew that wasn't what Kael was talking about.

"What is it?" I asked.

"I don't know…something in the air."

"It's called snow." The annoyed agent at Kael's shoulder waved his hands around as if we couldn't see the blizzard trying to freeze us where we stood.

I spread my fingers out at my side, and a malignant sort of energy soaked into my skin. "He's right. It isn't just the weather. Something is coming."

Mason looked over his shoulder. He had the car door open. They'd left it running, and I could see the warm air shimmering from within. "Demons?"

He was reaching toward a pistol at his side.

The biting wind suddenly stopped tugging at my hair, and I blinked. Through the lazily falling snow, a figure emerged.

My eyes widened as I took the person in. Huge wings arched from his back. The wings were leathery, but were white, nearly opaque, as if they had been formed from ice. The webbing shimmered, the way thin ice shone on a window pane when shot through with bright sunlight. Talons tipped the wings, as beautiful and sharp as frosted glass. My gaze finally landed on the man's face. I recognized him, though he was more ethereal and breathtaking than I'd ever seen him.

Renathe.

Behind him were at least a dozen other winged fae, beautiful and deadly as the winter storm which had been raging around us. With a grace I would have never managed in the ice and snow, Ren stepped forward. His face was a cool mask, but his silver-shot teal eyes glinted.

"Now, Mr. Anderson," he said. "I know you're not kidnapping my dear friends."

The agents at our side pulled out weapons. Ren didn't spare them a glance.

"This is not your concern, fae." Mason spat the last word. "Leave, or there will be trouble."

A vicious grin curved Renathe's lips. My friend's face was touched with something feral and fierce. He was no longer the charming and composed fae I knew, and seeing him like this put me more on edge. He wouldn't have shown up like this unless something was very wrong.

"Oh, little wolf," Ren said. "I'm afraid it's a little too late for that."

Mason's eyebrows pulled together. "What do you mean?"

Instead of answering the agent, Ren turned to me. The mocking smile fell from his lips, and his gaze grew hard.

"Olivia, he's coming."

Dark energy raked across my skin. My gaze slid over Renathe's shoulder.

"No," I said, pointing over his shoulder. "He's here."

Past the fae, with a group of demons assembled behind him, stood the dark mage.

CHAPTER 6

As I stared at Vehrin, it wasn't fear that gripped me in tearing, sinking claws...it was hatred. It burned through me, and in that moment, I wanted nothing more than to reduce the mage to ashes. He had brought havoc to the lion shifter pride, and he'd killed my friend, Sarah.

Magic licked around my wrist and flowed over my knuckles. I stared at Vehrin with a searing gaze. He didn't deserve to be breathing.

The agents flanking me and Kael raised their pistols. Ren leaned back, and the shifters fired. My ears rang with their volley of bullets.

It wouldn't do any good against the mage, but my heart still shuddered a beat of hope.

Vehrin lifted his arm, and the rounds fired from the agents bounced harmlessly off some sort of shield. As the mage lowered his arm, I narrowed my eyes. Was my vision playing tricks on me?

Kael had bitten that very same arm off during our last confrontation with Vehrin, but it was as if he had grown it back. Instead of a normal arm, however, writhing shadows formed the forearm, hand, and fingers. Ink seemed to spill from the stunted limb, as if the mage's veins flowed with dark matter rather than blood.

Someone said my name, but I was uncertain who. As I stared at the ebony swirls of Vehrin's new arm, something flickered in my mind. A voice spoke near me again, but a long-forgotten memory was already sweeping me away.

Sweat rolled down between my shoulder blades, though it had nothing to do with the pressing jungle heat. I clenched my fists against the power rolling inside of me. My magic used to be pure, and wholly a part of me, but for the past year, it had a swirl of darkness staining it. Like a piece of rotten fruit in a bowl, that stain was slowly corrupting my own magic.

I had believed it was a fluke, some fragment of twisted circumstance that had changed my fate, but knowing the man before me was now tainted with the same darkness, I knew better.

"Vehrin," I said.

His gaze lifted to mine from where he had been staring at his palm, as if he could see the malignant energy beneath his skin. He merely raised an eyebrow.

"This curse will eat us both up inside," I continued, "until nothing but shadow and hate and power swirl around our bones."

Vehrin grabbed the cotton fabric of his dark purple robe and pulled it tighter around his lean frame. "I've always liked the darkness," he muttered, as if speaking to himself.

My companion had always been drawn to a deeper shade of life and magic. He found wonder in death and disease, and that same fascination is what brought the curse upon him in the first place. One cannot cure death without a cost, even if his intentions had been, to some extent, honorable.

"There is too much power at work here. No being should have so much. It will break us, crush every ounce of humanity we have left, and mold us into something vile. We have to break this curse, Vehrin."

He had to understand. Relief blew through me when he gave me a small smile and nodded. "Yes. Yes, I know. But, how?"

I chewed at my lip. Could I give him information which had been passed down in my family since my ancestors drew their first breath?

Fingernails of dark magic scratched inside me, and I shuddered. I had no other choice. If I wanted to save myself and Vehrin, I had to divulge the secret.

I thought about the roll of fabric that I kept hidden beneath a loose stone on the floor in my sleeping quarters. The nondescript tan fabric held four keys formed with magic I was certain would be able to help us.

All I needed was for Vehrin to help me discover what they unlock.

"Come." I took his hand and led him toward my room. "I'll show you."

Breath hissed in through my teeth as the vision blew away with a cold wind. I'd wanted to scream at her, scream at *myself*, not to show Vehrin the keys.

My gaze refocused on his arm, at the swirl of dark magic leaching from the ruined limb. Clearly, a cure for the curse hadn't been found.

What about me? Was I poisoned, as well?

Pressure wrapped around my arm. "Let's go."

Mason tugged me sharply toward the open door of the black car.

"Ow! Hey!" My feet slid on the slick motel parking lot. I fought against his hold, but the wolf shifter's grip was steel. "Let me go!"

"You're coming with me." The agent's voice wasn't one that conjured up a sense of protection, like he wanted to whisk me away to safety. His tone was harsh and ragged. Possessive.

I leaned my body back away from him and pulled. "I said let me go."

Before he could slide me forward another inch, a hand landed on my shoulder.

"Get your hands off her." Kael thrust his arm out, and his fist connected with Mason's face with a crunch.

Mason stumbled back into the side of his car. Blood poured from what I was certain was a broken nose. He stared at Kael, and his lips pulled back, red staining his teeth.

The agent began to shake, and in the next moment, he

shifted into the biggest wolf I'd ever seen. A deep growl rumbled beneath his dark gray coat, and his frame still trembled with rage. He lowered his head and shifted his weight, ready to dash forward.

Kael shifted into his jaguar, his torn clothes falling to the ground. His spotted, golden fur stood out against the stark white of the snow. He paced back and forth in front of me, his muscles fluid in his long, graceful body. A sense of pride warmed me at the sight of him.

The wolf charged forward, and Kael leaped to meet him. An icy breeze kissed the back of my neck, and I tore my eyes reluctantly from the pair biting and tearing in the snow.

Vehrin had stalked closer while I'd been distracted. Renathe stood in front of me, his beautiful wings half-raised. I couldn't see his expression, but I knew he was readying for a fight.

Kael, are you all right? I said, using our mental bond that had connected when he'd shifted.

There was a sort of internal grunt from him as the car behind me groaned with a sudden impact. *Fine,* he said. *Just focus on Vehrin.*

I stepped up beside Ren and reached for my magic…or at least, I *tried* to.

It was as if I were trying to find something buried in thick mud. My magic was there, but I couldn't grasp it enough to twist it into the energy I needed. With every step closer the mage took, the farther away my magic seemed to retreat. Then, my stare fell on the key around his neck, and realization soured in my gut.

Vehrin could hinder my magic with the relic he was wearing.

I expected the dark mage to strike out and take advantage of my sudden weakness, but he didn't. Instead, he paused in the snow.

Vehrin was so different now than he had been in my

vision. He was younger then, and hadn't yet been swept away with darkness as he was now. The only part which remained the same were his cold, calculating, and unwaveringly obsessive eyes.

"It is time to quit running, Olivia." My name on Vehrin's lips still sounded foreign, and I was thankful he had never called me by the name he knew me as before. He reached his hand out, and swirls of shadow dripped from his fingertips. "It is time to accept our fate, just as I did long ago."

The dark mage's words gave me pause, and the vision of our ancient conversation flitted through my mind. "What do you mean?"

Vehrin smiled. "The answer is already within you, sweeping beneath your skin, tainting the marrow of your bones, and lacing your muscles with a delicious dark." His nostrils widened as he pulled in a deep breath. His gaze flicked to Mason's pair of agents. They had stopped firing their pistols, though whether it was because they had run out of ammo or had found it pointless, I wasn't sure. The mage's cruel grin grew as he pulled his stare from them back to me. "I can taste their fear. Can't you taste it, too? Don't you want their fear and screams and pain? You would thrive, Olivia, just as I do."

A horrible part of me *did* want it, and I barely caught myself from nodding.

"No!" I spat through clenched teeth. I didn't want to think about how I was convincing myself as much as I was trying to convince Vehrin.

A menacing growl shuddered through the air behind me. I spared a quick glance over my shoulder in time to see Mason leap at Kael and slam him into the snowy curb.

I gasped. *Kael!*

In my next breath, Vehrin's demons rushed forward to take advantage of our distracted group. Mason's agents shifted into wolves and charged forward to meet the demons, and I found a small part of myself thankful. With their hands, or rather, mouths, full with the demons, they couldn't help Mason end Kael.

Phantom pain flashed through me as the alpha wolf locked his jaws around Kael's neck.

The gold and green woven bracelet around my wrist unraveled, twisted, and hardened into my sword. This, at least, was something Vehrin couldn't touch. I took two steps toward Mason when something vile punched between my shoulder blades.

I landed hard. Cold snow numbed my cheek where I lay on the parking lot. Specks of light danced across my vision, and when I tried to take a breath, my lungs seized. My ribcage throbbed with pain as a pressure squeezed my body. Vehrin's deep laugh reached me. His dark magic constricted, choking the life out of me.

...Kael.

Hang on, Livvie. His mental voice was strained, as if he could barely get the words out.

There was a sudden whooshing sound, and I pulled sharp air into my lungs with a deep breath as the pressure fell from me. A figure knelt beside me, and I rolled to my back to find Renathe's teal gaze. Behind him, a wall of shimmering ice cut us off from Vehrin.

Ren helped me to my feet just in time for me to see a pair of fae grab Mason and throw him an impressive distance. He landed with a yelp, and though I could see he was still alive by the puffs of mist rising from his jaws with each breath, he didn't get back up.

With a tremendous crack, Ren's wall of ice splintered and fell to the ground like a shattered chandelier.

The dark mage remained standing in the same place. His demons were fighting, and falling, to the fae. One of the wolf shifters was down, and the other stood snarling beside his comrade with his hackles raised.

Are you all right? I asked Kael.

I got a mental nod in return.

I didn't turn to look at him, afraid if I saw his blood dripping to the snow, I'd change the course of action rising in my mind like a raging volcano.

I fixed my gaze on Vehrin, and my nostrils flared. Death. Destruction. Pain. It would continue if I didn't stop him.

My sword hadn't fallen from my clenched fingers when I'd hit the ground. I gripped it with a firm hold and rushed toward Vehrin with a yell. My magic may not be working, I could still punch through his gut.

As the mage raised his hand with a smirk, preparing to strike, strong fingers grabbed my jacket and yanked me back. Ren stepped in front of me and spread his wings just before a blast of something similar to dark smoke hit him. He grunted with the impact, then looked at me with wild eyes.

"Get out of here! Now!"

I shook my head. "He killed Sarah." There were many other reasons Vehrin needed to die, but for some reason, that one seemed the most important to me. Perhaps it was because her death was the most personal. The anger burning through me had me trembling. "I'm going to kill him."

Kael stepped up beside me and bumped my hip with his head. *You can't kill him, Livvie. He must be bound, remember? You'll only release his darkness on you or someone else if you kill him.*

A sharp yell fell from Ren's lips as Vehrin hit him with another blast of energy. The fae's frame shuddered, and I knew my friend wouldn't hold up shielding me for much longer.

"Find the fourth key, Olivia," Ren said. "It's the only way we'll be able to stop him."

Ren was right, and I wanted to cling to his logic, but the emotional side of me was beyond reason. I tried to rush around him, to take out the malicious man causing pain.

"Kael, get her out of here!" Ren yelled. He nearly stumbled under a third attack.

The jaguar at my side took my arm in his jaws. He didn't puncture my skin, but the pressure was enough to let him tug me away.

Come on. We'll live to fight another day.

I relented. After releasing my sword back into a bracelet, I ran with him. As we made our way through the snow, I glanced back. Mason was on his feet fighting against a fae. The fae were fighting against demons and Vehrin.

"The fae will die," I said.

They are stronger than you think, Kael thought back to me.

Kael's warm body pressed up against me as we ran. The influence the fae held on the weather didn't go far, and we rushed into a fierce blizzard.

Again, I looked back. My eyes squinted against the whipping snow, and the angry growl of my name howled on the wind.

CHAPTER 7

I TIGHTENED my fingers on the bags in my hands and pulled in my shoulders as I stepped out of the store and back into the frigid weather. Through the blustery flurry of wind and snow, I set my gaze on a small diner across the street. Glancing both ways and finding no one crazy enough to be driving in this mess, I made my way across the slick road.

The diner looked as if it hadn't changed much since the fifties, with its stainless-steel siding and big, flickering red sign that read "Pearl's". Faint light glowed through the frosted windows of the diner and hinted at the warmth within. I desperately wanted to go inside, but instead I skirted around the long building. In the back was a lone dumpster with snow banked against the side and sitting on top in a thick layer.

"Kael?"

I edged around the dumpster to find him sitting on his haunches, ears back and tail flicking. The jaguar was practically dripping with impatience.

"I tried to hurry," I said. "There was only one register open. It was lucky I went in there when I did. They were talking about shutting the store down until this storm passes."

Kael stood and shook his body like a dog, bits of snow

falling from his golden-brown fur. I set down one bag of assorted clothes. The rest of the clothes and odds and ends, I started shoving into the backpack I'd bought.

"I called for the balance on my card before I went in," I said. "It's weird. There was way more in there than there should have been."

Probably Renathe's doing, Kael said. He grabbed the bag in his teeth and moved behind the dumpster. Even though the area was seemingly empty, if someone happened to see a naked man behind the diner, they may call the authorities.

I frowned as I squeezed a pack of socks into the bag. Ren had put money in my account? "Great," I muttered. "Who knows how many dates I'll owe him now?"

There was a flash of irritation from Kael, and I started to hear his mental complaints about the fae before he shifted into human form.

Kael came out from the dumpster, and I eyed him openly. He wore jeans in a way that should be a crime. I'd splurged on a deep brown leather jacket, which he wore open, revealing the gray tee stretching across his chest.

He held up a beige scarf. "I'm not wearing this."

I shrugged a shoulder and snatched it from him. "Fine. Freeze to death." I stuck it in the backpack and handed the pack to him.

Kael slung it on his shoulder and took my hand. "Let's get inside, then, before I succumb to the cold."

He didn't have to tell me twice. I eagerly led our way to the front of the diner. A little bell jingled above our heads as we went through the front door. The warm smell of coffee and something frying in the kitchen made my stomach gurgle.

Pearl's looked like a place I could sit in for hours. The floor had black-and-white tiles, and directly across from us was a long counter with red stools. Booths lined the rest of the wall, and I led us to one of them. I slid into the bench seat, wedging my bag between my hip and the window. Kael shoved his backpack down by his feet and settled in opposite me.

The man looked exhausted. His eyes were red and his face a bit haggard.

"How are you feeling?" I asked. He'd been attacked by a giant wolf, after all. Not to mention he'd already been recovering from a gunshot wound.

He gave me a weary smile. "I'm fine. It just takes some energy to heal so quickly."

A woman came over to the booth. She grabbed a pen out from behind her ear. "Can I get you something?"

"Two coffees, please," Kael said.

"Sure thing." She gave him a *very* appreciative smile.

I narrowed my eyes at her as she walked off toward the kitchen. I didn't like the way she smiled at him. Who wears that shade of lipstick at work, anyway?

As she disappeared behind a swinging door, I shook my head. Since when was I the jealous type? Damn mating bond was messing with me.

"It's supposed to get easier," Kael muttered. He was picking at the corner of the menu.

Had he noticed my flash of jealousy? I bit my bottom lip and nodded. The last thing I wanted to talk about was the bond between us. Thankfully, the waitress—Heather, her name badge said—returned. She set the steaming cups in front of us.

"Anything else?" she asked. Her attention was completely on Kael.

"Not right now," Kael said. He swept his gaze up to me. "How about you, babe?"

The nickname threw me off so much, I could only shake my head. The waitress walked off without another word.

"*Babe?*"

Kael chuckled as he put an obscene amount of sugar in his coffee. "Just keeping you on your toes."

I pursed my lips. I suspected he'd only said it to throw off the waitress.

I took a sip of the coffee. It was nice and hot, but after the stressful day I'd had, it wasn't quite enough. "I wish I had something stronger," I muttered. I thought of my collection of bourbon back home in Connecticut.

"Maybe later," Kael said. As in, maybe when we weren't being hunted down by an evil mage.

For several minutes, we sipped coffee and sat in silence, both so physically and mentally exhausted we needed some time to wrap our heads around things.

Heather stopped back by to refill our cups. "How about a bite to eat?" She didn't seem as inclined to smile at Kael as she had been.

I felt a little bad about it. I wasn't that kind of person. Kael was sexy as hell, so of course he was likely to catch a lot of attention. There was nothing wrong with being admired.

I glanced at the menu, then smiled at her. "How about two big slices of apple pie? That sounds perfect."

"Sure thing."

As Heather walked back toward the kitchen, I noticed another employee staring at Kael. She didn't smile or look away when my partner saw her. Instead, she just stared. Kael narrowed his eyes, and his eyebrows pinched together.

"What's your problem?" I asked. He jerked his head toward the woman, who finally turned away to give her attention to an elderly man at another booth. "She's probably just staring at you because you're so handsome."

Kael quirked a smile. "You think I'm handsome?"

I shrugged and took a sip of coffee. Heather came back with our apple pie, and I eagerly reached for my fork.

"Livvie." Kael reached across the table and laid his hand on my arm. He dropped his voice. "We need to be more careful than ever. It's not just demons and Vehrin after us, but PITO is now, too. They have informants all over the place.

The last thing we need is to be dragged back to headquarters."

I took a few bites of pie and thought about Kael's boss. "Do you think Mason really wanted to keep the keys safe, or do you think he wanted their power? He seemed so angry there at the end."

Kael leaned back against the booth and crossed his arms, making the leather of his jacket creak. "I think perhaps Vehrin's hold on the world is starting to influence people. The stronger he grows, the more the darkness in him is going to affect others."

I went cold inside at the thought, and not even my warm apple pie could chase away the chill.

"Where should we go, Kael? We can't stay here." I waved a hand around me. "I don't even know where to start." I chewed on the inside of my cheek for a moment. "I had a vision."

Kael went still. "And?"

"It was of me and Vehrin back in the past." It felt so strange to talk about seeing the past, knowing it had been a vision of my ancient self. "We were, well I guess *are*, cursed. It's some sort of dark taint on ourselves or our magic. Anyway, I'd told him about the four keys, and how I knew a way to possibly stop the curse. I'm not certain how, though. The vision went away before I could find out." I tapped the end of my fork, making it clang against the plate.

I knew I had some kind of darkness in me, but learning for a fact it was the same darkness in Vehrin made me want to take a shower.

"We'll get this figured out, Livvie." Kael was leaning forward, his sincere gaze holding me.

I swallowed. "What if I can't be cured, Kael? What if I become...like him?"

Kael reached up and ran his thumb along my jawline. "You won't. I won't let you. I promise."

His promise warmed me, but I wasn't sure if good intentions were enough to save a soul damned with darkness.

Perhaps it was cruel, but I let Kael believe in his promise. "Okay," I said, and gave him a smile. I shoved the empty plate away. "We also need to figure out why Vehrin wanted that disc."

I had no idea what the relic was capable of that Sarah and the rest of the archeological team had found, but I was certain it would do more harm than good in Vehrin's hands, or else he wouldn't have wanted it.

Kael scratched at the stubble on his cheek. "There's a sort of cult in New Orleans that has long worshipped magical items, the more malevolent and cursed, the better. PITO has trouble with them every few years or so. They're unsavory, dangerous, and difficult to find, and would more likely try to kill us than help us, but without PITO's resources, they may be the only ones who could point us in the right direction."

I pulled on my jacket and glanced outside as snow continued to whip by the windows in a frenzy of swirls. "I'll take the risk if we can get out of this God-forsaken weather."

I reached into my bag to the inside pocket where I'd stashed more money than I'd ever held on my person at one time. I was uncertain if PITO would be able to put a hold on my card, or track me with it, so before I'd gone into the store for the items we needed, I went to the ATM and withdrew as much cash as it would allow.

I set the money on the table without waiting for the bill. I made sure to put down a good amount for a tip, because anyone who had to get out and work in this frigid mess deserved it.

As we headed toward the door, Kael started whistling Willie Nelson's "On The Road Again."

* * *

My dad had taken me to New Orleans when I was ten because he had some sort of history convention to attend. I'd had to stay in the hotel for a few hours at a time during the day, but when my dad wasn't busy, he'd taken me out exploring.

I'd loved every minute of the lively atmosphere, the sights, the food. As Kael and I made our way to the bed and breakfast we'd booked, I was excited to see not much had changed.

The streets were bustling, something likely typical for a late Saturday afternoon. Live music venues were beginning to fill with people embarking on a night of dancing, mingling, and drinking. One of the places we passed was playing some amazing old-school jazz. I paused by the doorway, wanting to soak it in, but Kael ushered me down the crowded sidewalk.

Delicious smells from restaurants and food carts boasting a plethora of seafood and spicy creole-inspired dishes filled the air and made my mouth water. I wanted to stay and enjoy the lively atmosphere of the awakening Bourbon Street nightlife, but my partner was impatient to get to the bed and breakfast.

We'd booked a room on Bourbon Street in a bed and breakfast called Brousse Guest House. Kael hoped we'd be able to avoid detection by staying somewhere besides a hotel, and an establishment on one of the busiest areas in the French Quarter was perfect.

Kael halted in front of our destination, and I peered with wide eyes at the building. "Wow."

The Brousse Guest House was a three-story beauty from the eighteen-forties. The white face of the building was bedecked with contrasting black shutters and wrought-iron-railed balconies. Flowers draped from planters outside beside the door. We were greeted by a very friendly woman named Lisbeth, who offered us some refreshment.

Kael politely declined, and we were shown to our room. When he shut the door behind us, I let out a low whistle.

Every piece of furniture in the room was antique, and there was a fireplace against a warm, brick wall. Wispy, white curtains were pulled aside next to double-doors leading to a balcony overlooking Bourbon Street.

I turned to Kael with a raised eyebrow. "And how exactly did you pay for this?" I wasn't insulting his bank account, but was merely curious how he'd managed to do so without fear of being tracked.

He grinned. "I have my ways."

"Whatever." I tossed my bag on the four-poster bed.

I spotted a phone on a spindly-legged table in the corner and contemplated trying to call Ren. I had no way of knowing if he'd survived the confrontation with Vehrin, but I was also uncertain if his phone was tracked. I couldn't risk it. Not yet.

Instead, I settled down on a seat in front of a mahogany desk. Kael's plan to visit the relic-worshipping cult wouldn't unfold until after dark, so we had a few hours to kill. Besides, a lot had happened in the past couple days, including the nearly twenty-four hours it took to travel to New Orleans. A break for rest was deserved. I dug in my pocket and pulled out the folded article I'd printed off while I'd still been under the so-called protection of PITO.

It was an article about Sarah and the stolen relic. I'd read it over and over again, as if hoping a new clue would leap out at me. I set it on the desk and smoothed it out, my gaze pulling from my murdered friend and colleague's face to the relic itself.

Kael came up behind me and squeezed my shoulders. "We need to talk." His warm breath brushed against my ear, and I shuddered.

I almost turned to him, but something strange started happening to the photo of the relic. I leaned closer to it, barely noticing Kael's fingers drifting down my arms. The photo changed, and another image emerged, wavering as if I were peering at it through water.

It was no longer a disc, but a box of some sort.

I knew that box.

My eyes shut, and a vision unfurled from my past.

I walked back and forth across the worn stone, my hand tight on the keys around my neck. On a pedestal between myself and Vehrin was the box we'd found. It had cost a great deal of pain and suffering to collect it, and I could almost feel the vileness of it spreading tendrils throughout the room, seeking out more victims.

"It isn't what I believed," I said.

Vehrin ran a hand through his black hair. "It has the cure."

My gaze flicked to the box and back to his face. "It would also unleash an evil too terrible to imagine. We could be cured, but it would put the world at risk. We cannot open it, Vehrin."

My companion's jaw worked for a moment before he let out a sharp sigh. He turned and strode from the room. I couldn't see his face, but I didn't miss the way his fingers curled into fists.

The memory faded, and I snapped back to reality. The box in the photo had returned to a disc once more. I turned so fast I nearly knocked Kael down, who—I realized too late— had had his lips on the side of my neck.

"The disc isn't a disc! It's a box."

Kael rubbed at the back of his neck and unclenched his jaw. "What are you talking about?"

Clearly he'd been trying to make a move, but I was too caught up in my most recent revelation to dwell on it.

I picked up the newspaper and tapped the picture of the relic. My heart hammered. Even no longer wrapped in ancient sight, I could still sense the malevolent forces within the box.

"It's a box that would destroy the world." I swallowed. "And it's already in the hands of the very person who wants to do just that."

CHAPTER 8

Kael slid the manhole cover with a grating screech across the pavement. I glanced around the dark street. Thankfully, we were in a less savory and more deserted part of town. The only place nearby was a bar with windows so dingy, I doubted anyone could properly see through the glass.

I got down on the road and swung my legs into the hole, ready to descend into the darkness. Kael crouched down beside me with amusement quirking his lips.

"What kind of crazy girl heads into a sewer this willingly?" he asked.

Shifting my bag around farther onto my back, I smirked. "Going underground is my specialty, you know." I eased myself down until I found the metal rungs of the ladder built in for service workers. "Besides, you're the one mated to the crazy girl, so what does that make you?"

Before he could answer, I descended. Thankfully the smell wasn't too bad. Perhaps this was used more as a storm drain than an actual sewer. I would have gone regardless, but it was nice to be able to take a deep breath without choking on the heavy scent of waste.

Kael dropped down beside me and clicked on a flashlight.

He stared at me for a moment, as if considering something. "We need to talk about that, by the way."

I fished in my bag for my own flashlight and turned it on. "About what?"

"Being mated."

My mouth popped open. "And you think now is the time? *Down here?*" Call me sentimental, but I figured a discussion involving a bond as deep and meaningful as a mating bond should involve some good food, a warm place, and a calm atmosphere at the very least.

"We have to at some point, Livvie. You can't avoid it forever."

I crossed my arms and lifted my chin. "I'm not avoiding it. The last time we tried to talk about it, we were attacked by a bear shifter. Maybe it's the universe's way of saying to put a hold on that particular conversation."

My partner let out a deep sigh but didn't press the issue. He was right, though. We did need to talk about it, and I admitted to myself I was putting it off. I just wasn't sure what Kael thought about the whole mating thing. Hell, I wasn't even sure what *I* thought about it. Obviously, there was an attraction between us, and I cared deeply for Kael, but was I ready for something that would last forever?

On the other hand, if I denied the bond, would that mean losing Kael? It was a hard thing to think about, and just the thought of never being more than a friend, or possibly not seeing him at all, made my stomach burn unexpectedly.

I cleared my throat, and the sound bounced off the dark, cement walls around us.

"Are you all right?"

I glanced at Kael. "Yeah." I made a show of wincing. "I've got a raging case of heartburn."

Kael rolled his eyes. "I told you not to get that dish at the restaurant, the one with the five-pepper rating."

"It was good," I said.

Kael scoffed as he glanced around. He was trying to figure out which way to go, and I took the opportunity to study our surroundings.

We stood on a concrete ledge that stretched the length of the tunnel. Beneath us, a small stream of water flowed. I could imagine it was raging when there was a heavy downpour, and I was thankful the weather outlook had called for clear skies. There were a few lights, but they flickered and didn't do much to light the dark space. The air was cool and damp.

I zipped up my jacket. "Do you know which way?"

Kael jerked his head to the right. "I think it's this way."

He started off. The path wasn't wide enough for us to walk side-by-side, so I had to be content to follow him. I glanced behind me as prickles scattered up the back of my neck. I could have sworn we were being watched, but Kael didn't seem concerned so I passed it off as unease.

"What kind of people would want to live in a place like this?" I asked. A sudden thought occurred to me. "They aren't giant rat people, are they? I don't think I could deal with that."

The shifter in front of me chuckled. "No. They live down here because they don't want to be found."

"Are you sure PITO won't come looking for us here? I'm sure Mason won't just give up and let us continue on our world tour."

Kael pointed out a fallen bit of pipe, and I hopped over it. "No, I'm sure he won't, but he won't think to look for us here. PITO only comes about once a year to this place. They mostly give warnings, but they rarely confiscate items. It causes too many problems and paperwork. These people down here are difficult."

They were too difficult for Kael's organization to handle? That certainly didn't bode well. "What kind of beings are they?"

"A mix. All of them worship cursed objects and ancient

artifacts they believe hold magic or some other kind of ethereal influence. There are witches, fae, vampires, even shifters."

I stopped, and it took Kael a few steps to realize I wasn't shadowing him. "Hold on. Did you just say vampires?"

Kael looked at me like their existence was obvious. I had a sudden urge to check the dark crevices of the curved ceiling for bats.

"Okay, vampires. Great. So, should I expect mermaids to start popping out of there?" I pointed to the water running below. "Maybe when all of this is said and done, I'll get a pet unicorn."

"Don't be silly. Aren't unicorns only in fairytales?" Before Kael turned to continue, however, I caught a sly grin on his face. It appeared I still had much to learn in this crazy world I'd been thrown into.

Shortly after I learned of the existence of blood-sucking monsters, we came upon a small opening. There was nothing that hinted this was the right way, no signs or runes, but Kael headed into the space.

"How do you know where we're going?" I asked. "Have you been here before?"

Kael was quiet for a moment. "No, but Aidan has. He told me about it once."

Regret and anger swirled through me, and I fell silent as I followed Kael. The concrete walls quickly changed into stone which grew more aged and crumbling as we went. I could sense unease from Kael as we made our way through the smaller tunnel. He really wasn't into tight spaces, and this time I couldn't blame him, especially with who knew what kind of monsters potentially lurking in the shadows.

"Wait." Kael held a hand up, and I halted. He started sniffing. "Do you smell something?"

I couldn't smell anything except the heavy, damp air. Kael angled his flashlight ahead of us and to the left. Two figures stepped out into the light. They made deep hissing noises while they put their arms in front of their faces. Kael lowered the flashlight.

"Apologies," he said. "We mean no harm."

The pair walked closer, their steps slow and shuffling. As they drew closer, I was able to see them better. They had human-like features, but their skin was gray, and they had eyes so large it reminded me of deep earth-dwelling creatures. Had they ever been above ground? I was so caught up in their appearance, it took me a moment to see they held long knives in their hands.

"What do you want?" one of them asked in a voice so low and guttural, I barely understood his words.

Kael took a step forward, his hands out to show them he wasn't a threat. "We have some questions concerning a powerful artifact and would like to speak to Xavier."

Xavier? Who was that?

For a moment, the pair of creatures—fae of some sort, I was guessing—merely stared at us with their big, pale eyes.

"Follow us." This one seemed to be a female, judging by her slightly higher voice. "And just know, if you try to harm us, there are more of us in the tunnels. We have been watching you."

We were led down the narrow path, the walls seeming to close in on us even more as we went. Kael was hunching his shoulders and ducking his head in front of me. The tunnel made several turns, and I hoped we wouldn't get lost on our way back out. Finally, we stopped in front of a door.

There was a symbol on the front, though I couldn't make any sense of the twisting pattern. One of our escorts slid a hand along a curve of the symbol and the circular doorway rolled to the side. They gestured us through, and when we stepped into the room beyond, my jaw dropped.

To call this a room was a vast understatement. It was *huge*. The walls curved upward into a domed ceiling that had to be several stories high, and the place stretched to the size of a football field. Monuments, columns, and alcoves broke up the space, and everywhere I looked, there were artifacts, treasures of gold, jewels, and statues.

This was no mere cult hideout. This place was a temple.

How had this place never been discovered?

A crowd started to emerge from the shadows clinging between the artifacts. There were witches, fae, and people that seemed human who I assumed were shifters. They all stared at Kael and myself with open suspicion and contempt. Their angry muttering quieted when a man walked from an open doorway in front of us.

The man was dressed in a sharp, dark blue suit that didn't appear as if it belonged in the underground place. His skin was pale and missing the subtle glow all living beings held. As soon as his bright, crimson gaze landed on me, I knew what sort of being drew near.

Vampire.

I had a sudden urge to flip the collar of my jacket up and hide my neck.

"Well, well, who do we have here?" The vampire's voice was soft as silk as he eyed us.

"I am Agent Rivera, with the Paranormal Intelligence and Tracking Organization. This is my partner, Agent Perez," Kael said.

I hadn't been aware he was going to make me out to be an agent, as well, and the unexpected title threw me. Luckily, I was able to hide my surprise with little more than a couple of blinks.

The vampire let out a long, exaggerated sigh. "Another inspection? And here I thought we weren't due for one for another six months, at least."

"We aren't here for an inspection. We have questions to ask on a matter unrelated to your…inventory."

"Really?" The vampire tapped a finger on his chin, then smiled. "My name is Xavier." He held out his hand to me.

His eyes had swept to me and were lingering so long, I felt it rude not to step forward to take his hand. Kael's gaze was latched onto me as I closed the distance with the vampire.

Xavier took my hand. "A pleasure," he purred. He laid a kiss on my knuckles. His lips were ice against my skin, and I fought the urge to shudder.

"Nice to meet you." I paused for a moment, still in shock at attempting to have a cordial conversation with a vampire. I gestured around me. "This is fascinating. How long has it been here?"

Xavier, obviously pleased about my interest, smiled widely. "This temple has been guarded by my ancestors long before the French set foot on the soil above."

"Really?" My curiosity was piqued. "Before the sixteen-hundreds?"

"Quite a while before."

My love of history, especially unknown history, had questions bubbling out of my mouth. "Who were your ancestors? Were they indigenous to this continent? Has this always been a temple or——"

Kael put a hand over my mouth. "We don't have time for a history lesson." He glared at me, and I scowled behind his palm. I knew we were on an urgent mission, but how could he not want to know more about this place? Some of the artifacts I'd spotted had to be centuries old. "We're looking for a key."

Xavier folded his hands in front of him. He had long fingers, and I couldn't help but notice his fingernails were so sharp they were nearly claws. "A key? Like the keys around your pretty friend's neck?"

I lifted a hand to the front of my jacket, afraid the keys had slipped out somehow, but they were still tucked safely inside. "How did you know?"

"I have a way of sensing powerful artifacts." Xavier

cocked his head as he stared at my chest. "One of them is rather curious. It pulses like a living thing, feeding off something, and giving life and power in return." He studied my face with a scrutiny that made me uncomfortable.

"Do you know of the key we speak of or not?" Kael asked.

The vampire finally tore his stare from me and turned to my partner. "I do."

"Is it here?"

"No, it is not here. Why do you want it?"

Kael was going to lose his temper. I could sense the tension rolling through him, so I stepped in before he said something rash.

"Surely a man such as yourself has heard of the events unfolding above ground."

Xavier raised an eyebrow. "A man such as myself?"

I smiled. "Knowledgeable, savvy, and very observant." A little flattery never hurt. Unfortunately, it seemed to fall on deaf ears.

"Whatever is happening in the world holds no sway over us here," the vampire said. His gaze swept over the others, his followers, I was certain. They had pressed closer.

"You're wrong," I said. "Vehrin, the dark mage causing chaos and destruction, will poison everything, even the deepest parts of the earth if he wins. We need the key so we can stop him before it's too late."

Xavier took a step back and lifted his arms wide. "We are protected by our gods." A reverence tinted his voice which hadn't been there before.

I glanced around, eyeing the artifacts and treasures, recalling what Kael had said about these people worshipping objects.

When the vampire looked back at me, something had changed in his face. The cordial, politeness had given way to a sharper, more intense look that made him seem dangerous. When he spoke, I noticed a pair of sharp fangs.

"You are as nefarious as this Vehrin you speak of."

Kael edged closer to me, wariness flooding through him. "How so?" I asked.

Xavier pointed a long finger at me. "No one should wear such a gift around their necks. To do so is blasphemy."

There were murmurs of agreement in the crowd. When had they surrounded us?

"Just tell us the whereabouts of the key, and we'll be on our way," Kael said. His voice was measured, cautious. Were we in danger? "Please, we are running out of time."

The brightness in Xavier's eyes seemed to dim a bit. "I will give you the information you need in exchange for the keys around Agent Perez's neck."

I took a step back. I couldn't do that, especially with one tied to my soul. "No."

A manic haze crossed over the vampire's red stare. "The keys are not for you to possess, but to be worshipped by many."

Kael's hand gripped my arm as he drew me farther away from Xavier. "You cannot have them. If you don't tell us where the key is, all of this will be destroyed."

"You cannot destroy a god," Xavier said. "Just as you cannot possess one. Hand over the keys."

The crowd pressed closer, murmuring, chanting, speaking in languages I didn't understand. It made my skin prickle, and the thumping in my heart warned me of danger.

In my next breath, magic swirled around my hands.

The vampire recoiled. "She has stolen the power of the blessed artifacts," he yelled. He bared his teeth, sharp fangs glinting in the light. "You are no better than a hoarding gryphon." He whirled, throwing his arm out toward us. "Kill them, and save the relics!"

Kael cursed under his breath as dozens rushed forward to end us.

CHAPTER 9

THE FRENZIED CROWD closed in on us, and I pushed my hands forward. Tingling magic flowed from my fingertips, and I didn't give a damn if Xavier thought it was blasphemous or who I might harm in the process.

Why couldn't things just go smoothly for us for once? We were the good guys, and yet the world seemed so against us. I wasn't sure if it had something to do with the influence Vehrin had on the earth, or if we were just lucky that way.

Several members in the crowd had retreated with cries at my attack, but most still pressed on. I noticed a few women with their arms raised and a slight shimmering in the air which seemed to deflect my magic.

Witches. They were conjuring up some sort of shield.

"Above us," Kael growled beside me.

I lifted my gaze to find several winged fae had taken to the air and were descending on us. Howls and shrieks and angry yells bounced off the domed ceiling. There would be no reasoning with these fanatics, not when they thought I had *gods* hanging around my neck.

Kael punched someone in the face, and kicked a fox shifter away from him. Sharp claws grabbed my sleeve, and I turned to blast a green-skinned fae who had needle-like teeth. She rolled into the oncoming attackers, but they merely jumped over her and rushed forward.

There was no way we could keep up with this onslaught. We were going to be killed.

Darkness swirled and eddied inside of me, and the closer the attackers came, the more it purred for release. I didn't want to rely on the side of me which relished in shadows, but I had no choice. I drew it forward from where I kept it locked within me, and it was like pulling in a breath of fresh, cold air. The dark magic filled me, made me feel powerful and strong. I locked my gaze in front of me, where the majority of the crowd had gathered.

"Kael, get behind me." My voice was cold and hard. Surprisingly, Kael did as I said and moved behind my back.

I pulled in a deep breath, then released an enormous blast of energy. The relic worshippers flew backward, tumbling through the air like leaves on a blustery autumn day. I could almost taste their pain and fear as they hit the ground. Their agony was sweet, and their cries and groans were like a lullaby. I wanted to hum with their anguish and dance in their blood.

The dark power begged for more pain, more screams.

Then, there was a brush of warmth against my conscience. Kael. He still stood behind me, and a sense of caution and strength floated down our bond. I pulled in a deep breath, and shoved the dark power back to the recesses of my soul.

It had been the curse talking and wanting more agony. I couldn't give into it, not if I wanted to remain true to myself.

We had to get out of here. Xavier had moved several yards away, out of the danger zone, and was urging his uninjured followers to finish us off. I looked behind me to find the doorway we had entered through was blocked by angry cult members. My jaw cracked as I ground my teeth in frustration and glanced around. My eyes landed on a clay vase with splinters of gold running through it, and an idea came to me.

I grabbed Kael's arm and tugged him toward the artifacts. "This way. We'll hide behind the relics. They won't want to risk harming their gods."

"Good idea."

As we ran toward the columns, Kael put an arm on my shoulder as if ready to yank me out of harm's way at any moment.

We passed into the columns and put most of the treasures between us and the still recovering crowd. Xavier was shouting something, but I couldn't understand his words over the pounding of blood in my ears. A swift glance over my shoulder showed a group of the vampire's uninjured followers were hot on our trail.

There was no doubt in my mind if we were caught, Xavier would kill us, or worse. I had absolutely no desire to become a vampire, or someone's dinner.

Our feet pounded on the age-smoothed stone and sent strange echoes bouncing amongst the treasures and relics. I couldn't help but flick quick glances over them as we ran, and a part of me wished I had time to study them.

The angry mob behind us was drawing nearer. I shrieked as a blast of energy from a witch smashed into the stone wall to our right. We ducked and stumbled. The pair of us recovered quickly, but we'd lost some ground.

The way curved up ahead, and we followed the turn. How much longer would we be able to outrun them? This place was a maze. A group could have popped out in front of us at any second. Perspiration rolled between my shoulder blades. I could make out their voices, their footsteps growing closer.

Suddenly, Kael yanked me into a dark alcove. My back hit hard stone as he pressed against me, shoving us as far into the shadowed space as he could manage.

It was a horrible time to dwell on such things, but I

couldn't help but notice the way Kael was pushed against my body. His chest rose and fell in quick breaths that tangled with mine. This close, I could smell his scent of citrus and rain, tinged with sweat. I lifted my gaze to his, and he held my stare. Our breaths stilled as a group ran past.

A gasp flew up my throat as I tilted back and the pair of us fell. My backside hit the ground hard, and Kael barely caught himself from squishing me. The wall we'd been leaning against swung closed.

I climbed to my feet, tailbone throbbing painfully. The room was shaped like an octagon. Each wall had a small alcove which held torches, the flames sending flickering light around the space. The stone on the floor was polished to gleaming, and in the center was a dais, the sides covered in bronze-colored pebbles.

My eyes grew round at the object resting atop the dais. "Is that what I think it is?" Kael didn't answer, and I stepped closer to what was undoubtedly a unicorn skull. I'd seen horse skulls before. History had been paved with battles and workloads atop the backs of horses, so finding their remains on digs was common. This skull, however, had a spiraling horn protruding from the center of the forehead. The entire skull was a mesmerizing cacophony of gold, silver, and bronze, instead of the yellow of aged bone.

"Seriously?" I said. "Is there anything in this world that doesn't exist?"

I paused as footsteps pounded on the other side of the wall, then walked closer to the skull with Kael at my side. The hushed atmosphere of this place told me it was held in high reverence. This could be their most prized possession, or most worshipped god, in Xavier's case. We came to a stop beside the dais.

"I've heard of the existence of unicorns," Kael said. "I've never seen one, though." He reached toward the skull.

An uneasy feeling twisted in my gut. "Kael, don't touch it."

His fingertips brushed the horn as soon as the words left my mouth, and the floor gave way beneath us.

We hit a slanted floor and slid downward. The stone was rough, scraping at my arms and legs as we tumbled and rolled. Finally, we hit level ground.

"I told you not to touch it." I groaned. That was the second time I'd fallen in the span of about ten minutes. What was with this place?

"Oh, so you're allowed to be curious, but I'm not?" Kael climbed to his feet and reached down to help me up.

I adjusted my bag and brushed off my pants. "Let's leave the risk-filled curiosity to the professionals, shall we?"

Kael smiled, and I could tell by the twisting of his lips he was about to say something smart, but I held up a finger.

"What is that?" I asked. I tilted my head. There was an odd rushing noise.

My partner's eyebrows drew together. "It sounds like—"

Along the walls of the small room, stones crumbled, and bursts of water poured outward, filling the space at our feet.

Kael's head whipped back and forth as water hit the top of my boots and started soaking my socks.

"There!" he said. He pointed to an opening on the far side of the room.

We hurried through the doorway and into a long stretch of tunnel. As the water rose, my heart sank. This was a trap, and I could only hope we made it to the other side before the water got too high. It would have been easier if we had a straight shot, but our path was broken up by large sections of stone jutting out here and there, forcing us to duck under and climb over objects.

My body trembled as the cold water reached my knees. A large section of stone rose up before us, too high to climb.

"We have to try going under," I said.

Kael nodded, and I pulled in a deep breath before diving under the water. My hands quickly found an opening. I kicked my legs and was soon on the other side. Kael burst out of the water beside me and urged me on. My muscles burned as we rushed through the water toward the end of the tunnel. The water was at my waist, making it difficult to hurry and wearing me out.

Then, we reached a wall.

Kael dove under the water, no doubt trying to see if this was merely another object. The current had stopped, but the water still rose around me. He resurfaced, and I quickly read the look on his face.

"It's a dead end," I said. My voice shook with cold and fear. I looked around us, frantic. We had nowhere to go. We were trapped, and the water was rising higher. I turned my wide gaze to the man beside me. "Kael, we're going to die."

The water sloshed as he pulled me close. He didn't deny my statement, and he didn't make a promise that we'd make it out alive. He grabbed my face, his palms impossibly warm as they pressed against my cheeks.

"It's all right." His voice was soft, not holding the tone of someone with one foot in the grave. "I'm here, okay?"

I bit my lip and nodded. I didn't look down as the water reached my chest. Instead, I lifted my arms out of the water and wrapped them around Kael, holding his gaze.

It was in that moment, with death breathing down our necks and the water rising around us, I realized I really and truly loved Kael. I had been fighting something that, deep down, I had already accepted.

A soft smile touched Kael's lips, as if he knew my thoughts, and then he kissed me. It wasn't a hot and passionate kiss, but sweet and unhurried. I savored the feel and taste of him, wanting to cling to it as long as I could, which, I realized, would only be a couple more minutes.

I pulled back with a cry. "I'm not ready to go. I haven't had enough of you yet."

Kael swallowed, then nodded. His hand cupped the back of my neck, and he searched the space again. There was nothing but dark stone. Then, he paused and squinted. His gaze swept back to me.

"Do you trust me?" he asked.

"I mean, I didn't always...."

His fingers drifted across my cheek. "Wait here."

He disappeared under the water. I waited for one second, two, three. My heart raced as the flood rose over my shoulders. Water hit my face as Kael swam up out of the water and slammed his shoulder into the rock wall on my right. I caught the unmistakable sound of scraping stone.

There was a weak spot in the wall.

Kael ducked under the water again, swimming down, then back up to give himself momentum. He hit the stone again, and I could have sworn a wisp of fresh air brushed my cheek.

I turned toward the wall, intent on using my magic to blast through, but when I tried to summon it, my vision blurred. I had no energy. I'd used too much power earlier.

I tilted my face back as the water reached my chin. "Kael, hurry."

I took a deep breath, and cold water passed my mouth. Then, I closed my eyes. We were completely under. Kael's efforts continued, and after some time, my lungs began to burn. Small bubbles burst past my lips as I began to lose my battle with the water. I couldn't hold my breath much longer, and I was certain the same could be said of Kael.

The water abruptly shoved at me, and I was caught in the current. My body tumbled and rolled, then the water fell away. Kael was coughing somewhere near me, and I drew in my own ragged breaths. Mud squelched under me as I sat up.

It all happened so fast, it took me a moment to process that he'd broken through the wall. In front of me, water continued to pour from an opening in a small hill a few yards away. I glanced around to find nothing but grass and some trees. Judging by a slight glow in the darkness a distance away, we were somewhere outside the city.

Kael crawled over and rolled to his back beside me. He fumbled around until he found my hand, then held it, giving it a good squeeze.

"You…okay?" he asked, still breathless.

"Yeah." I reached over and patted him. "Good job, shoulders."

We laid there for several minutes, catching our breath and coming to terms with the fact we were somehow still alive. Thank goodness for Kael's keen sight, or he would have never spotted the weakness in the wall.

"Those people are psychopaths," I finally said. "That was completely useless. We didn't learn anything."

Kael rose up on his elbows and shifted to face me. "Actually, Xavier gave me an idea. Remember how he said you were as bad as a gryphon with your relic hoarding?"

"Yeah," I said slowly.

After a moment of hesitation, Kael said, "I happen to know a gryphon here in the States. It's a long shot, and more likely to fail than this fiasco was, but it's the only option we have left."

I turned to look at the sky. There were no stars, only an endless dark that somehow seemed more intense than the night sky should have been. The air held a sense of wrongness, heavy with malice and foreboding.

"All right," I said. "Let's go find this gryphon."

I tried to sound optimistic, but there was a sinking feeling in my gut. All this time spent chasing leads was only going to give Vehrin a bigger hold on his mission to destroy the earth.

We weren't any closer to finding a way to defeat the dark mage, and time was slipping through our fingers.

CHAPTER 10

I YAWNED into my fist as Kael pulled the Toyota Corolla away from the small motel with the cheesy cactus-shaped sign.

We had walked our soggy selves back to the bed and breakfast after surviving a fight with a crazed cult and nearly drowning. We'd had our things packed up within a half hour and boarded the first flight to Dallas.

Kael's acquaintance, the gryphon, lived about two-hundred miles west of the city. We rented a car, but had only made it halfway before we were both too exhausted to go any farther. Luckily, the Grinning Cactus Motel had been right off the highway.

I pulled my gaze from the overly happy cactus sign and onto the stretch of road in front of us. "So, how do you know this gryphon? He doesn't work for PITO does he?" I certainly wouldn't feel safe if that were the case, given Kael's own friend had turned on us.

"No, she doesn't work for the organization." Kael cleared his throat, his stare glued to the highway stretching out into the Texas desert. "I know her personally. Well, not so much anymore, but…" His words drifted.

"Oh," I said. I cut him a sideways glance. Why was he

being so weird? Then it clicked. "*Oh.* So, this gryphon woman is an ex?"

Kael glanced at me. "How did you know?"

I gestured at him. "Open book."

He muttered something, then sighed. "Listen, Livvie. We have a bit of a troubled past. Me and her, I mean."

"Well, technically we have a troubled past, too." I gave him a grin. He smiled, but it was slight. "Sorry. Go on."

"I'm not sure if she will talk to me, let alone help us out. This may be a wasted trip."

I mulled over his words as I grabbed my to go cup of coffee from the cupholder and took a sip. "Why wouldn't she talk to you?"

Kael gave me a cautious look as his fingers drummed the steering wheel.

I fought the urge to roll my eyes. "You're allowed to have exes, Kael."

Still, a petty slice of me hoped she looked like the frumpy bear shifter who worked the front desk at PITO.

"Things didn't end well with us. She wanted me to move in with her here in Texas, but I wasn't willing to give up my position and responsibilities with PITO. She didn't take it well when I left." He winced, as if at some memory, and I wondered if she perhaps had hit him with something.

"How long has it been?"

Kael rubbed the back of his neck. "Four years?" He looked to me. "Do you think she's over it by now?"

I shrugged. "It depends on how badly you broke her heart." He went quiet. I tugged at a loose thread on the hem of my T-shirt. "Did you love her?"

"I'm mated to you, aren't I?"

I lifted my eyes to Kael. His intense gaze held so many words and meanings, I was certain I'd be swept away under the current crashing into me. What had he meant? Was he saying he loved me?

I turned and peered out the window to hide my delighted smile. The thought of being mated was still unnerving, and I wasn't certain yet what exactly I was going to do about it, but his unspoken profession had my heart thrumming. I swear I could feel Kael smile through the bond.

Kael, ever in the habit of driving like a maniac, got us to our destination in record time. We turned from the main highway, and after twenty minutes, my partner steered us onto a small, unmarked road I would never have noticed. The land rose and fell slightly, with scarce trees, but it was enough to hide any sign of civilization.

The gritty dirt road crunched under the tires as Kael slowed to a stop in front of a wide gate with a high fence stretching out of sight on either side. On the front of the gate was a large yellow sign with black letters that read 'No trespassing. Violators will be dismembered.'

I raised an eyebrow at Kael. "Seriously?"

"I wouldn't put it past her," he grumbled, mostly to himself, as he climbed out of the car.

The gate was held shut with a thick chain and a heavy padlock. Kael was strong, but there was no way he was going to be able to break through. Maybe we could crash the car through it?

Kael bent down and started upending rocks near the post the chain was wrapped around. Then he picked something up from the ground and grabbed the lock. The chain fell from the post with a clang.

Kael returned to the car with a self-satisfied grin. "Four years, and she never moved her hidden key."

"Maybe she wanted you to return so she could dismember you," I said.

He chuckled, but I wondered if I was perhaps guessing correctly.

We drove through the gateway, and I watched out the window, waiting for a scorned gryphon to come swooping in to tear Kael, and myself, apart. There was nothing but scraggly vegetation and the winding road. Finally, a building rose up. It was steel and long, with curved sides so it was a half-cylindrical shape.

An aircraft hangar.

Beside the building was a small house, rather plain, with dingy siding that used to be white but time and the elements had aged to a dirty yellow. There were no vehicles parked nearby. Maybe she only flew planes? By the looks of everything, paired with the sign on the gate, she wanted to be unbothered and unnoticed. It didn't bode well for us.

Kael parked the car and I went with him to the front door. I stood behind him as he knocked, then we waited. Finally, the door opened to reveal a woman.

Her eyes locked on Kael, and I hardly saw anything of her before she said, "Oh, hell no."

Her statement was promptly accompanied by the slamming front door.

I turned to Kael and patted his arm. "I don't think she's over it."

Kael growled and banged on the door again. "This is important. Open up." He waited a beat, then added, "Please."

The front door slowly opened, and the woman leaned against the doorframe. Her gaze ran up and down his body. I didn't think it was so much an appraisal as much as she couldn't quite trust her eyes that he was on her doorstep.

"It's been a while. What do you want?"

"We've had a long drive. Can we come inside?"

At the mention of "we", the woman shifted her gaze to me. My small hope she might look like a troll evaporated under her coal-black stare. The woman was beautiful, with long dark hair, lightly tanned skin, and the body of a runway model. She pursed her full lips as we waited.

"Fine," she said. "Come on."

We followed her inside, and I took a moment to study her

home. It was small, but comfortable and not nearly so derelict as it appeared on the outside. She had papers, mostly maps and charts, scattered on surfaces. Forgotten cups had been left here and there, along with various books. Admittedly, it looked like the sort of place I could make myself at home in. Maybe Kael's ex was someone I could get along with, despite their history together.

She led us into a kitchen with sky-blue cabinets and white curtains, then gestured for us to sit at the round table in the corner. We sat while she busied herself at the counter.

"I just made a pot of coffee." She glanced over her shoulder at me. "Hope you like it black. I don't have anything fancy to put into it."

"Black is perfect, thank you." I gave Kael a questioning look. Did I seem like someone who liked fancy coffee?

I studied her as she tipped the coffee pot. She certainly didn't seem into the finer things in life with her cargo pants and plain blue shirt, but she pulled off the casual clothes with a finesse most women couldn't hope to accomplish. Even her hair, with a slight wave at the nape of her neck that told me she pulled it into a ponytail often, was perfect.

"Here you go." She set a cup in front of me, slid one to Kael, then joined us at the table with a steaming cup of her own.

Kael glanced down at his mug. It was bright pink. "You didn't poison this, did you?"

The gryphon shifter gave him a mirthless smile. "Don't be silly, Kael. If I was going to kill you, I would have done it before you stepped through the door." She swept her attention from Kael to me, then frowned. "I'm sorry. I'm being rude. I'm Ziba."

I took her outstretched hand. "I'm Olivia."

She smiled as she sat back, and this time, it seemed to have lost a bit of frostiness. Maybe she was just shocked to see Kael after so long. "Nice to meet you. How do you know Kael?"

"We work together."

"At PITO?" she asked.

I hesitated. "Not exactly."

Ziba tilted her head as she studied me, dark hair spilling over her shoulder. "What do you mean?"

"That's part of why we're here," Kael said.

Before he could explain further, Ziba narrowed her eyes and leaned closer to me. Her gaze suddenly flashed as she looked between Kael and me.

"You're not working together." She stared at me, and any bit of warmth I thought she had given me was snatched back. "You're his mate." Ziba straightened, and her eyes went a little wide as she studied Kael. "You mated with her?"

"I did," he said. "But that isn't the point."

The woman turned back to me. "What kind of shifter are you? You don't have the eyes of a jaguar."

"I'm not a shifter," I said. "I'm a...mage, of sorts."

The glare Ziba pinned on Kael could have frozen a lake. "You're mated to a glorified witch? What did she do, cast a spell on you?"

I was stunned into silence. Whatever had gone on between these two in the past, it must have been ugly for her to be so insulting.

Where Ziba's words had been cold, Kael's were granite. "Don't talk about Olivia like that."

The gryphon relented and gave a little laugh. "I'm just surprised. You had always been so against anyone who wasn't a shifter, especially magic-wielders."

Ziba was trying to get a rise out of me. Fine. I could play. "Oh, I know. He was completely stubborn and prejudiced when we first met."

"And now?" Ziba took a sip of her coffee.

I didn't take my eyes off her as I reached over to squeeze Kael's forearm. "I'm here with him, aren't I?" Satisfaction warmed me as I noticed her fingers clench her cup a bit harder. It wasn't until I caught the slight flicker of loss in her eyes that I came to my senses. I should know better than to claw at old wounds. I pulled my hand from Kael and back to my own space. "Look, I don't know what happened between you two in the past, but I'm sorry if it makes this meeting difficult. We came to ask a favor of you, if you would be so kind as to help us."

Ziba looked to Kael. "Is that so?"

Kael gave a short nod. His eyes darted between Ziba and myself as if he were worried we were about to start scratching at each other across the table. "We are out to bring down Vehrin, a dark mage bent on wreaking havoc on the world."

"I thought you were all chummy with mages now."

"I know you've seen what is going on, Ziba. His power is staining everything."

Ziba's finger tapped a few times on the porcelain of her cup. "Business has been slow lately. The weather patterns have been too unpredictable. Blizzards in the southeast, hurricanes off the coast of the northwest, even flooding. Is that because of him?"

"Yes, it is. We're out to stop him." Kael gestured between us.

"Why you two?" Ziba asked.

I set down my coffee. "Because we're the only ones who can. Because we've been tied together since the beginning."

Ziba lifted her chin, clearly not at all cool with the destined lovers' vibe I was giving her about Kael and myself. "And what does that mean?"

Kael gave me a nod. I told Ziba most of our story, how I was the reincarnation of an ancient sorceress, and Kael was my guard and lover in the past. I told her of Vehrin, and the keys we'd fought to find. I kept the explanation brief, and left out the part where I was as cursed as Vehrin, and I didn't mention the fact my soul was bound to one of the keys.

"We need the fourth key to bring him down," Kael said

when I was finished. "We came here hoping you would have some kind of knowledge of its existence."

Ziba had been silent through my story. Now, a ghost of a smile touched her lips. "Yes. I know exactly what you're talking about."

My heart thumped. "You do?"

She flipped her perfect hair back over her shoulder and grinned. "I'm descended from those who are entrusted to protect it. I could take you right to the relic."

"You can?"

Her smile deepened. "Yes, of course. For a price."

CHAPTER 11

I FOUGHT a glare under Ziba's secretive smile and wondered what she could possibly want from me. She wouldn't ask for me to break the mating bond with Kael, would she? Could I do it, if it meant having the chance to save the world?

"What price?" My tone was sharp as I already prepared for something I would be unwilling to pay.

The gryphon shifter scooted away from the table and set her coffee cup on the counter. "According to your story, you're an accomplished archaeologist. I have something I wish for you to translate for me. It's a scroll. Do this, and I will give you the information you need."

I fell silent for a moment. That was all she wanted? I really needed to quit jumping to the worst conclusions. "Sure," I said. "I'd be happy to help."

Kael held up a hand and pinned Ziba with a hard stare. "Hang on. What kind of scroll is this? Where did you get it?"

He had a point. What if it was cursed? I couldn't handle anymore bad luck on my end.

Ziba crossed her arms over her chest. "Not that it's any of your business, but it has been passed down in my family for years. Most of my brethren collect treasures of gold and ivory.

I enjoy these things, as well, but I also covet knowledge. The scroll never interested my family, but I would like to know what it says."

I scooted my chair back and got to my feet. "I can't say for certain I'll be able to translate it for you, but I'll certainly give it a try."

"Let's hope you can, or you will get no information from me. The whereabouts of the key is something my brethren are trusted with, and I will not part with the information lightly." Ziba's gaze flicked to Kael. "Not even to old friends."

Ziba left the kitchen and gestured for us to follow her down a short hallway. Kael let out a groan as she reached a door at the end.

"You have it in there? Do you even know where it is?"

I wasn't sure what he was talking about until Ziba stepped into the room. My eyes grew wide. It was as if I had stepped into one of those hoarding shows, with a museum flair. There were boxes everywhere, most labeled in messy scrawls with words like "Scandinavia platter," "Italian pottery," and one very disturbing box that read "blood skulls."

Although morbidly fascinated by that one, I thought it best not to ask. Aside from the boxes were shelves on one wall overflowing with books, maps, and loose bits of paper. Ziba crossed the cluttered room to one of the shelves. She moved aside a stack of old encyclopedias and pulled down a narrow, wooden box.

There was a small desk crammed in a corner with an office chair that had definitely seen better days. Ziba pushed aside notebooks, stray pencils, and what looked to be some sort of old woodwind instrument, then set the box down. She tilted the lid back to reveal a scroll with tasseled ends nestled inside.

"You can sit here." Ziba pulled out the desk chair. "We'll leave and let you have some privacy."

Kael seemed hesitant, though whether it was to leave me alone or to have to spend time with his ex, I was unsure.

I gave him a nod and smile. "I'll be fine. See you in a bit."

Ziba shoved at Kael. "Come on. We have catching up to do, anyway. It's been too long since we sat together and talked."

There was a forced lightness in her tone which told me she was trying to seem more at ease with the current situation than she felt.

A sense of irritation flared down our bond from Kael. The door shut behind the pair, and I couldn't help but be annoyed, as well. I took a deep breath and told myself to be patient with Ziba. The woman had lost Kael. I could understand her being caught off guard by us showing up. How would I feel if Kael left me?

I shook the thought from my mind and dropped into the office chair. It creaked in protest, and I grabbed the edge of the desk as the old chair listed backward a few inches. Once I was certain it wouldn't dump me on the floor, I turned my attention to the scroll.

I picked it up with light fingers and slowly unrolled it. Bits of dirt fell from the thin parchment, as if it had just been pulled from the earth it had once hidden beneath. Judging by the browned and brittle paper, the scroll was very old. My eyebrows rose as I flattened it out on the surface of the desk.

The scroll was written in something similar to Old Persian cuneiform, but the symbols, which were supposed to be read left to right, didn't make sense, somehow. It was almost as if they were backward, but when I tried to decipher it from right to left, that wasn't correct, either. The angles of the characters themselves also didn't quite seem right.

"I wish Sarah were here," I muttered. She had always been the expert on deciphering ancient languages.

A sour knot formed in my stomach. She could have helped me, if Vehrin hadn't killed her to get that box disguised as a disc. I rubbed my temples and stared at the paper. Somehow, I had to translate the scroll. If I didn't, we wouldn't get the information we needed to defeat the dark mage.

I stared at the symbols, and my heart jumped. They suddenly shimmered, the angles and curves of the text shifting into runes I recognized. It was the ancient language I conversed in long ago.

I grabbed a notebook and pencil and wrote as fast as I could. I only managed to catch a brief glimpse before they changed back into the Persian-like cuneiform. Still, what I had written down was enough for me to use to decipher the rest into at least a close interpretation.

I wasn't certain how long I sat in Ziba's storeroom of treasures, but by the time I put the pencil down, my eyes were burning and my back was sore from bending over the desk. The paper I had written on had sentences quickly scrawled, scratched through, and arrows showing exchanges of words or phrases. It had been difficult and left my mind numb, but I was fairly certain it was as accurate as it was going to get.

Carefully, I rolled up the scroll and nestled it back inside the box. It was strange I was able to interpret it when it belonged to Ziba, yet she had been unable to decipher the relic. Was it simply because my ancient self had a better knack for languages, or was it some sort of magic-fueled destiny?

I tore the paper I'd written on out of the notebook and made my way around the stacks of boxes toward the door. As I walked down the hallway, Ziba's angry voice reached me.

"…left without saying anything, and then you just show up out of nowhere, with a mate no less? How do you expect me to react?"

A pang of guilt hit me. If Kael had told me about his history with Ziba, perhaps we could have handled things differently.

"I told you I was leaving, Ziba. My loyalty to PITO was not something I was willing to just toss away."

I paused in the hall. Letting my presence be known would be the proper thing to do, but a part of me was curious. And the saying went curiosity killed the cat. Not the archeologist.

There was a sharp sigh and the staccato beat of fingernails tapping against the table. After a moment, Ziba spoke again. "You had been unwilling to leave PITO to travel the world with me, yet you seem content to do so with this witch."

"Olivia is not a witch," Kael growled.

"Semantics."

Anger rippled through our mating bond. "Do not speak about my mate in such a way. We would never have worked out. You know this. You were too free-spirited, too careless. One of us had to keep our feet on the ground now and then. And to answer your question, yes, I am willing to leave PITO for Olivia. It goes back farther than you know, before us even, in ways I cannot begin to explain. If I have hurt you in the past, then I apologize. I never meant to hurt you, but I do not regret any decision I made that brought me to my destiny. To her."

The entire house fell silent. My rapid heartbeat was the only sound I heard. *His destiny?* I leaned against the wall before my legs gave way, and I fell to the floor in a puddle of romance-induced mush.

My god.

I had admitted to myself in that flooded tunnel in New Orleans how much I loved Kael. I knew he cared for me deeply, as well. We had always been tied together in some way, even if we hadn't known it at the time. A part of me feared he would resent that he never really had a choice in the matter, but the way he had just spoken to Ziba, as if our destined relationship were a dream realized instead of a duty to uphold, cast away any remaining doubt and cemented together all of the hope and love and faith I had in him.

Kael was my mate.

A tingling warmth flowed through me, dancing along my

veins to settle in my heart. I could practically feel Kael settling into my skin, his soul binding to mine more tightly than it already had been.

My mate.

"What are you grinning at?"

Ziba's sharp voice snapped me out of it. I pulled in a deep breath to gather myself, then stepped into the kitchen.

My gaze swept to Kael to find a wide grin on his face. He looked like he wanted to rush over and crush me in a hug. Thankfully, he stayed put. It was difficult enough for me to refrain from running over and attacking him, myself.

I forced myself to look at Ziba. Whatever anger she'd had was masked under cool indifference. I held up the paper.

"I translated the scroll."

A spark of interest lit her dark eyes. "Oh?"

I laid the paper on the table, and Ziba and Kael bent over to peer at it. "It's a rough translation. The script was so ancient, I'm afraid I failed to capture the nuances and poetry of the language correctly, but it's close enough, I think." I ran my finger along the paper. "It says the bearer of the scroll—which is you, Ziba—will have a part to play in saving the world from the cursed ones, that life must become death, so death may become life."

Ziba picked up the paper and stared at it for a moment longer. Then, she folded it up and stuck it in her pocket. "Thank you, Olivia." Her gaze flitted to Kael and back to me. "I'm sorry for my behavior since your arrival. I was just…a bit shocked. I'll gladly take you to the key, myself."

I smiled. "You will?"

"Yes. You have helped me a great deal by translating the scroll. It's only fair I uphold my end of the bargain. We can leave first thing in the morning."

Kael braced his hands on the table to fix her with a glare. "And where exactly are you going to be taking us?"

"To the birthplace of my kind, where we guard the lost treasures of this world."

A grimace creased Kael's face.

"What?" I asked. "Where is that?"

Kael shifted to face me. "Gryphons were born in ancient Persia. What is now modern-day——"

"Iran," I finished for him. I turned to Ziba. "You want us to just go to Iran? It's impossible. We won't be allowed past the border."

Iran was a war-torn country. There was no way we would be allowed in, not by Americans or Iranians or any other government who had a foothold there.

Ziba's lips lifted in a smirk. "Clearly, you've never flown with a gryphon before."

Kael let out a groan that didn't bode well. We were leaving the U.S. in the morning to go after the fourth key, held in one of the most mysterious, yet volatile regions of the middle east.

It was a dangerous mission, but I couldn't help but think what damage Vehrin could cause if he made it there before we did.

"Alright," I said. "What's the plan?"

CHAPTER 12

THE BACK DOOR shut with a sharp snap. I winced under the early morning sky and wished I had more time to douse my exhaustion in caffeine. I'd only gotten through one cup when Ziba had informed Kael and me it was time to leave.

As Ziba's long, dark hair swayed over the back of her T-shirt, my stomach swayed with unease. The day before, she'd said I'd clearly never flown with a gryphon. How exactly did one fly with a gryphon? What we were we going to do, sit on her?

Gravel crunched under our feet, and the large, metal hangar loomed above us. To my extreme relief, a small cargo plane was parked in front of it. It was an older model, likely World War two era, with a twin engine and a round nose that had three large scratch marks painted underneath the words *Sky Cat*.

"We're taking the *Cat*?" Kael asked.

"Yep." Ziba patted the olive-colored plane and looked to me. "Had this baby for ten years. C-60 Lodestar. Bought the old girl off a man who was taking her to the junk heap."

I eyed the plane. "Did it belong there?" The last thing I

wanted was a ride in a shady piece of machinery thousands of feet in the air.

Ziba grinned. "Not anymore. Fixed her right up."

The plane had to be close to fifty feet in length, with a wingspan close to sixty. I glanced around, half-expecting some hidden crew members to come from the shadows of the hangar.

"You're not flying this by yourself, are you?" It definitely seemed too big a plane to fly alone.

"Of course, I am."

I swept a dubious gaze to Kael, who shrugged.

"Ziba has always had a way with aircraft. She can fly anything, knows how to fiddle with engines and other mechanics to make them fly faster and longer, and capable of being flown solo. She'd make a fortune if she ever put those skills to good use."

Our pilot shrugged. "What's the fun in that?"

I tilted my head. "So, if I were to drop a hot air balloon in front of you, could you fly it?"

Ziba waved a hand. "I prefer something faster." She walked toward the tail of the plane and opened a door. "All aboard."

She waited for Kael and me to climb in, then shut it behind us. She walked up the middle toward the cockpit. On each side of us were wooden crates held close to the body of the plane with thick netting. I shuffled closer to them and saw the names of various vineyards labeled across the crates.

The gryphon shifter noticed me studying the cargo. "It's ironic. I'd been getting ready to head to the middle east, anyway. Some sheikh hiding out in Iran has a penchant for American wine."

Was it just some fortunate coincidence this woman, someone Kael knew, had been heading right to the location we needed to be? Or could it be everything in our lives was predetermined, like the way Kael and I had already been twisted together? The mystery didn't do anything to lessen the dull headache pounding at my temples.

Kael grabbed my elbow and twisted me to face him. "Livvie, you okay?"

"Yeah. I just didn't sleep well last night." I flicked my gaze over his shoulder as Ziba headed to the cockpit and lowered my voice. "I kept having these dreams, but whenever I woke up, I couldn't remember any of them. I just had this sense of dread hanging over me."

Kael's calloused fingers scratched the edge of my jaw as he cradled my face. "One day this will all be over. No more running after dark mages or cursed keys."

I smiled. "Sounds delightfully dull."

"I think we could both use some delightfully dull in our life."

Our life. The way he said those two words, as if our future was already in front of us, safe and set in stone, had me leaning up on my toes and pressing a kiss to his warm lips. I would have stayed there longer, with his warm mouth on mine as I edged closer to him, but Ziba's voice called out from the cockpit.

"Sit down and strap in."

Kael shifted me over to a long, narrow bench built into the wall opposite of much of the cargo, where we settled down and strapped in. The engines murmured, then groaned to life. I leaned back into the vibrating steel of the body. I glanced over at Kael, and he gave me a wink that promised more kissing later. I smiled.

The ground dropped beneath us as we tilted upward and into the sky. I leaned my shoulder against Kael.

"Do you know how long it will take to get there?"

"Ziba said less than a day, if the winds stay down."

It didn't seem right, given the distance and size of the plane. "Won't we need to stop somewhere to refuel?"

Kael jabbed his thumb toward the gryphon. I could only

see her shoulder through the narrow opening leading to the cockpit. "Ingenius aircraft engineer, remember?"

I tried to wrap my mind around how it would be mechanically possible to do such a thing, but my brain just wasn't built for technological sciences. Nor could I figure out how Ziba was going to get around air traffic control to fly right into Iran. But something told me Ziba wasn't about to offer up any information on how she planned to pull that off.

Eventually, the plane leveled out. I lay my head back and stared at a pheasant-shaped vineyard logo stamped on a crate across from me. The steady whir of the twin engines pulled at my eyelids.

The stone walls pressed in around me, and though I could hear the calls of birds and monkeys from the window to my left, I felt utterly alone. There was nothing in the room except for me...and the box.

It sat at my feet, seemingly innocuous with its pale wood and four plain locks, but at its heart was a corruption viler than anything this earth had seen. Shadows seeped from beneath the locked lid, tendrils wrapping around my ankles. They called to me, those swirls of darkness, and promised power and freedom. All I had to do was unlock the lid. I gripped the keys hanging around my neck so tightly they dug into my palm.

Freedom.

The world was like cool water to parched lips. How I longed for freedom. Freedom from the curse, freedom from this place, and freedom to be with him.

The curling shadows beckoned me, and inside the box, the dark power reached for me. I wanted to open the lid, to cure myself and be free. I had the keys. It would be so easy and would take a matter of seconds. Perhaps, if I only opened it for a moment...

There was a sudden presence at my back. I didn't need to turn to know he was there. He knelt behind me, wrapped his arms around my body, and drew me against his broad chest. I pulled in a steadying breath. He smelled like a bright morning after a thunderstorm, fresh and full of hope.

"No." His voice was quiet, but firm. "You do not need it."

My gaze fixed on the box. "It's the only way to break the curse." If only I hadn't stolen what wasn't mine...

"You know the cost of the cure."

Death. Destruction. The very world as we knew it would be destroyed.

The shadows were retreating, but I could still feel the dark promises they'd left on my skin. Healing. Power. Freedom.

I unclenched my hand from around the keys. I had come so close to giving in to temptation and opening the box. "I fear I will try."

"As long as I am here, you will never lose your way." His rich, soft voice caressed my ear before he pressed a kiss to my neck.

I smiled. "You may need to be near a lot more."

His arms tightened around me. "I will never leave your side again if you wish. Not three steps away, or two, or one." He hugged me, and I wanted to stay caged in his arms forever.

"Vehrin will grow suspicious, if he isn't already." I glanced at the box. "He has been acting strange lately. Distant. What if he knows about us?"

My relationship with my guardian was forbidden. Bloodlines had to remain pure, for shifters and sorcerers alike. It was the reason I'd been paired with Vehrin, though we had yet to make any final vows of bonding. The curses we drew upon us had put a hold on that fate. Still, if he knew, he might take matters into his own hands.

"I will fight for you, my love."

I twisted in his arms to find his golden gaze full of promise and conviction. "I know you would." It would be so easy to take his hand, walk down into the jungle, and run away with him. Then, I thought about the dark curse clinging to my bones. "Perhaps we should focus on one battle at a time."

I rose up and pressed my lips to his. The back of my neck prickled as if someone were watching. I broke our kiss and turned to peer toward the open doorway, but I saw no one. I drew away from him, picked up the box, and climbed to my feet.

"I need to hide the box. I'm making plans to conceal it, and the keys, but I need time to think."

"Meet me in our clearing later."

I watched as the man I truly loved bent to retrieve his golden-tipped spear. He gave me a grin before leaving the room to resume guard duty outside of my door.

I set the box down and peered out the window toward the darkening sky heavy with rain. A crack of thunder echoed through the room.

Thunder shook through me and rattled me awake. I blinked away the blurriness, and my gaze focused on Kael. His hands were tight on my shoulders and lines were etched in his brow. He stopped shaking me.

"We have a problem."

"A problem?"

Kael unbuckled me and pulled me to the cockpit.

How long had I been asleep? Below us, an endless sea of rocky hills and gray-brown mountains stretched in every direction. We'd already reached Iran.

Impossible.

I squinted at something strange, a wisp of smoke along the ground. "What's that?"

Kael barely managed to keep his feet as I slammed into him in the tilting aircraft.

"Damn it!" Ziba yelled.

It took me a heartbeat to realize we'd nearly been blasted apart with a missile.

Ziba peered over her shoulder at me. "You need to do something before we're shot out of the sky by some very angry military personnel."

I braced my hand on the ceiling above me and curled my fingers around a ridge of metal in an effort to keep steady. "I thought you were making a delivery?" The bottles of wine rattled slightly in their crates behind us.

"I am, but it isn't exactly legal."

The entire plane buzzed like an angry hornet as Ziba tilted the wings again.

"Can't you take her higher?" Kael asked.

Ziba scoffed. "Why? So if we get hit we have farther to fall?"

In the next moment, the entire aircraft shuddered. Vibrations rattled up my legs, and Kael cursed as he rocked back and hit his head. One of the engines made a sputtering noise.

Ziba's knuckles were white on the yoke as she tried to steady *Sky Cat*. "It's now or never!"

My heart hammered as I stared out the window to find no less than five missiles soaring straight toward us.

CHAPTER 13

Our lives were a heartbeat away from exploding into oblivion, and every fiber of my body reacted. Magic burned through me, and my pores tingled as energy bursting from them. Light shot outward in a display of last-ditch survival and punched through the sides of the *Sky Cat*'s steel body.

Wind whipped hair around my face. The sharp, blaring beeps of an alarm went off in the cockpit.

In front of us, my attack collided with the missiles. We were enveloped by bursts of smoke and shrapnel, the metal pieces punching into the plane. The *Cat* gave a sudden and hard jolt. My knees buckled from the impact, and I smacked onto the floor.

Ziba's arms shook as she fought to steady the plane. "We've been hit!"

I clenched my teeth. I'd missed one of the missiles.

One of the engines sputtered, and my stomach flipped as we suddenly dropped several feet. Ziba looked over her shoulder at us. "We're going down!"

Our group had missed one death only to skip right to another. We were going to crash.

Kael gripped me and hauled me up from the floor. The

plane keeled up, and he slammed into my chest. He caged me in his arms and looked to Ziba. "Can you get us out of here?"

I barely heard him over the wind bringing in thick smoke through the damaged plane. Ziba loosened her grip from the yoke and quickly unbuckled. She stared at Kael for a moment. The nose of the plane tipped down, and Kael braced a hand against the wall as he tightened his hold on me with his other arm.

"Ziba?" he asked.

Ziba brushed past us and rushed past the crates of wine to the cargo door. The plane gave another shake. Without a backward glance, she opened the door and jumped out.

My heart plummeted with the plane.

Ziba had abandoned us.

"She left us." My muttered words were drowned out by the dying sputters of the engines. I glanced up at Kael to see if he'd heard me, but he stared through the cockpit.

I followed his line of sight to see rock outcrops zooming closer. I twisted my fingers in Kael's shirt. My mind raced as I tried to come up with a way to save us.

The plane gave a sudden, sharp jolt, and my stomach flew to my throat. Kael lost his grip, and we both slid into the cockpit. I let out a loud cry as my body hit the edge of the pilot's seat. Kael smashed into me. The sound of clanking bottles and breaking glass was drowned out by a screeching cry.

Shredding metal on rock tore through the air, and the *Sky Cat* gave a final jerk.

Then, everything went still.

For several minutes, I lay listening to a hushed hiss of the plane's final breath. Smoke filled my nostrils and stung my eyes.

Somehow, I was alive.

I shifted. Kael's weight pinned me down.

"Kael?" I nudged at him, but he didn't move. Only the mating bond between us told me he was alive.

How exactly we were alive remained a mystery to me. No one would have survived a crash at that speed.

I glanced around. The body of the plane was bent and gnarled. The crates of wine had broken free of their netting. Kael and I were covered in glass, wine, and splintered wood.

I gave my mate another shake with my free arm that wasn't being crushed by his weight. He let out an indiscernible mumble, but remained still.

Sighing, I tried to string together the last, frenzied moments of the plane falling. How on earth had we managed to survive?

The plane...I could have sworn it had been slowing down in its fall.

Metal suddenly screeched above me. I glanced up to find something punching through the cockpit. Steel twisted and bits of glass rained down on me as the side of the cockpit was torn away by claws. My eyes grew wide when the rest of the creature came into view.

It was a massive gray and brown eagle. Its shining beak curved down into a sharp hook I was certain could tear into me with ease. The giant bird's bright yellow eyes focused on me, and as it grew closer, I yelled.

Kael jolted awake and jerked his face up toward the creature. No longer having his weight pinning me down, I inched away from the massive bird. He studied the creature for a moment, then turned to me with not an ounce of panic on his face.

"It's all right," he said. He gave my shoulder a squeeze. "It's just Ziba."

Ziba? In the aftermath of the crash, I hadn't even thought to wonder about her whereabouts. She had jumped out of the plane. She had abandoned us.

Or had she?

I turned from Kael to the creature, and the pieces clicked into place. Gryphon shifter. Not some monster here to tear into me.

Kael rose to his feet and helped me up. He jerked his head toward the opening Ziba had made. I reached up and grabbed hold carefully so I didn't cut myself on glass and sharp metal. Kael helped heave me up and out. After a moment, he followed, a blue bag slung over his shoulder.

After climbing down from the wrecked *Sky Cat*, I gawked openly at Ziba's gryphon form. I had thought she was beautiful before, but it was nothing compared to what stood before me at that moment.

Ziba had the head, chest, and front legs of a great eagle. The gray and brown flecked feathers melded perfectly into the nearly silver body of a sleek lion, and she folded a pair of wide wings against her flanks. She was huge, the size of a large horse, and I could see why she had jumped from the plane. If she had shifted inside, she wouldn't have been able to get out.

I suddenly recalled the screeching roar I'd heard as we fell. Ziba must have been the one to slow the plane. Guilt stabbed me for thinking she would have just abandoned us.

Ziba sat on her haunches, tail flicking with impatience as Kael climbed down and strode over to me.

"You okay?" he asked.

I nodded. "Feel a bit banged up, but nothing serious."

He had a few cuts on him, likely from the broken bottles of wine. He seemed to have gotten the worst of it.

I looked to Ziba. "Are you all right?"

Ziba's gryphon form nodded, and then she shifted. I should have been used to seeing shifters change back to their human forms, since I'd spent countless times in the gym at PITO, and it wasn't unusual for them to be naked from time to time, but seeing Ziba's sudden, and perfect, naked form was a bit jarring. She seemed perfectly comfortable as she closed the distance between us.

"I'm fine," she said. "Just glad I was able to slow the plane a bit."

Kael, to his credit, kept his gaze on the rough, stony ground as he held out the blue bag he'd taken from the plane. "Here," he said.

Ziba took the bag and pulled out a set of clothes. As she dressed, I glanced around to study our crash site. We were on the side of a mountain, the range itself stretching off on either side into more hills and cliffs. There didn't seem to be anything around except rock and gray skies.

"How far off course are we?" I asked Ziba as she tugged on a pair of hiking boots.

She flicked her hair back over her shoulder and glanced around. "Right on course, actually." She frowned as her gaze fell on the ruined *Sky Cat*. "Guess I won't be getting paid for that cargo."

The way she turned sharply away made me wonder if she was more regretful about the loss of the wine or her plane.

"I'm sorry," I said.

Ziba shrugged. "It is what it is." She gave me a smile over her shoulder. "Don't worry about it. We better get going before the people who shot us down come to investigate."

Without a backward glance, she led us farther into the mountains.

The rough terrain was difficult to navigate. Most of our way was made up of sharp rocks that made it difficult to keep our footing and a brisk wind that whistled in through the crevices we encountered here and there. Ziba walked with the confidence of someone who knew the way, which was fortunate. We took so many twists and turns, I never would have been able to keep track without getting hopelessly lost.

I certainly would have walked right past the crevice where Ziba suddenly stopped.

"This is it," she said.

The path looked barely big enough for either her or me to squeeze through, let alone Kael.

"Are you sure?" Kael eyed the crevice dubiously.

Ziba rolled her eyes. "Yes, I'm sure. Look." She pointed down to the rough rock face. There, at knee level, was a single, small rune. It wasn't one that I recognized, neither with my archaeological skills or my ancient mind.

"You've been here before?" I asked.

"Yes," Ziba said. "I used to live here when I was a child, but my mother was forced out, along with myself." She didn't elaborate as she pursed her lips. "The scroll you translated for me is my key back." She gave my arm a squeeze. "Thank you again, Olivia, for helping me."

"No problem," I said. How could the scroll be the key to helping her back into her home? It had said Ziba would have a part to play in saving the world from the cursed ones. Would she be welcomed back as some sort of savior?

Kael crossed his arms. "You didn't tell us you wouldn't be welcomed here, Ziba. We don't need to walk into yet another place where they wish us harm."

The gryphon shifter sniffed dismissively. "You have nothing to worry about. Besides, it's my blood they want, not yours."

Without another word, she pulled a pocket knife from her bag, swept it across her index finger, and crouched before the strange symbol etched at the mouth of the crevice. She pressed her finger to the rune and let her blood soak into the stone.

Around us, the mountain seemed to groan. The crevice shifted and widened with the sound of scraping stone. The earth trembled beneath our feet, and then suddenly everything went silent. The space was now wide enough for two people to walk abreast.

Ziba gave Kael a satisfied smirk. "Ready?"

Without waiting for an answer, she made her way into the crevice. Kael and I followed.

My magic murmured inside me, as if warning me to be cautious. I brought it farther from my core so it settled just beneath my skin, giving my palms a subtle glow. Kael seemed just as on edge. His eyes swept the sides of the rocky walls flanking us, and he tilted his head now and then as if attempting to catch the sound of any incoming danger.

The crevice opened up ahead, and light spilled across the stone beneath our feet. Ziba paused, her shoulders rose and fell in a deep breath, and then she stepped into the light.

My mouth fell open as we stepped up beside her. The mountain terrain opened up into a massive bowl, the cliffs stretching up toward the sky. Every side was lined with large columns, the spaces in between broken with open doorways. Ancient glyphs of gryphons, lions, and falcons were etched above the open spaces.

I twisted my hands around the strap of my bag as my gaze fell on the people who now surrounded us. Most of them wore long, white robes, some with deep hoods pulled up. Many of them paused to look at us, but thankfully, none seemed to be hostile.

I kept expecting angry gryphons to descend upon us, but instead, a single robed man approached.

Ziba ducked her head in reverence. Kael did the same and I followed suit, afraid to offend the elderly man.

He stopped before us and gave a small smile. He didn't ask who we were or why we were there.

"Welcome," he said. He swept an arm out to the enormous space. "To the City of Wings."

CHAPTER 14

THE CITY OF WINGS.

As soon as the thought passed through my mind, a loud screech rang out. I tipped my gaze up. Five gryphons appeared over the rim of the massive bowl formed by the ring of mountains.

The gryphons flew toward our group. Kael stepped closer to me as they landed before the elderly man who had greeted us. They shifted and each immediately reached over to a small alcove on our right, where they pulled out neatly piled white robes. Only when they were dressed did they address the man.

A young man at the front lowered his head in reverence, as Ziba had done. The elderly man was obviously someone important, and I would bet he was the one to ask about the fourth key.

"We observed the crash site. While it is being investigated, no one was able to follow them here." The young man flicked a golden stare at me. He wasn't hostile or angry at our intrusion. If anything, he seemed curious. Then, his eyes swept to Ziba. "It has been a while."

"You may go." The elderly man lifted a dismissive hand, and the five gryphon shifters gave more bows and left.

The minutes stretched on as we waited, and I began to wonder if the man had forgotten us. Then he sighed and folded his hands inside his robe. The stare he pinned on Ziba wasn't hard with anger, but stern nonetheless.

"You have returned, Ziba. You were banished along with your mother when she stole what was not hers. To steal from our sanctuaries is a crime. Why are you here, when you know returning means death?"

I shared a quick look with Kael. Ziba hadn't told us her life would be in danger if she returned to her homeland.

Ziba reached into her bag and pulled out her scroll. She raised her chin and held the scroll out to the elderly man. "I have translated the scroll. I know what it means." She took a deep breath. "My mother paid for her crimes, many years ago. I have come to make up for the transgressions."

The man fixed her with a level stare. "You know the price?" His stare swept to us and back to Ziba so swiftly I wasn't certain if I'd just imagined it.

"Yes, I do."

"Very well. Ziba, you will accompany me to the council, along with the scroll, and speak your case to them."

Ziba nodded, but then hesitated. "What about my friends?"

"Your companions will be taken somewhere to freshen up and have their wounds tended to."

I hadn't even given a thought to all of the scrapes and bumps we'd received in the crash. I was too focused on other matters, like the key.

"Sir, we've come to—" I stopped short when Ziba gave a small shake of her head. We desperately needed to get the key before Vehrin found it, but I trusted Ziba's judgment. Perhaps she would ask this council about its whereabouts.

The man, who I realized hadn't told us his name, stopped a young woman with her hood pulled up. He spoke to her quietly, then gave us a smile.

"This is Ayla," he said. "She will look after you until Ziba has spoken to the council. If you need anything, simply tell her, and she will do her best to accommodate you."

"Thank you," I said.

The young woman swept her arm to the left. "This way, please."

Kael and I followed her along the rim of the bowl the mountains had formed. We passed by huge columns and countless doors that lined the edge, and stayed away from the center where most of the people were gathered to talk. As we walked, I glanced back, but Ziba and the man were gone.

"I'm afraid I didn't catch his name?" I said to Ayla.

She didn't pause as we continued. "He has no name, nor do the other members of the council. They set aside their earthly ties when they ascend to their position. We simply refer to them as elder or councilman."

We finally entered a small doorway to a room that was furnished plainly, but would be comfortable enough. There were a pair of beds against one wall and a low table in the center. There were no chairs, so I assumed most around here sat on the floor to eat. At least the beds looked comfortable, piled with brightly colored blankets.

"I will return with water and medicine for your wounds. Is there anything else you require?"

"No," Kael said. "Thank you."

Ayla gave a slight bow, her hood slipping farther over her head, and then left. After a moment, I turned to Kael.

"What is this place? These people seem very...cultish."

Kael walked over to one of the beds and lowered himself onto it with a small groan. He must have been hurting more than he was letting on. "This is a holy city, a place where they protect valued treasures. The don't worship treasure like the cult in New Orleans. They simply believe it is their duty to preserve and protect relics and ancient rarities."

"Sort of like a museum," I said.

"Yeah, sort of." Kael gave me a smile and held out his hand. "Come here, mate."

His words sent a shiver of pleasure through me.

"You like saying that, don't you?" I took his hand, and he pulled me down beside him.

"Yes, and you like hearing it."

I stared down at our entwined hands and ran my thumb beside a small cut across his skin. "I never thought I would be someone's *mate*."

Kael chuckled. "Disappointed?"

I scoffed. "Hardly." I tipped my face up to stare at him. "There is no one else I can imagine being with, Kael. Truthfully, you were already mine." I smiled. "It just took some extremely strange circumstances to find each other."

"That's an understatement," he muttered as he bent down to press his lips to mine.

As our kiss deepened, reality swept over me. I heard the sound of *Sky Cat*'s dying engines, the groan of metal as we fell to the earth, the painful certainty I'd felt that we would not survive the crash.

I pulled in a shuddering breath and eased back.

Kael cupped a hand on the back of my neck. "What's wrong?"

"We almost died," I said.

He gave me a small smile. "We seem to do that quite a bit."

"A habit I'd like to kick."

Kael wrapped his arms around me. The feel of his strong arms, the warmth of his body, and his familiar scent went a long way toward soothing the sudden unease that had taken hold of me.

"One day, this will all be behind us, Livvie, and we can get on with our boring lives together."

Boring. I'd kill for boring right now. I'd love to have a life without dark mages, ancient keys, and being cursed.

The warm ease I'd felt cooled in my gut. *Cursed.*

Defeating Vehrin wouldn't do anything to lift the curse latched to my soul. Darkness swirled within me, and no matter how much I tried, I couldn't see a way to rid myself of the malevolent power.

The vision I'd had on the plane had shown only one way to free myself of the curse, and it would do more harm than good to try.

Kael drifted fingers across my cheek. "What are you thinking about that has you feeling so lost?"

I sighed and leaned into his touch. I'd almost forgotten our bond meant he could feel what I was feeling. "I just wish I knew more about this curse. Why do I have it? Where did it come from? If I knew, perhaps I could find a way to rid myself of it."

My mate shifted his stare to the doorway and dropped his voice. "No more talk of curses."

Ayla returned with a another meek-mannered woman behind her. Together, the pair cleaned our scrapes and applied a spicy-scented ointment where necessary. They left water and a plate of fruits and cheese before departing. We spent the next several minutes devouring the food.

When the plate was empty, Kael drew me into his arms again. "Don't worry, Livvie. We'll get things all figured out."

I didn't have the heart to tell him I wasn't so sure my curse was curable, so I buried my worries in another kiss instead. Just as his tongue swept across my lips, someone cleared their throat nearby.

Ziba was standing in the doorway. She gave us a smile, but I hadn't missed the cold glint in her eye when I first noticed her.

"The council would like to speak to you," she said.

I stood from the bed and hurried over to her. "Did you ask them about the key?"

"I did." Ziba backed out of the doorway as Kael joined us. "And they have an answer for you."

"What is it?"

"You will have to discuss it with them."

I exchanged a glance with Kael as we followed Ziba. Why was she being so vague? Were we going to receive bad news?

The council waited in a circular room not far from where Kael and I had been waiting. The floor and walls were stone, but had been polished to a gleam which reflected light coming from the sky above. Perhaps the council wanted to be able to fly straight here in their gryphon forms, so they'd chosen a room with no ceiling.

There was no table or chairs. The council, seven members total, stood on the opposite end of the room. All were clad in white robes with their arms folded into their sleeves. Only the elderly man we'd first encountered had his hood down.

"Come closer," he said.

Ziba led us to him, bowed her head, and stepped aside. The man's gaze focused on me. His eyes were golden, like the piercing stare of a hawk, but their color was pale and watery.

"You are the witch?" he asked.

Irritation rang through Kael, and out of the corner of my eye, I saw him whip his head toward Ziba.

I sniffed. "I'm not a witch."

The elder, who I assumed was the leader of the council, cocked his head to study me. "No, no you're not, are you? You are something else." He lifted a wrinkled hand as if he were going to touch my face, then drew it back. "A darkness lives in you, a malevolent power that should not dwell inside any living being."

My pulse quickened. "What do you know about it?"

"Why are you here?"

I swept a quick glance to Ziba. "Did Ziba not tell you?"

One of the other council members strode forward. Most

of her face was covered in shadow from the hood, but I could see the frown weighing down her lips.

"Ziba told us you seek a powerful relic. A key, to be precise. It has been entrusted to our protection for centuries. Why would we give it to you?"

Kael stepped forward. He gave a reverent nod of his head. "My name is Kael Rivera. I worked in an organization whose mission is to track and protect such magical objects. Trust me when I say we have no ill intent. Vehrin, a dark mage, will destroy the world if he goes unchecked. We need the remaining key if we are to stop him."

"You already have relics in your possession, yes?" A new voice boomed around the space, and a heavy-framed figure stepped forward. I had expected the council to be completely made up of elderly members, but this man sounded as if he were the same age as myself. "Show them to us."

I hesitated, but tugged on the chains around my neck and pulled out the pair of keys. "Vehrin was able to get the third key," I explained. "He also has a box, and if he has all four keys, he will be able to open it and unleash hell upon this earth."

The council muttered to themselves, though whether at my words or the keys I held before them, I was unsure.

The head of the council held up his hand, and the murmuring ceased. He fixed me with his pale gaze. "If you want the fourth key, you must go into the pool of reflection."

"What is that?" I asked.

"The pool of reflection will give you what you truly need." The elder motioned toward a small, open doorway on the left side of the wall.

Kael gripped my shoulder and twisted me to him. He lowered his face to mine. "I don't like this, Livvie. You don't know what's in that room."

"It may be the only way they'll give us the fourth key. I

have to go." I gave him a smile. "Besides, mate, where's your sense of adventure?"

He cocked a smile back at me. "You have enough sense of adventure for both of us." His hand drifted up my arm, and he growled. "I love hearing you call me mate." His molten stare told me he wanted to show me just how much he loved it.

I turned away from him with my stomach fluttering. What I wouldn't give to have some extended alone time with the man I'd come to love.

I sighed and looked to the elder. "All right. I'll go."

I started to step toward the doorway, but the elder held out an arm. "You may not take any worldly possessions."

I frowned, but didn't argue. I pulled off my bag and gave it to Kael. The council wasn't satisfied, and the elder pointed to my bracelets, the braided one which would turn into a sword and the one with the snowflake charm Renathe had given me. I pulled them off, making a mental note to check in on my fae friend when we left this place. I dropped the bracelets in Kael's hand.

"The keys," a robed woman said. "Leave them."

I wrapped them in a fist. "No, they stay with me."

"Then you may not enter the pool of reflection."

I bit my lip. Not only were the keys dangerous, but the one from the Amazon was bound to my soul. I couldn't risk giving it to them.

"I'll hold onto them," Kael said.

I relented with a nod. He would protect them with his life.

Facing the council, I held my arms out to the side. "Anything else?"

"You are permitted to enter," the eldest said. "May you receive what you truly need."

I glanced back at Kael and gave him a wink. He smiled, but it didn't erase the worry creasing his brow. He leaned close.

"Be careful. I don't like you going in there without anything to defend yourself."

I took his hand and let a small spark of magic warm at my fingers. "You and I both know that isn't true." I gave him a smile before turning away.

There were runes etched across the top of the doorway, though my ancient mind didn't recognize the symbols.

What did I truly need?

If we had the fourth key, we were one step closer to defeating Vehrin. As I stepped through the doorway, though, my magic churned within me, and I couldn't help but wonder if there was a way to rid myself of the vile curse.

The council room fell silent behind me, and as I cleared the doorway, my breath was stolen from my lungs. I stumbled forward, a soundless gasp in my throat as an icy sensation seized me.

My heart raced with panic as I struggled to breathe. Then, my boots hit water and air rushed back into my lungs.

My lips parted as I stared at the pool of reflection, the promise of answers heavy in the atmosphere.

The only problem was, my mind couldn't decide between what I needed, and what I wanted.

CHAPTER 15

IN THE OVERBEARING silence of the room, all I could hear was blood pounding in my ears. Shards of light from the pool that took up most of the space reflected off the sharp angles of the dark rock walls, and the surface of the water was smooth as glass, with swirls of silver and white.

Statues bordered the rim. Some were made in the likeness of gryphons, while others were robed figures. All of them had their stone eyes downcast toward the water.

I shifted the toes of my boots against the pool. The movement hardly made a ripple across the surface.

"Hello?" My voice didn't echo, but instead seemed to be drawn into the rock walls. I hadn't really expected anyone to answer me, but I was at a loss as to what to do.

The pool of reflection. Hmm.

Slowly, I crouched to peer into the surface of the pool. Oddly enough, there was no reflection of myself, or even the walls. There was nothing but the silvery swirls in the water.

I chewed on the inside of my cheek, then dipped my hand into the liquid. It was warm, and had more substance than typical water. When I lifted my hand back out, my skin was dry.

"Well," I said, standing. "In I go, I suppose."

I cautiously stepped into the pool and it rose higher as I walked toward the center. The water finally ended at my waist, pressing in on me to fit my curves like a blanket. When I lifted my arm, silver threads lined with droplets fell back to the surface, as if the pool were hesitant to let me go.

Drawing in a deep breath, I tried to focus on what I needed.

The room buzzed with energy, and indiscernible whispers echoed around me. I twisted and tried to find the source, but there was nothing other than the water and the still statues staring at me.

Wait. Staring at *me?* Weren't they staring at the water before?

Goosebumps rushed to the base of my skull, and before I could twist around to see if all the statues were staring at me, I found myself in a different place.

The twisting canopy above is so thick it blocks out much of the sun. The scent of damp earth clings to my nostrils as I dig my fingers into the fertile soil of my homeland. Across from me, Vehrin mirrors my position.

This has to work. With more power, I could do so much in this world.

An incantation mumbles from my lips, words as ancient as the rainforest around us. The earth hums beneath my fingertips. I can feel Earth's energy, the power she holds in the soil, in the roots of the palm trees and the rain-scented air around me.

I pull at the buzzing energy and draw the power into myself. My teeth grind together as the earth resists, unwilling to surrender her hold. Vehrin groans with his own struggle. With my nostrils flaring, I use the magic I was born with to take the power of the earth into myself.

Pain seizes me, scores my flesh, and rips through my muscles. I give one final tug, and my own screams meld with Vehrin's.

I blink up at the shifting canopy. The ground is wet beneath my back, and twigs poke at my skin. I sit up.

The earth's power settles into me, along with something deep, and something dark.

As I snapped back to the present, the unusual hold of the water was the only thing that kept me from falling to my knees.

The curse.

My past self had stolen power from the earth, and it had brought the curse along with it.

I pivoted in the water and glared at the statues, as if the vision, and the knowledge along with it, were somehow their fault.

"Wait," I said. "That's not what I needed."

I was here for another reason, but the water and staring statues seemed to draw on my conscious. I tried to fight against the pull as another vision flickered to life in my mind.

My eyes burned with unshed tears. I'd had enough spill onto my cheeks over the past few days.

I had never felt so utterly lost and alone in the world.

My mate was gone, and it was the fault of the man standing before me.

"You killed him," I spat. My hands opened and closed as I imagined them constricting around Vehrin's neck.

Vehrin hardly reacted except for a narrowing of his eyes. "You are a traitor. You were promised to me and no other, and yet you bound yourself to a mere guard. I did what any man with honor would do to one who would engage in such transgressions with his betrothed."

I bared my teeth at him with all the menace my mate would have shown. "I will not bind myself to such a monster."

"I am no more a monster than you." Vehrin waved his hand toward me. "You've taken human sacrifices in an attempt to cure the scourge across this land. We stole magic from the earth in an attempt to grow powerful enough to stop the disease and bloodshed."

My heart deflated. I couldn't protect the man I loved. I couldn't save my people. "Yes," I said. "And now we are as doomed as the rest of them."

"We could change that..." Vehrin's voice shifted from condescending to low, soothing tones. "...if you give me the box. Opening it is the only way to save ourselves." He took a step toward me, his hand out.

I retreated. "No. Unleashing that sort of darkness would destroy the earth."

"But we would survive it. That kind of darkness would make us strong. You know this. You feel it. Pain. Anger. Loss. We can feed from such things, and become all the more powerful. Maybe even powerful enough to break the curse."

Loss. It didn't make me feel stronger, only more helpless against the curse. And feeding the darkness...that's what the curse wanted. We'd never be free from it so long as we gave in to its desires.

Vehrin stared at me, a frenzied sort of hunger in his gaze. "Give me the keys and the box."

He was a murderer. He had killed the man I loved, and any hope I had along with him.

"It's too late. They are already hidden. You will never find them, Vehrin."

Vehrin yelled and flicked his hand. I slammed into a wall, and pain shot through my skull. I almost welcomed the agony. It was almost enough to make me forget the misery I would have to endure without my mate.

"I should have known you were too weak-minded for this endeavor. I thought when you got a taste of the earth's power, you would understand what we could become."

I lifted my head. "What are you talking about? We didn't want to become anything. We only wanted enough strength to save our people, Vehrin."

He sniffed. "Save our people. Those peasants have forgotten how to worship their betters, their gods. We will be superior again, with the very power we stole."

My eyes grew wide. "You intended this all along?" I sat up with a wince as my mind raced. "The curse. It's your fault. I only wanted to help, to heal our people, and you..." My words drifted as Vehrin crouched in front of me.

"I saw an opportunity, and I took it. When are you going to realize this is not a curse, but a gift?"

I sat in silence as he stood and walked from the room, leaving me with nothing but my thoughts and crippling loneliness.

With angry tears rolling down my cheeks, I dug my fingernails into the stone floor beneath me. Vehrin was wrong. The dark power inside us was no gift, and I was going to make him regret the day he helped put the curse upon us both.

My head pounded with the impact of the memory, and I was surprised at the anger constricting my throat.

The curse was Vehrin's fault. His greed and lust for power had twisted my ancient self's good intentions into something vile and wicked. We had stolen power from the earth, but Vehrin had been the one to cause the twisted, dark power to coil inside of us.

I rubbed my temples in an effort to massage the ache away, then glanced around. I gasped.

The statues were leaning forward, looking as if they were ready to either speak to me or eat me alive. I took a step back and glanced down.

The water was gone. There was nothing in its place but dry stone.

I blinked several times, and the heaviness that had seemed latched to me since the moment I stepped into this place lifted.

The key.

I had come to find answers on obtaining the fourth key.

I twisted this way and that, but there was no sign of it.

Where was the key?

My heart pounded.

The elder had said the pool of reflection would give me what I truly needed.

Had answers to my past been what I needed, or had I sabotaged my chances to get the key by subconsciously wanting light shed on the unknown?

My gut twisted with guilt at the thought that I had possibly messed things up.

Then, a sense of panic that wasn't my own rang through me. I looked toward the doorway.

Kael?

I hurried from the dry hollow in the floor where the pool had been. As I passed above the rim, silvery water filled the space once again. I hesitated, wondering if I could try again, but a harsh yell from Kael sent rushing through the doorway.

I'd barely gone three feet from the door when rough fingers gripped my arms and cold, sharp steel pressed against my throat. I glanced down at the curved blades resting against my skin, then up to see Kael being held by another pair of robed figures.

My mate had a black eye already forming on his face. His arm shook with the effort with which his fist gripped the pair of keys. His eyes flicked down to the braided bracelet that had fallen to the floor near my feet. There was no sign of the charm Renathe had given me.

"We now have our answers on who you truly are, mage."

I turned to stare at the line of the councilmen. The lead elder was closest. Ziba was standing next to him.

She had a smirk on her face that suddenly had my blood boiling.

"You were correct, Ziba," the elder said. "She is indeed cursed, and as such cannot be allowed to leave the city. Not only that, she is a thief, as well. She's stolen that which belongs to the earth, and the earth's relics."

Another of the councilman, a woman, stepped up to Ziba. She placed a hand on her cheek with all the affection of a forgiving mother. "Thank you for bringing this abomination to us. Welcome home. Your price is now paid."

I sliced Ziba apart with a glare. "Ziba, you—"

One of the guards knocked me sharply in the side of the head with his elbow. I stumbled to the side.

"Olivia!" Kael tried to rush forward, despite the blades threatening to cut his throat.

I held up a hand. "You will let us leave this place," I said. Magic began to crackle at my fingertips. "And you will give us the key we need."

The elder smiled. "I do not think so. Those treasures you claim will aid you are not for you, or anyone else to use."

"If you won't give it to us, we have no choice but to take it."

The councilman pointed toward me. "Once a thief, always a thief. How do we deal with thieves in our midst?"

It was at that point I realized there were many more in the chamber than there had been earlier. Most looked to be guards of some sort, with curved blades cinched around their waists. They shook their fists and called out in anger.

Then, their harsh yells turned to sharp, piercing cries.

In seconds, the room was filled with gryphons, and every one was bent on tearing me and Kael apart.

CHAPTER 16

THE ROOM ECHOED with angry shrieks, the beating of enormous wings, and the raking of great claws against the polished stone floor.

Kael bellowed as he fought against the hold of his guards. A ripple of pride ran through me at the sight of him outmaneuvering the men and tossing them to the side. His gaze locked with mine, and the fierce determination on his face gave me the push I needed to take action.

I drew deeper on my magic as the gryphons neared. The bright energy sparked at my fingertips and danced around my fists. A deep brown gryphon reached toward me with tearing claws, and I released a sphere of power directly into his chest. He fell back, but another gryphon took his place.

Through the flurry of wings and shouts, I heard Ziba yelling to the councilman. I couldn't make out her frenzied words, but it didn't matter. I doubted she was pleading for our lives, not after throwing us to the beasts. She may plead for Kael's life, given their history together, but I was something much less to her. A mage. A witch. A cursed being.

I dodged another gryphon's attack and used a blast of

magic to knock its legs out from under it. As it landed, I noticed my green and gold braided bracelet beside it.

My sword.

If I continued to use my magic, I would get low on energy, and I needed to keep as much of my power as I could. Vehrin would not have forgotten the fourth key, and while my life was in danger now, it would be nothing compared to what would come if Vehrin were to arrive.

I took a deep breath and dashed toward the recovering gryphon. An indignant shriek from its wide beak threatened to puncture my ear drum as I ducked under its head. I tucked into a tight roll and managed to snatch up the bracelet. When I got to my feet, my sword was in hand.

I held the blade aloft as I retreated from the angry gryphon. My back hit something, and I whirled only to find Kael standing there. He had managed to get a hold of one of the guards' curved swords. I grinned.

"What's so funny?" he growled.

I jerked my head toward the weapon in his hand before turning back to the advancing gryphon. "Do you know how to use that thing?"

Kael scoffed, but said nothing. His weapons of choice were always pistols or rifles. Or, when he shifted, he was lethal with claws and sharp, tearing teeth.

"Don't worry," I said. "I've got your back."

A flicker of annoyance melded with a flash of amusement through the bond.

We drifted apart as the gryphons moved in for the attack. Despite my teasing, Kael did well with his curved blade. I slashed mine toward the gryphon. The creature lifted up on its hind legs to avoid the attack and flapped its great wings. I squinted under the blast of wind, but I managed to keep my footing.

With another cry, the gryphon leaped forward in an arc. I quickly shifted my feet, and just as the gryphon was reaching for me with spread claws, I twisted. The gryphon missed, and as it passed with wings aloft, I swept my sword across its exposed side.

A pitiful sound came from it. I held my weapon up, ready for a counterattack, but the gryphon twitched and shifted.

A woman crouched on the floor in the gryphon's place. An angry, red line traced down her ribcage. Blood ran from the wound to puddle at her feet. When her pale face lifted to mine, it wasn't hatred there, but fear.

Cursed, those eyes said. *Intruder. Thief.*

Monster.

I wanted to retreat from the woman's gaze, but something about her fear spoke to something within me. I could use that fear. Eagerness sped through my veins as I stepped toward her. Her terror would make me stronger. I could use that power to steal the key, kill these weak shifters...

I halted and blinked several times. My breath shook, and as I stared at the woman still crouched and bleeding on the ground, I saw someone else.

I saw the lion shifter I'd killed in Africa, and her son I'd left without a mother. I'd left the chief without his mate.

Would I cause nothing but pain and loss everywhere I went?

I really was wholly and truly cursed.

The clamor of angry gryphons and my fighting mate continued around me, but I couldn't pull myself to the present.

All I could think about was the damage I'd done, and the lives I kept destroying.

"Olivia, watch out!" Kael's warning broke through to me.

I whirled to find him, but only fell into darkness.

* * *

COLD STONE PRESSED against my cheek, and deep, rumbling growls rolled over me.

The back of my head gave a painful twinge as I pushed myself into a sitting position. The cell I found myself in was poorly lit by a single torch flickering on the other side of the thick bars.

Kael paced back and forth a few feet from me in his jaguar form, his tail twitching and threatening growls coming from his chest. Blood stained his spotted, golden coat along his rolling shoulder.

"You're hurt," I said.

Kael whipped his head toward me. *You're awake.* His voice was soft in my mind. He walked over to me and bent to rub his head against my cheek.

I wrapped my arms around his warm coat. "Why are we still alive? I thought they wanted to kill us?"

They have a different fate for us, it seems. Kael sat back on his haunches, and a deep sigh huffed through him. *Livvie, they have your keys.*

My heart jumped. If they had my keys, then they had the bond to my soul. They could control me, use my power to taunt and torture and kill whoever they pleased. My throat tightened as I stared at Kael, his golden eyes reflecting even in the poor light.

They could use me to kill my own mate if they wanted.

Kael stood and curled his neck over my shoulder. *No one owns your soul but you.*

His hot breath sent surprisingly delightful shivers through my body.

I gently pushed him away before I gave too much thought to the fact that, if he shifted now, he'd be naked, and we were alone. Kael tilted his head in what I was certain was smugness.

"What sort of fate do they have planned for us?"

"One you won't be satisfied with at all," came a familiar woman's voice.

Ziba.

Kael charged against the bars as she rested against the wall beneath the torch. She crossed her legs, perfectly at ease.

Hatred rose in me like bile. I got to my feet and did my best to ignore the painful throb at the back of my skull. Someone must have knocked me out.

I wrapped my hands around the bars and bared my teeth in a way that would make Kael proud. "You bitch. Why are you doing this?"

Ziba picked at her fingernails. "It's my destiny, just as the scroll revealed. Remember? The bearer of the scroll will have a part to play in saving the world from the cursed ones." She pointed her finger at me. "Starting with saving the world from you."

I bristled, mostly because I wondered if she was right. "And what about the part where it said life must become death, so death may become life?"

A wicked smile touched Ziba's red lips. "Well, I guess you have an answer on your fate, don't you?"

We hadn't escaped death. It had merely been postponed.

"You would kill Kael?"

The gryphon shifter's smile faltered as she glanced down at my rumbling mate. "I cannot beg for what is not mine."

Kael snarled at Ziba. *She is lost,* he said.

I put my hand on Kael's shoulder and stared at Ziba. "He says you're lost."

Ziba lifted her chin. "I was lost for years. Now I'm finally home."

As she started to leave, I shoved my arm through the bar in an attempt to stop her. "Wait! What exactly are they going to do to us?"

"The gods have put their earthly treasures under our protection," Ziba said. "Thievery against the earth is a great affront to the gods. There will be a sacrifice to appease them."

She smiled again. "I hope you're ready to have your soul cleansed by fire, mage."

I covered my ears as Kael's roars chased Ziba's retreating form.

* * *

AN HOUR PASSED before Kael finally calmed down. He apologized, knowing his incessant roaring hadn't done anything to help my headache. He'd curled up, and I'd laid down against him, listening to his pounding heart.

I'd nearly fallen asleep when Kael suddenly climbed to his feet. A guard stepped in front of our cell.

"Here," the guard said. He shoved my bag through the bars. "You will leave the earth as you walked through our doors."

"What about my keys?"

The man's face darkened. "Those were never yours."

I wanted to tell him that yes, in fact, they had been, long before one of the keys had been given to the gryphons for protection, but saying so wouldn't do any good.

The guard left, and I pulled out a spare set of clothes for Kael. As he changed, I rummaged through the bag and found a bottle of water. I twisted off the cap and chugged half of it before handing it to Kael. He put the cap back on and tossed it into my bag without taking a drink.

"I won't let them kill you," he said. Pain lashed through our bond, as if he could already feel the loss my absence would bring.

I wrapped my arms around him and gave him a squeeze of reassurance. "I'd hardly let them kill me, either."

Kael's voice was barely more than a whisper. "Can you use your magic to get us out of here?"

"Yes, but it won't do any good. We still have to get the keys. All of them."

"And how exactly are we going to do that?" Kael took a hold of my shoulders and leaned me back so he could stare at me. "Olivia, they're going to *burn us to death*. I've heard the guards talking about building a pyre. They're going to tie us to it."

"Hmm. I should have brought marshmallows."

Kael scowled. "This isn't funny. I won't watch you die."

"We've survived a raging fire on a Scottish mountain, a pack of corrupt wolf shifters in England, traps, mazes, a murderous cult, betrayal, and three encounters with Vehrin. I think we can handle a horde of angry gryphons." I paused, thinking. "Or is it a pack of gryphons? A pride?"

"A flock, actually."

Kael and I whipped our heads around to find the leader of the council. His hood was down, and he had a small smile on his face. "Are you ready to atone for your sins?"

My pulse quickened. I could sense the keys. Their magic pulsed through the air, and the one bound to my soul called to me.

Two guards let us out and kept blades at our backs as the elder led the way through the dark corridor. I had to let Kael know the gryphon leader had the keys, but I couldn't risk trying to whisper it to him.

I grabbed his hand. The elder glanced back, but given the circumstances, it wasn't an out of place gesture. Slowly and deliberately, I traced the word "key" into Kael's palm, then I traced an arrow pointing toward the elder. Kael gave my fingers a squeeze, and I hoped it meant he understood.

If something went wrong, he would know where to find the keys.

We followed the elder as the corridor slowly started to rise. Up ahead, I could see light and hear voices. The nearer we got to the doorway, the louder the voices became. When we stepped out of the corridor, my eyes widened.

The crowd was enormous. Every member of the City of

Wings must have come to watch our execution. My gut twisted when my gaze fell on the cleared path leading to a rise with a pyre waiting atop it.

"Bind their hands," the elder said.

Kael protested as the guards forced his hand from mine. I let my wrists be bound tightly behind my back, then turned to look at my mate, letting him know with a nod and a swell of confidence that, if things went too far, I would put a stop to this before they set flame to the wood.

The guard at my back gave me a hard shove, and I started down the path. The crowd yelled and jeered, calling me a thief and an abomination. They hated me and Kael both, without even realizing we were there to try and save the world.

We were poked and prodded up the stairs. I stared at the square stack of wood piled before me, and my mind raced as I tried to come up with a way out of this that wouldn't end in the slaughter of innocent lives.

Hot anger ripped through Kael, and I spotted Ziba coming to stand beside the elder.

"You will pay for your betrayal, Ziba." The cold promise in his voice made me shiver. For once, the woman didn't seem to have anything to say.

I waited for some sort of speech that would list crimes pointing to our guilt, or our need for redemption. No words came. The elder simply held up his hands, and the guards moved forward.

Two of them lifted me toward the wood that would soon be aflame. My heart jumped. I had to do something. I had to—

A thunderous boom echoed through the massive bowl and rang through the surrounding mountains. The ground beneath us shook.

"Stop this, girl, and accept your fate," the elder said, his gray eyebrows drawn together.

I looked at him, bewildered. "That wasn't me."

Another boom shook through the City of Wings, this time accompanied by black swirls cracking into the rock.

Screams and cries rang out as the inky shadows smashed into the crowd.

I swallowed as I peered around. I couldn't see him through the growing chaos, but I knew he was here.

Vehrin had come for the fourth key, and without my own keys in my possession, the dark mage may soon have everything he needed to destroy the earth.

CHAPTER 17

FIRE LICKED my wrists as magic burned away the ropes binding my hands behind my back. I turned to the elder as Vehrin let loose another volley of attacks that crashed into the frenzied crowd.

"Give me the keys."

Sharp cries pierced the air as many of the shifters took on their gryphon forms. The elder gazed around the City of Wings before he settled his pale golden eyes on Ziba.

"Take them to the temple, Ziba."

Ziba's mouth popped open. "But…the key. You can't—"

"Sacrifices must be made." The elder's words were hard, low, and heavy with an indication I didn't miss.

What did he mean by sacrifices? That he had to sacrifice the key in order to save this ancient city from the dark mage? Or was another sacrifice called for?

Ziba glared at me as if I had been the one to make the decision for the elder. After a moment, she nodded. She pulled a knife from her pocket and moved over to Kael. I stepped forward, magic flaring at my fingertips, but she ignored me as she cut through the ties biting into his wrists.

"Come on," she snapped. She started down the steps, leading me away from our imminent death on the pyre.

"Wait." I took a step toward the elder and held out my hand. "The keys. Now."

The entire platform shook as an explosion of shadow and ash plummeted into the pyre. The wood cracked as it burst outward. Kael was there in an instant, his arms wrapping around my head protectively. Another shudder, and the stone beneath our feet gave way. Our small group was sent rolling and tumbling into the crowd of people who hadn't taken flight on gryphon wings.

Vehrin knew exactly where I was, and it wouldn't take him long to get to me, even in the chaos he'd created. As soon as he found out I didn't have the keys…

I pushed against Kael, and he helped me up. Where had the elder gone?

"Over there," Kael said.

Ziba helped the elder to his feet. He coughed and brushed at his white robes, as if them being dirty was something he couldn't tolerate.

The crowd swelled and nearly bowled us over. The elder shoved Ziba toward us. "Take them to the temple. I'll meet you there."

"I'm not going anywhere without the keys." The crowd swallowed the elder as soon as the words left my mouth. I started forward.

Kael clutched at my bag. "Wait. I'll go after him. Go with Ziba to the temple."

I turned to Kael, but didn't get a chance to argue. Ziba was already pulling me away from him.

"He'll be alright. Let's get out of here."

I watched a moment longer as my mate disappeared into the crowd to chase after the elder. I swallowed. He would be fine. He'd get the keys and meet me at the temple. Besides, I still had to get the fourth key.

"Okay, lead the way," I said.

I stayed close behind Ziba as we snaked our way through the center of the bowl in the mountains and toward the northern edge. Several times, I nearly lost my footing as people jostled me, and I earned more than a few bruises in our hurried trek.

"Wouldn't it be easier if you just turned into a gryphon and flew us there?"

Ziba looked over her shoulder to glare at me. Instead of speaking, she gestured upward.

I followed her pointing finger, and my heart sank. I hadn't noticed the gryphons being struck down from the sky by Vehrin's twisted magic. Their sharp cries of pain bounced from the surrounding cliffs.

I halted. "We should stay and help." I watched with twisting guilt as a small gryphon—a child, most likely—cartwheeled from the sky. Magic raged in me at the sight. "They'll all be killed."

Ziba grabbed my arm tightly. "Put that magic away or you'll paint a bulls-eye on your head," she hissed. "Do you want that key, or not?"

A sharp sigh flared my nostrils as I let my magic go. She was right, but leaving the gryphons to their fate still churned my stomach.

The temple was marked with a pair of wings above a round doorway. We had left the crowd far behind and, after a short climb, had reached our destination. Both of us were out of breath as we ducked into the building.

I had expected mounds of treasure and relics, as it had been in the place in New Orleans, but this room was small and empty.

"This is your temple? I thought this was a holy city?"

Ziba frowned. "We have many temples here, but this is our most sacred. It holds our most precious treasure."

I stepped farther into the room. It was a perfect square,

hardly more than ten feet across. The floor was smooth stone the color of sand, except for a strange pattern etched near the wall opposite us.

I made my way closer and studied the unusual markings on the floor. The shallow pattern was continuous and didn't seem to make up anything in particular as it snaked its way toward the wall and disappeared into a small hole in the stone.

Lifting my gaze to the wall, I found a mural of a gryphon with outstretched wings. The image carved in the stone was so old it was difficult to pick out any details but the vague shape. Ziba stepped up beside me to examine the gryphon.

I walked the edge of the room in search of the key, but found nothing. Finally, I stood near the doorway and narrowed my eyes at Ziba who was watching me with a smile.

"Okay, I give. Where's the key?"

The mountain rumbled around us and dust shook from the ceiling. I braced a hand on the edge of the doorway.

Ziba's eyes danced with an edge of delight. "You will never get that key. You have no right to it."

"I have every right to it," I said through clenched teeth. I shuffled my feet apart to steady myself as the mountain groaned. "It was my ancient self who sent it here long ago. I sent all the keys away, to protect them from Vehrin."

The gryphon shifter laughed. "Being cursed has certainly messed with your brain. *Your ancient self.* I've heard the lies you've fed to Kael. It's no wonder he was tricked into mating with you."

"I didn't trick him." I didn't bother telling her we were mated because of our love for one another. I didn't owe this woman any kind of explanation. "Why would you bring me here if you weren't going to give me the key?"

"As my elder said, sacrifices must be made." Ziba stared at me with murder in her sharp gaze. She reached behind her and pulled a small pistol from her waistband. "It isn't as theatrical as I would have liked, but it is what it is. It will still serve the same purpose."

My pulse quickened as she raised the gun. "Why are you doing this, Ziba? I haven't done anything to you."

"I'm destined to stop the cursed ones." Ziba stared, and her eyes shone with triumph and promised glory. They shone with redemption. "Life must become death, so death may become life."

If I summoned my magic, it would draw Vehrin to this place, and to the final key, but as a smile quirked Ziba's lips, I knew I had no choice. She started to squeeze the trigger, and I flung both of my hands forward.

A shot rang out, but my magic was already upon her. I heard a pop as the bullet was swallowed in the energy I sent flashing forward...and straight through Ziba's chest.

The gryphon woman hit the ground with a thump. Her eyes, which a moment before had been alive with victory, were now dull and empty.

I'd killed her.

My breath shook as I walked over to where she lay on the strange pattern in the floor. She'd betrayed us, but she had been someone Kael had once cared for, and it felt wrong. I curled my shaking fingers tightly and forced the rest of my magic back inside.

Blood ran from the gaping wound in Ziba's chest and flowed down into the shallow pattern. It filled the curving spaces and followed the pattern like a macabre maze, right to the little hole in the wall.

I gasped and took a step back as the bottom of the mural carved in the stone wall began to glow an eerie red. The light traveled up the stone, highlighting lines, angles, and curves I hadn't noticed before. The entire gryphon sparked into such detail it didn't seem real. The tips of the feathers almost seemed to be shifting on a breeze, and a red heart pulsed in the stone creature's chest with unnatural life.

My heartbeat skipped faster. I pulled my eyes from the gryphon, then glanced down at Ziba's lifeless form before looking back up to the creature once again.

Life must become death, so death may become life.

I grimaced. Ziba had been right. The scroll had been her destiny, but not in the way she had predicted. Her blood, her death, had brought the mural to life.

There had to be a reason for it. I chewed on my lip as I thought. The key had to be hidden nearby. Why else would this be here?

My head whipped toward the doorway. Footsteps thudded closer, and my pulse quickened.

Vehrin.

I turned back to the gryphon, my eyes locking on the pulsing, ruby heart. I closed the distance to the wall and pressed my hand to the gryphon's heart. It gave beneath my touch and sank into the stone several inches with a grating sound.

Then the wall began to crumble. I gripped the handle of my bag and retreated, fearing the entire room may collapse, but a quick glance around showed the rest of the temple remained intact.

The mural fell apart, and loose stones rolled to the floor, stirring up debris and partially covering Ziba's body. I waved a hand in front of me to clear away the dust as the stones and broken bits of mural settled.

I went back to the wall, eager to grab the key and get out of the temple before Vehrin found me.

But I stopped short when I realized the room was nothing but an empty alcove.

"It's gone," came a man's voice from behind me. I pivoted at the sound of the elder's voice. Kael stood in the doorway. He had one arm wrapped around the elder, who sagged heavily against my mate. Blood ran down the man's face from a wound on his head. Crimson soaked his white robe at his side, as well. The elder's eyes were nearly as dull as Ziba's had been in death. He was barely alive.

Kael held the pair of keys in his other hand. Relief flooded through me at the sight of both Kael *and* the relics.

My relief was short lived as the elder's words ran through my mind again.

It's gone.

What was gone? His people? The City of Wings? There had been those moments where the mountain had seemed about to come down on our heads, after all.

I walked over to Kael and the elder. Kael handed me the keys, and I quickly put them back around my neck. He hefted the slipping elder up and leaned him more heavily against his body.

"What's gone?" I asked.

The elder took a deep breath. It rattled beneath his stained robe. "The key. It's gone. It hasn't been in our possession for over five hundred years." He lifted his gaze to me. "My people, they had to believe in something, that we were doing something worthwhile. They couldn't know our greatest relic was gone."

I peered over my shoulder at the empty alcove. All of this strife, suffering, and death, and the key hadn't even been here.

I shifted my attention back to the elder as another tremble groaned through the mountain. "Okay, then. Where is it?"

The elder moaned, and Kael eased him to the floor. He was dying, and we didn't have an answer.

I clutched at the snowy fabric of his robe and gave him a shake. "Tell me where it is!"

"The dragons," he said. "The dragons stole it."

CHAPTER 18

KAEL SWORE colorfully as I stared at the elder. Images of massive, winged lizards breathing fire and singeing the flesh from their victims' bones burned through my mind.

Dragons? We had to confront *dragons* to get our hands on the fourth key?

Judging by Kael's disgruntled expression and impressive cursing, I imagined it wouldn't be an easy thing to do.

"Where are the dragons?"

The elder's eyelids fluttered before he focused back on me. "You are not worthy of the keys, or their power. The curse writhing within you makes you unfit for such a gift."

Kael knelt down beside the man, anger hardening the line of his jaw. "She is worthy because she has darkness within her, yet still wants the best for others, and this world. What you see as a weakness only makes her strong. Suspicious, isolated zealots such as yourself are the ones who are weak."

The elder's breath rattled as his chest rose and fell slowly. "Perhaps so." He glanced over my shoulder.

My stomach churned as I stared at Ziba's still body, very aware that Kael was gazing at her, too. Her blood still darkened the pattern on the floor.

"Eventually, we must all descend back into the marked earth," the elder muttered. He drew in another rasp, then his head lolled to the side, and he fell silent.

His final words clung to me. *We must all descend back into the marked earth.* Why did that seem so important?

The mountain around us groaned and trembled again. I blinked against the dust shaken loose from the ceiling. A couple stones from the mural rolled across the floor behind us.

I leaned over and closed the elder's eyelids. He may have wanted to sacrifice me to appease some gods, and was a fool to think I wasn't there to help, but he was still a leader and a religious man. He had only wanted to protect his people.

I stood and turned to Kael. He was staring at Ziba's body. His face held no expression, and my own emotions were such a mess, I couldn't get an accurate read on his.

"We have to get out of here," he said. His nostrils flared as he started toward the doorway.

"Kael..."

He reached back and took my wrist. "Come on. We need to leave before Vehrin finds his way to this temple."

Was he angry about Ziba? I wouldn't blame him, but I didn't know how to make it right. I tried to tell myself it was self-defense, but in all honesty, I could have just as easily sent her flying against a wall, unconscious. Instead, I'd killed her.

I tried to speak to Kael again, but my words turned to ash in my mouth as we left the temple. My lips parted around a shaky gasp.

"Oh my God," I breathed.

The City of Wings was nothing more than ruins.

Rocks and boulders from the protective bowl of the mountain now lay scattered throughout the gryphons' holy city. A mixture of smoke and unsettled dust choked the air. Cries and shrieks echoed around the mountains. My heart raced at the sight of the bodies, both human and gryphon, that lay broken among the destruction.

So many had died in such a short amount of time. They were innocent. These people had done nothing wrong.

I lifted my gaze, drawn like a magnet to a malignant force across the city. Through the chaos and death, my eyes locked on Vehrin. I couldn't pick out the details of his face, but I didn't have to see his features to know a smirk was on his lips.

Anger burned through me, and magic lashed inside me for release. I wanted to strike him down, burn him where he stood, make him scream.

Vehrin needed to pay for what he did to the City of Wings.

"Not now, Livvie," Kael said. His tone was firm, leaving no room for argument.

"Is there a better time?" I snapped. I pulled in a deep breath. "Look what he did. All those people…" My throat tightened. I should have stopped to help them instead of following Ziba to the temple, especially now that I knew the key had never even been there.

Kael cupped my shoulders. "We can't win this fight, not now. If he gets too close to you, his key will lessen your powers, remember?"

I looked out across the bowl. Vehrin was already making his way toward us through the wreckage. I lifted a hand to the keys around my neck. Kael was right. While I had magic of my own, the keys gave me more power, and if Vehrin lessened that power, he may be able to take the keys…and the command of my soul.

"Where are we supposed to go?" A quick glance around showed no escape. We could only go back down into the city, bringing us closer to Vehrin, or back into the temple, which would be a dead end.

Even if we managed to get out of the city without getting caught, how were we going to get out of the country? We couldn't exactly go traipsing through Iran.

Vehrin was getting closer, with demons flanking him. There were dozens of the vile creatures, their eager chirps and clicks melding with the agonized cries of the wounded.

We would have no choice but to fight.

Magic twisted around my hands and up my arms. Beside me, Kael lifted a curved sword he'd found in silent agreement. As much as he'd wanted us to flee, there would be no escape for us today.

My heartbeat ticked away the minutes it would take for Vehrin to reach us. His demons screeched eagerly as they raced across the ruins and bodies. It wouldn't be long. I shifted my feet and prepared for the onslaught of claws, teeth, and dark magic.

Someone chuckled nearby.

I swiveled, met Kael's confused face, glanced around, and then looked up.

My eyebrows flew up at the sight of Renathe. His white wings were folded behind him, and he was lounging on a rocky outcrop as if he had nothing better in the world to do but watch my impending doom. A crooked grin spread across his face.

"You make a final stand look simply breathtaking," he said.

It took a moment for my mind to come to terms that my fae friend was actually with us. "What are you doing here?"

Ren straightened and pulled something from his pocket. "I couldn't sense you anymore." He opened his hand to reveal my bracelet in his palm. It was broken, but the charm he'd created, and used to track me, was still intact. "I thought I'd come check up on you."

I pulled my stare from Ren and looked toward Vehrin. He was close enough for me to see his face, and his demons were only seconds away.

"As glorious as it would be to see you in battle—" Ren

hopped down lightly beside me "—perhaps a quick exit would be best."

In the next instant, Renathe slashed his hand through the air. A great wall of ice erupted from the earth, blocking Vehrin and his minions. Just as it had done when the agents had tried to take us back to PITO headquarters, though, it quickly began to crack under Vehrin's power. Dark fissures spiderwebbed across the surface. It wouldn't hold for long.

Ren's arms wrapped around my middle. "Up we go."

I screamed as his powerful wings lifted us into the air. "Wait!" I reached down toward Kael, whose form was rapidly growing smaller as we flew upward. "Kael! We can't leave him!"

My heart lodged in my throat as an image of the demons breaking through the wall of ice and overtaking my mate seared through my mind.

Then, two more fae, both with wings the same color as Ren's, dove toward Kael. Another fae flew to hover beside us, his wings outstretched protectively. I didn't look away from my mate until the pair of fae had taken a hold of him and hoisted him into the air. Just as they reached me and Ren, the wall crashed down.

We crossed the lip of the bowl formed by the mountains as bursts of dark magic chased after us. A black mass exploded into the fae who was guarding us. He fell from the sky, but Ren didn't stop.

"Wait, Ren! He fell!"

Ren tightened his grip on me. "He isn't the first, and won't be the last if we don't get out of here. Hold on."

I clutched my friend tighter as we soared through the air. I buried my face in his shirt, partly to block my eyes from the wind, but mostly so I wouldn't have to see the total destruction of the City of Wings one last time.

* * *

I WASN'T certain how long we flew, but by the time we landed, I was chilled to the bone. Ren settled me on the rocky earth, and though I was sitting, the roar of wind refused to leave my ears.

"Give yourself a moment," Ren said. He crouched beside me. "The dizziness and rush will fade."

The other two fae landed beside us and dropped Kael a bit more roughly than was necessary. He scowled at them and hurried over to me.

He lifted his hands to my face. They were so warm against my skin. "Are you okay?"

I nodded. "Yeah, I'm fine."

"You're freezing." Kael glared at Ren.

My friend rolled his eyes. "Apologies that I forgot to grab a heater while I was rescuing you." Then, he studied my face and frowned. "Perhaps we could build a fire."

Kael scoffed and gestured to the rocky, barren landscape around us. "Out of what? Rocks?"

One of the other fae did, indeed, start to gather rocks. He stacked them in a small pile in the center of our group. Then, he looked at me expectantly.

"What?" I said.

The fae smiled. "You are Ren's little mage, yes?"

I narrowed my eyes at Renathe. "I'm not anyone's little mage."

Ren grinned. "He only means you're my friend who possesses magic."

"Sure," I muttered. I looked back at the other fae. "I still don't know what you think I'm supposed to do with a pile of rocks."

The fae leaned down and touched my forehead. He ignored Kael's low growl and said, "Your magic is of the earth, and as such, the rules of earth are yours to bend. Set fire to the rocks."

It seemed completely ridiculous, but I was freezing and willing to give it a try. I held my hands down to the rocks as magic flowed over them. At first, nothing happened, but the more I concentrated on imagining the rocks burning, the more I was certain it would work. The rocks began to warm, then grew hot. Finally, tiny flames licked their sharp edges and grew to cover the pile.

I sat back with a sigh, feeling completely drained. The fae gave me a small smile, then went to join his companion.

Kael shuffled behind me and drew me against his chest. The fire was already beginning to thaw my bones.

"So, what's been happening back home, Ren?"

Renathe settled across from us, his wings tucked neatly at his back. "PITO is in chaos. Some are making an effort to search for supposed traitors like Kael, while others say the organization is corrupt. Many have left."

"PITOs division likely worked right into Vehrin's plans. The agency can't help stop him if they aren't working together."

A dark light settled over Ren's expression. "There are many things working into the dark mage's hands. Crime has quadrupled in many cities, the weather continues to cause disasters, and there are outbreaks of sickness across the world. Friends and allies are distrusting of each other. People are afraid to leave their homes. There have been riots and sudden food shortages. It's a mess."

My heart broke at Renathe's news. "All of this so quickly?" It hadn't been so long since we'd left. How could so much damage have been caused so fast?

"If Vehrin isn't stopped soon, the earth as we know it will perish." Ren grabbed a loose rock from nearby and tossed it onto the already burning pile. Surprisingly, it caught fire, as well. "How has your mission been going?"

"The fourth key wasn't with the gryphons as we'd thought. It turns out it was taken years ago. By dragons."

Ren exchanged a glance with Kael, one that told me he was less than thrilled at the news. "The only dragons in existence are in China, and they are even less welcoming than gryphons."

"Perfect," I said flatly.

"Don't worry," Ren said. "We'll get it figured out in the morning. Until then, you and Kael both look like you could use some rest."

I gave him a small smile. "We did almost die today."

Ren laughed. "An unfortunate pattern for you, it seems." He stood and joined his fellow fae, falling into a low discussion.

"Let's try and get some sleep," Kael said. He eased me onto the ground beside him. It wasn't exactly comfortable, but I was so exhausted, I didn't really care.

For a few minutes, we lay in silence. The escape from the temple had happened so quickly, I wasn't certain how things were between Kael and myself. I thought of Ziba, and my eyes began to burn.

"I'm so sorry," I said. My voice shook, and I sniffed.

Surprise flashed through Kael. "About what?"

"No matter what I do, I cause pain and destruction everywhere I go. I...I killed Ziba, Kael. She was going to shoot me, and I was trying to protect myself, but I could have done something different. I could have—"

"Stop." Kael squeezed me tighter. "Don't do this to yourself, Livvie. Ziba was twisted with thoughts of redemption and loyalty. She betrayed us both. It wasn't your fault, and if you have any thoughts that I have any ill will toward you because you protected yourself, you're crazy." He leaned over so his breath was hot in my ear. "I love you. Nothing will ever change that."

Tears rolled down my cheeks. "Some things might change that."

"What do you mean?"

If I didn't tell him now, I'd choke on the words. Admitting the extent of the darkness in me would be like ripping thorns from my skin, but I had to let him know who he'd tethered himself to.

"When people are suffering, or are in pain, or afraid, I…a part of me wants to feed off it. I want to use those negative feelings to make myself more powerful. I know I shouldn't want to do such a horrible thing, but something inside of me also yearns for it." I pulled in a shaky breath. "You've mated a monster, Kael, and I'll never forgive myself for it."

Kael grabbed my shoulder and shifted me around to face him. "That isn't you. That's the curse talking. I *know* you're not a monster. Deep in my soul, I know it, Livvie."

"I'll never be able to be rid of the curse."

He wiped at the tears on my cheek. "You don't know that."

"I brought this curse upon myself, in a past life. Vehrin was there, too. I only wanted more power to help my people, but Vehrin was selfish, and he twisted it into something dark. Now we're both doomed. I'll never be rid of it. It will consume me until I'm nothing but greed and power."

Kael went silent, and I feared I may have pushed him away. But after another moment, he finally spoke. "If Vehrin brought it on you, perhaps we can find a way to use him to end it."

It was a happy thought, the possibility of being free of the curse, but I wasn't sure how I'd be able to do it. "It's a sweet idea, Kael, but how?"

"Let's get some sleep. You're exhausted, and the last thing you need is to be thinking of this stuff. Things will work out."

Kael kissed me, which I returned with as much enthusiasm as I could muster. Then, I rolled onto my side with my mate at my back, his arm caged protectively around me.

The fire burned strangely around the pile of rocks, and I

played idly with the gritty bits of debris on the ground in front of my face.

As my eyes grew heavy, I started to trace my finger through the dirt, and I felt the earth humming against my skin.

CHAPTER 19

I'D FOUND a half-smashed granola bar in the bottom of my bag, and I stared at it with guilt. I knew the other four men around me had to be hungry, too. Kael's stomach had rivaled the growling he tended to do when Renathe was around. They had all chivalrously insisted I eat it.

"I can share," I said.

Ren scoffed. "Don't be ridiculous, Olivia."

I looked to Kael. "Is there something you can hunt?" I knew he held no qualms over eating wild prey while in his jaguar form.

"I doubt there's anything out there."

We sat in a rocky, mountainous region, and while we were still in Iran, we had thankfully not been discovered by Vehrin or anyone else.

Kael nudged my shoulder with his own. "Just eat it. We won't starve."

They weren't going to let up so, disgruntled as I was about being the only one privileged enough to have food, I ate the squished granola bar.

I stared out at the horizon as I chewed. It was a beautiful morning, even if the landscape was a bit desolate and cold.

The sky was clear, and there was no sign an entire city had been razed to the ground by a mad mage. I crinkled the wrapper and stuffed it back into my bag.

"So, tell me about these dragons." My tone was light, but inside swirled a mixture of fear and awe. I held my hands out to the rocks I'd set ablaze. They hadn't gone out all night. "Do they breathe fire?"

"Not much is known of them." The fae who spoke hadn't said much to me since our rescue. At least the other one had given me the hint about using the rocks to make fire. "They are an ancient race, and it's said there are only a dozen or so left in existence."

"Are they shifters?" I wasn't exactly confident about the possibility of going up against a creature that wasn't at least somewhat human. Ren had wings, but at least he acted like a gentleman...most of the time.

"Of a fashion." The man didn't elaborate.

Perfect. Mysterious, possibly not human *or* shifter dragons held the fourth key, and we were the lucky ones who had to go after it.

"It's said they are volatile and very territorial," Kael added.

Renathe grinned at Kael, stretching his wings. "Takes one to know one, shifter."

My mate scowled. "I'm not volatile." His close proximity to me, especially with three other males present, didn't make it necessary for him to deny the second part.

I patted Kael's knee, trying to soothe the ire my fae friend was trying to work up. "If they're so dangerous, how are we supposed to get the key from them?"

I didn't think I could handle another situation like the slaughter Vehrin had set loose on the lion shifter pride or the holy city of the gryphons.

It was the fae who had spoken to me the night before who

answered. "Your only hope is for the dragons to listen to you, if the mage does not get to them first."

"That's assuming Vehrin will know where to find the fourth key. As far as I know, the gryphon elder was the only one who knew it had been stolen," I said.

The ground crunched beneath Kael's boots as he stood. "It isn't a chance we can take. Knowing Vehrin, he'll likely follow us there, somehow."

That was probably true. He had an uncanny way of being able to find the keys without having to jump through all the hoops we had to maneuver through. Which must have meant he was using our hard work to blaze the path for him.

"All right." I got to my feet beside Kael and took his hand. "How are we supposed to get to China?"

"I'll take you," Ren said.

I quirked an eyebrow and studied his wings. They were beautiful, like frosted glass on a bright winter day. "You're going to fly us all the way to China?"

All three of the fae chuckled.

"No, my silly sorceress," Ren said. "We will fly you out of Iran and into Turkey. From there, we will catch a flight to Hong Kong."

"We?" Kael didn't seem happy to be traveling with the trio of fae. I supposed old habits died hard and his prejudices were still something to overcome.

Ren gestured to his brethren. "They will be leaving once we make it across the border. It is time to gather our kind and make preparations. Only I will travel with you to Hong Kong."

"Why?" I asked. He'd never bothered to join us on our travels before.

"This fight will involve fae, witches, and shifters alike. Standing to the side is no longer an option."

To my surprise, Kael nodded. "It's time to make a stand."

"Agreed." Ren's grin was fierce and eager.

Inside, my magic purred. I couldn't tell if the power within was ready for the fight, or eager for destruction.

"Okay." I picked up my bag. "Off to Hong Kong."

* * *

"Is it always this crowded?" I asked. Once again, I had to practically smash up against Kael to keep from being trampled as we made our way past the towering buildings of Hong Kong.

"Yes," Ren said. We followed him as he made his way deftly through the crowd. He seemed to know exactly where he was going. The fae knew a great many things, and I often wondered how much he kept from me.

Kael stiffened as a woman screamed somewhere behind us. We didn't turn. Not this time. The packed streets were teeming with a tension people didn't seem to understand and was primed for outbursts of violence. Four times since our arrival, fights had broken out. One man had tried to steal my bag. His nose would never look the same. I rubbed my sore knuckles and caught my mate's grin of amusement.

"Something funny?"

He just laughed and slung his arm around my shoulders.

The three of us made our way through the dangerous streets and finally found a train station. We waited while Renathe bought our tickets.

"We're heading to Lijiang, in Yunnan province. From there, we'll make our way to Jade Dragon Snow Mountain," Ren said.

I took my ticket. "Is that really where the dragons are?" I muttered. "That seems a bit too obvious and easy."

"It will be anything but easy," Ren promised.

I was skeptical, but got on the train. I just hoped he was right. We couldn't afford any mistakes.

The trip to Lijiang was quiet after the chaos of the city. I tried my best to nap a bit, but my racing mind had me on edge. How was I supposed to convince dragons to give us the key? I hadn't been able to convince anyone else of our good intentions.

Could all these people sense the curse of darkness in me? Had I been unknowingly sabotaging our mission all along?

"Livvie."

I blinked. "Huh?"

Kael and Renathe were staring at me. I must have dozed off.

"We're here," Kael said. He gave my arm a tug. "Come on."

Ren headed to a desk at the train station as we waited on a nearby bench. He came back with a pamphlet and sat beside me.

"Here," he said, handing it to me. "Take this tour up into the mountain. It's the only one still operating. The rest have quit. There have been earthquakes in the mountains, but apparently this company cares more about money than safety."

"Lucky us," I muttered.

Ren continued. "From there, leave the group and seek out the dragons."

I jerked my face to Ren. "What do you mean? You're leaving? I thought you didn't want to stand on the sidelines anymore?"

"I won't be. I'll be working to gather more fae." He stared out the window. The massive mountain loomed beyond the glass. "I have a feeling this will be the final stand. The earth cannot withstand Vehrin's hold much longer." Ren looked back to me. "The dragons do not want to be found, and the way will not be an easy one."

"Is it ever?"

Ren smiled. "Here. I fixed it for you." He held out the

bracelet with the charm he'd made for me. "I'll find you before it's all over. You can do this."

I fastened Ren's gift around my wrist beside my braided sword bracelet. "You're a good friend, Renathe."

He stood. "You really surprised me, Olivia Perez. That isn't an easy thing to do." He gave Kael a nod, then left.

"Well, then." I held the brochure up to Kael. "Ready to go for a hike?"

* * *

THE TOUR GROUP that headed into the Jade Dragon Snow Mountain was small. There were only seven of us total, including the tour guide who seemed incredibly bored and not at all concerned about earthquakes. We made our way up the mountain, and when the group stopped at a small resort for food and rest, I knew it was time to leave.

"Do you think they'll come looking for us?" I asked as we made our way from the safety of the paths and walkways, and into the wild.

Kael held a branch out of my way as I passed. "I doubt they will put much effort into it."

I stared into the forest. It was surprisingly thick given the resort wasn't too far away. "Do you think there are tigers out there ready to eat us?"

My mate smiled. "Maybe. Or pandas."

I couldn't help but laugh at the thought of being taken out by something that looked like a giant teddy bear.

As we hiked up the mountain, I kept an eye out for any sign of the dragons. For hours and hours, we trekked. The mountain was beautiful, if a bit chilly, and it held a sort of peace that told me Vehrin had not yet touched this part of the world.

It was late afternoon when Kael urged me to stop. I sat heavily on the ground with burning muscles and a sense of failure. We were hopelessly lost. I didn't know the way to the dragons, much less back to civilization.

Kael lowered himself to the ground beside me. He lifted a hand and massaged the back of my neck. I moaned as his fingers worked into the tense muscles.

"Don't worry. We'll find it."

I tilted my head back as his fingers traveled up to massage through my hair. "I just wish I had some kind of clue to their whereabouts. We can't search every inch of this mountain."

My stomach rumbled loudly.

"Let's have a bite, then we'll figure out our next move." Kael took the bag from my shoulder and set it beside his own.

My gaze dropped to the ground, tracing the shapes of fallen leaves and twigs, then focused on a bare patch of dirt. As I stared, I couldn't help but recall the feel of the earth against my palms as I pulled the power from it so long ago.

I started to run my finger through the dirt, getting lost in the sounds of birds chirping in the branches and Kael rummaging through the bags.

Where are the dragons? I thought, staring out at the trees. The soil was cool against the pad of my fingertip, and dirt collected beneath my nail.

"What is that?" Kael asked.

I tore my gaze from the mountain forest to find Kael looking down with pinched eyebrows.

My lips parted. Where there had been nothing but a bare patch of dirt moments before, there was now a strange sort of symbol. I studied my dirt encrusted finger. Had I done that without even realizing it?

I stared at the symbol. "I don't really know. I think...I think *I* did it, but I didn't know I was doing it."

Kael crouched beside me. "What does it mean?"

I swallowed and hovered my hand above the symbol. There was a tugging sensation, as if my hand and the earth were magnets. I pressed my hand to the marked earth, recalling the words the elder had spoken. *We must all descend into the marked earth.* The soil grew warm and my entire body tingled. Something slipped into my being, a hidden knowledge I'd just unlocked.

I faced the northwest. "That way," I said. "The dragons are that way."

We gathered our bags, granola bars in hand, and headed out.

I studied my hand, and couldn't help but wonder, if the earth was willing to help me find the dragons, did that mean it was willing to forgive my transgressions?

Or was I being led to retribution by death at the hands of the dragons?

CHAPTER 20

THE SUN BEGAN its descent toward the horizon and blanketed the terrain around us in a dusty gold. Our way had grown steeper with each passing hour. Large rocks and boulders jutted out of the ground like giant, jagged teeth. Trees grew around them, their exposed roots clinging to them as if to push the offending stones back into the earth.

"Are you sure this is the right way?" Kael asked. The man hardly looked winded, despite the hours spent traversing up the mountain.

"No," I said. "But I *feel* that this is where we should be going." I waved a hand in front of me. A tingling warmth still clung to my skin from the mark I'd drawn in the earth.

"Why would the earth want you to find the dragons?"

I had to give it to my mate, he managed to ask that question without implying he was worried for my sanity.

I gave him a small smile as I stepped over a fallen log. "I'm not really sure, but I guess we're going to find out."

A sigh hushed past my lips as I stared up at the endless trees. How much farther would we have to go?

"Wait." Kael reached out and clutched my shoulder. He cocked his head and squinted.

"What is it?"

A deep rumble growled around us, and the ground started to jump below our feet. I gasped, one hand flying out to clutch Kael as the other wrapped around a small tree. Leaves shook free and rained down around us as the branches rattled overhead. The ground rumbled a few more seconds, and then everything went still.

For a long moment, we stood in silence. Kael's golden-brown gaze pierced the trees in search of a threat. An unrecognizable magic buzzed through the air. It was coming from the direction in which I was being led.

Kael released me and straightened. "Vehrin is already almost here," he growled.

I started back up the mountain and shook my head. "It isn't Vehrin."

"Then who is it?"

I pointed up our path. "The ones we're going to meet, I think."

"I don't think dragons have magic," Kael said.

"To me, it's incredible dragons even exist. Who's to say what they are and aren't capable of?"

Kael pursed his lips at my suggestion and fell silent.

The thought of gnashing teeth and searing flame was bad enough, but the possibility they could conjure magic made confronting them even more dangerous. Clearly, given the earthquake, they didn't want us here, but would they pause long enough to listen to our plea?

They had to. I'd give them no choice.

Another fifteen minutes had passed when the ground began to shake again. This tremor was more violent. My legs couldn't hold me upright, and I fell to my knees. Kael tried to get to me, but was pitched off balance and teetered backward.

I flinched as trees cracked around us. We were too exposed here. A tree could fall on us at any second. I glanced around for someplace to hide. Then, a rumbling, crashing sound drew my attention.

A large boulder was rolling down the hill…straight at us.

There was no time for us to jump out of the way. I raised my hands and released a blast of energy. Bits of rock and grit peppered my face as the boulder shattered into thousands of pieces. The earthquake ceased soon after.

I flopped to my back and pulled in shaky breaths. Kael leaned over me. His fingers brushed debris from my face before he rested his palm against my cheek.

"Are you alright?"

I swallowed. "This is getting dangerous."

"Yes, it is." Kael's face was hard. He didn't like seeing my life at risk.

"We have to keep going." I pulled his hand from my face and squeezed his fingers. "We can't afford to turn back."

Kael closed his eyes and nodded. "I know." When he opened his eyes again, I could see the burden in his gaze.

We were both in so much danger, but we had no choice. If we didn't try to get to the dragons, there would be no hope for anyone.

I sat up and grabbed Kael's face. "When this is all done, I want a vacation. Somewhere sunny, with beaches and unlimited margaritas."

Kael pulled my face close to his and kissed me. "Anything for you, mate," he murmured against my lips.

My stomach fluttered at his words. Not only because he called me "mate", but because I could hear the promise in his voice. Kael would do anything for me.

"I love you, Kael."

He smiled. "I love you, too."

And he really did. I could feel it through our bond, a strong warmth that wrapped around me like a blanket. At that moment, I wanted to just sit with him and be together, but reality struck me as a tree branch, damaged in the earthquake, crashed to the ground several feet away.

"Better get going before the mountain comes down on our heads," I said.

Kael helped me up. "Looks like there's a bit of a flat clearing up ahead."

Eagerness to be on flat ground again, even for just a couple of minutes, had my legs pumping up the hill. When we reached the clearing, I stopped short.

We were not alone.

Two people stood in the clearing, if the pair could really be called people. They wore a sort of stiff tunic of shifting shades of green. Wide, silver belts encircled their waists. Their arms were bare, and their forearms were covered in thick scales that shone even in the poor light of early evening.

The man had long, dark hair pulled back in a ponytail, but the woman's hair framed her face. Both watched us with glowing, pale green eyes that had dark slits for pupils. The woman's nose wrinkled, and her lips parted to reveal short fangs.

The magnetic pull I'd been feeling was so intense my bones nearly rattled.

The man, who watched us passively, was the first to speak, but I didn't recognize the language.

"I'm sorry," I said. "I don't understand you."

They exchanged a glance, and the man tried again. "Who are you, and why are you on this mountain?"

I took a step forward with Kael shadowing me, hovering behind my shoulder. "We've come to find the dragons. We're all in danger, and wish to speak to them."

The man held his arms out wide. "Congratulations, you have found us."

These were the dragons? So, they were shifters, after all, though I could see why the fae had said they were shifters "of a sort." For the most part, they looked human, but aside from the scaled arms and unusual, slit pupils, there was something... unearthly about them. Or perhaps it was that they were more of this world than I could have possibly imagined, a species here from the beginning, forged in time from the birth of Earth herself.

I glanced at Kael and saw the same confusion in his gaze I knew was in mine. Surely, there were not only two dragons left in this world? The fae had said a dozen.

"We would like to speak to all of you," I said.

The woman hissed and looked to her partner. "Make them leave. She doesn't want them here."

She. So, these weren't the only ones, and her words indicated they had a leader.

"May we speak to the one who leads you? It cannot wait."

The woman started forward, but the man held out an arm. "They have asked to go in, and they may..."

A beat of triumph pounded in me.

"...if this one—" The dragon shifter raised a pointed finger to me. "—can best me in a duel."

My eyes widened. He wanted me to fight him? I studied him more closely. He was long and lean, but his frame held firm muscles and a grace which suggested he was quick on his feet. The corner of his lips lifted in a smirk.

I glared. Who did this guy think he was? He may be one of the last members of a nearly extinct race, and likely a seasoned warrior, but I was no weakling.

"Fine," I said. I flicked a glance at the woman beside him. "But just you."

"Of course," the man said. "She will be busy with your friend."

Without another word, both dragon shifters leaped forward.

Kael didn't reach for the pistol Ren had given him. Instead, I heard the roar of his jaguar. Uncertainty flickered through me before I decided to call out my sword. I didn't want to use my magic, not unless I absolutely had to do so. I had come to warn them of the dark mage. It would be difficult to convince them if I held the same powers he did.

The man drew a sword from his back, and relief flashed through me. There would be no magic from him, either. He swung the sword down at me. I swept to the side and blocked, steel ringing on steel with a loud clang. He struck again, and I parried the attack. We circled each other in a deadly dance of blades. I didn't want to harm the man, not when he could lead us to the rest of the dragons, so I stayed on the defensive.

As my arms began to burn, however, I realized this wouldn't work. He had said the only way was through him. If he defeated me, he would turn us away. I couldn't win if I didn't fight for it. I let out a slow breath, then I tapped into my ancient knowledge of weaponry that was as twisted in me as the threads of my bracelet were around my wrist.

I knew I had him as soon as he retreated a step. I didn't relent. My sword flashed in my hand, spinning this way and arcing that way. Soon, he was on the defensive. I saw my opening, and I hit my mark.

He jumped to the side, but not before my blade slashed at his arm. Sparks jumped from his scales as if I had struck steel.

The clearing fell silent. Kael stood with his back to me and faced the woman, a rumbling growl in his chest.

One of the dragon shifter's shining scales had turned a dull gray.

My sword twisted back around my wrist. "I'm sorry," I said.

He looked up at me. "No one has ever managed to strike me before."

The woman snarled and strode toward me with the promise of pain in her gaze.

"Lina, stop," the man commanded. The woman went back to his side, though she didn't seem happy about it. He smiled. "Apologies. My mate is as fierce as she is beautiful."

I suddenly found her ferocity hearty-warming. She was only protecting her mate. I stepped up to Kael and placed a hand on his spotted coat. "As is mine."

A huff rippled through him. He retreated a few steps to shift back and tug on some clothes from our pack.

The man dipped his head. "As promised, I will take you. Be warned, however, that once you set eyes on our home, you may never be allowed to leave again."

I didn't have to glance at Kael to know he wasn't fond of the idea. I could sense his caution through the bond. But we had no choice. It was a risk we had to take.

"All right," I said. "My name is Olivia. This is my mate, Kael."

The man gestured to the woman beside him. "This is Lina. I am Hagen. This way."

Hagen led us out of the clearing and back into the forest. My muscles quivered at the sight of the steep incline, but I persisted. Occasionally, Kael would reach up to steady me once our way changed from merely walking, to climbing up the cliff. Could these shifters change into dragons and fly?

When I finally reached the top and hefted myself over the ledge, I found Hagen and Lina standing beside a bridge.

It was made of rope and wood, and it stretched to cliffs in the distance. I walked over to it and glanced down. There was nothing but swirls of mist far below. The ropes of the bridge were aged green with mildew and frayed in many places. The wooden planks looked so brittle I was certain they would crumble to splinters if the wind blew too hard.

"I'm not walking across that death trap," I said.

Hagen grinned, showing fangs. "Suit yourself." He started across the bridge as if he'd walked over it hundreds of times.

"I won't let anything happen to you," Kael muttered beside me.

I wanted to point out that he wasn't capable of sprouting

wings, but he was just trying to help. After a steadying breath, I stepped onto the bridge.

As we made our way across, the boards creaked and the bridge swayed, but everything stayed intact. A heavy mist continuously poured from the cliffs in front of us like water, spilling down to fill the ravine under our feet.

Halfway across the bridge, I shivered as a ripple of energy ran over me. I stumbled as my feet hit something more solid and peered down to find a stone bridge where the wooden planks had been. Behind us, there was nothing but a thick wall of fog.

When we stepped off the bridge, we found stone steps leading up through an archway.

Thank God for steps.

Hagen still led the way, with Lina behind Kael, the two dragons closing us in. As we ascended the steps, a loud screech sounded from somewhere in the distance. Kael was on edge. I could sense every ounce of his being ready for a fight. My magic fluttered beneath my skin.

The heavy mist clung to my skin and clothes, leaving me damp. It seemed like hours that we followed the dragons through the fog. Finally, the mist started to creep away behind us. Hagen stopped.

"Here it is," he said.

When I stepped up beside him, my mouth popped open.

Mountains rose before us, higher than I recalled seeing on the map. It was dotted with lights of dwellings and hanging lanterns. Stone bridges connected the buildings scattered about the ledges of the monolith. There were pagodas, pavilions, houses, and at the top near the summit, a palace.

But it wasn't the beautiful architecture and sparkling lights, or the impossible gardens and fountains that caught my eye.

It was the people.

The *dragons*.

All shapes and sizes. Some with horns and great wings.

Others more serpentine, with scales that glittered as their bodies twisted. They mingled on the cliffs, around the houses, and in the gardens with the shifters in their human forms.

As I stared at this city of dragons, I was at a loss for words. The fae had said there were only a dozen or so dragons left in the world. He'd been wrong.

There were hundreds.

The only question was, would they see us as friend...or foe?

CHAPTER 21

I HAD EXPECTED the leader of the dragons to meet us, as the gryphon elder had done upon our arrival in the City of Wings. Instead, we were shuffled to a nearby guard post.

I stared with curious fascination at the dragon twisted along the curving roof of the building. It returned my gaze, and its forked tongue flicked between rows of fangs as if it were tasting the air around me.

As the dragon started to lean down from the roof, its ruby scales glittering like fire, Kael grabbed my shoulders and urged me into the building after Hagen.

"Wait here. I'll go announce your sudden visit." The dragon shifter turned to his mate, amusement dancing in his eyes. "Be nice."

Hagen left, leaving us alone with Lina.

My muscles ached from the trek up the mountain. There was no furniture in the square room, so I dropped my bag to the floor and leaned against the wall. Lina watched us carefully, though she had the same anger in her unusual eyes that she'd had in the forest.

Kael stood quietly, so I thought I'd break the silence to try and quench my curiosity. "We were told there were only a dozen or so dragons left in existence, yet I saw hundreds, and so many different kinds."

The woman didn't seem willing to engage in conversation, at first. Then, she crossed her arms and said, "We won't let the world know of our kind or our numbers. This mountain is a refuge for us. It has become too dangerous to live elsewhere. Imagine if humans caught on to our existence? We would be hunted, enslaved, and who knows what else."

It was likely true, but I shook my head. "Humans like me aren't as observant as you might think." I'd gone my whole life without knowing I shared the world with shifters, fae, and other beings until I'd met Kael.

"You are not a shifter?" Lina said.

"No, I'm not."

Lina glanced at Kael. "And yet, you are mated to one. You seem human, but…there is something else about you." She cocked her head and squinted as she stepped closer. "What exactly are you?"

I wouldn't admit to her I was the reincarnation of a sorceress. I had to keep that information close until it was absolutely necessary to divulge. Instead, I gave her the truest answer I could. "Your only hope."

The dragon shifter's eyebrows scrunched, but she didn't pry for more information. The room fell silent again, until a deep rumble from the mountain across the ravine broke through the quiet.

Another earthquake.

Lina frowned, a look of concern crossing her face, but it was quickly masked by anger. I wasn't certain what sort of magic was at work in this place, but I could sense the tangible force of it swirling like dust motes in the air. The magnetic pull I'd felt had disappeared as soon as we'd entered the city.

The earth had revealed the sign to me and led me here, but to what purpose? If it was for retribution, I hoped any punishment would wait until after we defeated Vehrin.

Hagen suddenly strolled back through the door and waved us forward. I couldn't help but notice the dull, gray scale amid the glow of the other scales which covered his forearm.

I'll do no more damage here, I promised. If I left behind destruction as I had with the lion pride and the gryphons, I wouldn't be able to live with myself.

Outside of the guard post stood eight dragon shifters, all with the same scaled arms and strange, reptilian eyes. They carried slender katanas, and as they moved closer to me and Kael, I found they walked with a dangerous, fluid grace. It reminded me a bit of the way Renathe and his fellow fae moved, but there was something different about the dragons I couldn't quite put my finger on. It wasn't the wild, animalistic aura Kael would sometimes have, but rather something ancient and earthly.

Kael came to my side, and together we followed Hagen, with the guards half a step behind us.

"They know something," Kael muttered. "They wouldn't have so many guarding us if they didn't see us as a threat."

I didn't care if they saw me as a threat, as long as they would hear me out.

As we started up more steps, a soft groan left me, but my exhaustion fled to the back of my mind once I took in the sights.

Countless gardens perched on wide ledges that time had chiseled into the face of the mountain. Stone statues cloaked in lichen dotted the gardens, and colorful koi swam in pools beneath pink lotus blossoms.

We traversed over bridges, under which streams danced and flowed into waterfalls down the cliffs. Night had fully fallen, and everywhere, soft, warm lights glowed to keep the dark at bay. The city was peaceful and serene, but with a hard edge that warned of the warriors dwelling within the mountain.

It was the most beautiful place I had ever seen, and the world didn't even know of its existence.

After many twists and turns, we made it to the summit. A small palace was perched in front of us, the crown jewel to such an amazing city. It held the same traditional architecture as the buildings below. Heavy, wooden beams lined the front and the large, overhanging roof was made of ceramic tiles. The building's red face glinted in the sunlight, and was trimmed in bursts of gold.

Two dragons sat outside the arched gateway in the front. Talon-tipped wings curved from their backs, and their horns shone white, a stark contrast against their black scales. I didn't have to ask to know those were the kind of dragons which could burn me to a crisp. They stared as we approached, silent and cold. Hagen merely nodded as we passed them, but I could sense their searing gazes on my back.

We passed under the gate and through an open doorway. Flickers of energy sparked across my skin. It was the magic I'd been sensing, and the bearer of it had to be near.

The walls in the massive room were warm and rich, and the floor shone like molten gold. There were no trinkets or treasures along the walls, but weapons of every shape and size. The palace was fit for a warrior king, but it was a woman who stepped from the shadows.

Her bare feet glided across the gleaming floor. Her lavender dress billowed above her ankles, and energy curled around her small frame. My own magic shifted inside of me at the sight of her, on edge as she approached.

The woman had no scales on her forearms, and though her hair was dark like Hagen's, the pupils in her amber eyes weren't slit like the dragons'. My gaze dropped from her face to the jade-colored key around her neck.

The fourth relic.

"Were they alone?" she asked, peering at Hagen who had

stepped off to the side. He nodded. She swept her gaze to me. "Who are you?"

I took a deep breath. How many times had I given this speech, only to have the person listening not believe a word I said, or not take me seriously? This time, I had to say things differently and hope it would work.

"My name is Olivia, and this is my mate, Kael. We're here to ask for help."

The woman narrowed her eyes. "Help with what?"

"There is a man—a dark and powerful mage—wreaking havoc on the earth."

"I know of the mage." The woman's tone was short, and hard. "We have heard whispers of his deeds throughout the world. We've been trying to stop people from coming up the mountain in the hope it would dissuade him." She glared. "Though apparently we haven't been trying hard enough."

The earthquakes. This woman had been causing them as a defensive maneuver.

"What are you?" the woman asked. She studied me, and though she was a head shorter than myself, I couldn't help but feel small beneath her shrewd gaze. "I can sense the magic inside of you, so do not try and twist your words with me."

My magic seemed to know how to answer even before I knew myself. Power spilled from me and dripped down my fingertips. I curled my hands, but energy still swirled around my wrists.

"I'm the reincarnation of an ancient sorceress, one who used to be aligned with the dark mage Vehrin, before he betrayed me and killed my lover." My words were my own, but the tone of my voice was like a cold breath from the past, vengeful words whispered from a long-forgotten grave.

Kael put a hand on my back, and the warmth of his touch helped to fade the sudden darkness swirling inside me.

The woman walked around me, studying every inch of my body. "Yes. You are nearly as ancient as myself."

I blinked in surprise. "You're a sorceress?"

"A witch," she said. "The dragons call me Jade, because my true name is not something many can pronounce."

If she was a witch, then where was the ruler of the dragons? Was she an advisor of some sort, a person trusted enough to hold the key?

"I was expecting to speak to the leader of the dragons," I said.

The woman flashed a fierce smile. "I have watched over the dragons for eons. I do not lord over them, but offer guidance and will do everything in my power to protect them." She gave me a hard stare.

"I did not come to harm them." I reached into my shirt and pulled out the pair of keys. "I need the fourth key. *Your* key. Vehrin has the third. I need to recover it, and the box he has in his possession. If he manages to get all four keys and open that box, he will unleash hell upon this earth. And if he gets the fourth key, he will be able to take the two I have."

Jade stared at the keys on my chest. She reached out and hovered a hand over the relics.

"The gold one holds your soul," she said.

I swallowed. "It does."

The witch touched her own key. "This one has similar capabilities, except where your key has one soul, this one is able to bind many."

A chill ran through me at the thought. If Vehrin managed to get his hands on it, not only would he be able to open the box, but he would be able to steal numerous souls and ruin so many lives. He could control thousands.

Suddenly, the witch seized my wrist in a strong grip. I winced as her nails bit into my skin.

"There is something corrupt and devious in your veins," she said. "I can sense it, writhing in there, waiting for release."

She squeezed harder, and the malignant power in me reacted. It flowed and lashed, clawing to be free. The witch's eyes grew to dark, unseeing pools, and I could have sworn I felt her magic sinking into me.

I cried out in pain and fell to my knees, but Jade didn't relent. Kael's shout rang through the room. Out of my peripheral, I saw Hagen and another guard grab hold of him. He growled, fighting them, but they let him go no farther.

The magic screamed in my ears, begging to hurt the one who was doing us harm. We wanted to make her pay, make her scream, make her bleed.

No. I won't hurt anyone. Not again.

I clenched my teeth so hard I thought they'd break. Pinpricks scattered across my skin, sharp and biting as a thousand needles. Fire coursed through my veins. My mind blurred under the strain, and still I held on.

Finally, when I was certain the darkness would rip me to shreds, the witch released me.

My hands slapped the floor as I gasped for breath on all fours. Kael was calling my name, and then his hands were on me. He spoke, but I couldn't hear what he was saying through the rush in my ears.

He eased me back into a sitting position. Fierce anger mingled with concern through our bond. When I was able to hear again and had blinked the blurriness from my vision, I looked up at Jade.

"You have much power wrapped in those shadows," she said. "It is of the earth, the oldest and most alive force in existence." She paused, tapping her chin. "I will not ask you how you acquired it. Judging by the curse on your soul, I'm certain you regret having such power."

I climbed to my feet on shaking limbs. Adrenaline sent tremors through my muscles, and my pulse raced.

That power. I'd almost unleashed it on the witch.

"I am a seer," Jade said. "Among other things." She stared at me, then frowned as I wobbled a bit. "I am sorry, but I had to know your intentions. Though darkness lives within you, I can see it is not who you are. You fight the curse, and it has not overtaken you...yet."

"I don't want power," I said. "I don't want anything except to see Vehrin defeated so I can live my life as normally as I can, for as long as I can."

Kael squeezed my fingers. "We want to be rid of the curse," he said. "If we can use the keys to take down the mage, perhaps we could find a way to cure her."

The witch nodded slowly and fingered the key at her neck. "This relic is our greatest treasure. We took it from those hoarding fools so it could be protected. To give it up would require a heavy price."

My heart skipped a beat. "Anything."

"You can *borrow* the key," Jade said, her amber eyes locking on me. "But when you defeat this dark mage, I want it back. Along with the key that holds your soul."

CHAPTER 22

"THE KEY WITH HER SOUL?" Kael barked. He stepped in front of me as if he were afraid the witch would snatch the keys from around my neck. "Are you nuts? You can't have that!"

Blood pounded in my ears. She wanted the key bound to my soul? If she had it, she would be able to control me.

I stepped out from behind Kael and glared at Jade. "Why do you want it?"

The witch stared at me, and in her amber eyes, I saw a flicker of sadness. "I want nothing more than to ensure the survival and happiness of those I love." She gestured out the open doorway. "These dragons are my friends, my family. Their kind used to be scattered throughout the world, content to live their lives and be left alone. Over time, discovery, technology, and greed have forced them to retreat from many nations to this place they now call home."

She walked toward a tapestry I hadn't noticed and ran a finger along it. It was expertly spun with threads of a hundred different colors. Half of it depicted the very scene I'd first set eyes on when we reached the city, a place of serenity and beauty. A jagged line cut down the center, and the other half showed a city of blood and death, with flames flickering up the columns of the palace and bones littering the cliffs.

"As I said, I am a seer. If I do not try and change what is coming, this will be our fate." She turned back to me with accusation in her gaze. "A fate you will bring to us."

I bit back a retort, because I couldn't say for certain if what she had suggested was a lie. It would not be the first time I'd left ruin in my wake, even if it had only been because the mage had followed me there.

"This mage of yours is a threat to our survival, and while I know you have no ill intentions, there is no guarantee you will not become a twisted being like him. After all, the same curse within him dwells within you, as well."

Kael's growl shivered over me. "She will *not* become like Vehrin. We're going to get rid of her curse."

Jade shrugged a slim shoulder. "Perhaps, but we do not know for certain. I cannot risk it. Think of my proposition as a safety net for my people. I'm assuming whoever holds the key ensnared with your soul can control you and your power. With the key in my possession, I can assure you will not be able to follow in Vehrin's footsteps."

I crossed my arms, covering the keys behind my sleeves. "And how do I know you aren't just going to use the relic, and me, for power?"

Magic crackled around the witch. "I am not a deceiver." She took a deep breath, and the static energy abated. "I can assure you, Olivia, I would only use the key if *you* were threatening the world."

I turned to stare at the tapestry, my gaze sliding from the scene of beauty to the harsh and violent future the seer had envisioned.

"I'm not sure," I said truthfully. Handing my soul over to a woman I didn't know was not a decision I could take lightly. How could I give such a big part of myself away? Besides, what about Kael? How would it affect him if I were to give the key to my soul to a stranger?

"The decision is up to you," Jade said. "But I will not give you the key, otherwise."

It frustrated me that the witch couldn't just help us, but I could see why she wanted to protect her own.

A shrill screech bounced from the palace walls, and we turned to find a small dragon flying in through the open doorway. She landed roughly on the gleaming floor, her tiny claws raking against the surface as her wings fanned out. She was a small species of dragon, roughly the size of a cat, and a beautiful midnight blue. It only took me a moment to see the bright red blood dripping onto the floor beneath her.

Jade hurried over to her as the dragon shifted into a young woman with big, wide eyes. She barely looked seventeen. Hagen hurried from the room, then returned to drape a silk robe around her as the witch checked a wound running down the length of the girl's arm.

"The mage," the girl said. "He's reached China."

Kael and I stepped closer, exchanging a glance. We knew he would come, but we hadn't thought it would be this soon.

The girl continued, wincing as Jade ran her fingers over the wound. "A third of Hong Kong is burning. The rest of the scouts didn't make it. Demons are ravaging their way through the city."

Vehrin no longer cared about hiding, it seemed. If he had demons killing people out in the open, the world truly was on its way to a devastation it would never survive.

The girl grabbed Jade's shoulder. "The mage and his army will be here by tomorrow."

Ice dropped into my stomach, and I glanced at the tapestry, and every stitch of destruction, burning flame, and rotting corpse depicted threaded into my mind.

"You did well, Mara," Jade said. She helped the young

woman up. "Go to the others and tell the generals to meet me here within the hour."

Mara nodded, the wound on her arm already healing, and hurried out the door.

"How can we help?" I asked.

Jade studied me. "Get some rest and make a decision." She turned to Hagen. "They've had a long journey. Show them to the baths, then put them in one of the southern rooms and make sure they have meals brought to them."

I didn't want to go hide in some room, but my stomach growled at the thought of food and getting clean sounded heavenly. Perhaps we could hold off a few hours. "Thank you, Jade."

The witch leveled me with a stare. "Do not take too long to make your decision. You are running out of time. Tomorrow, there will be war."

Without another word, she strode down the long stretch of the room to a small table with burning incense. She began a low chant.

I hoped whatever the seer found, it would be good news.

Hagen was silent as we followed him past screened doorways and wooden columns, then up a small flight of stairs. Kael and I had both taken turns having quick baths, and now I was eager to rest.

"Here." The dragon shifter gestured to a closed door. "If you need anything, I will have a guard posted down the hall. Otherwise, I bid you goodnight." His voice was tight with strain.

I opened my mouth to thank him, but he was already walking away. No doubt he was eager to return to his mate and make preparations for the impending attack. With a sigh, I slid the screened door open.

"Wow." I'd figured Jade would put us in a nondescript, out-of-the-way sort of room. I hadn't been expecting the chamber we were given.

The walls in the large room were a light wood that made the space seem brighter. Steam curled up from a small pool in one corner. Had someone filled it, or was there a natural hot spring beneath the palace? Either way, I was tempted to shuck my clothes off and sink my weary body into the water.

Instead, I studied the rest of the room. There was a bed, not huge, but covered in plush blankets and pillows. It faced a wide balcony that was open to the night. There was a light tapping at the door, and I let Kael answer it. I made my way to check out the balcony view.

My palms tingled as I found a sand garden. There were a few large stones rising from the sand, and a simple wooden rake leaning against a twisting juniper. Something about it made my heartbeat pick up, but then Kael called my name. He set a tray of food down on a small table, and the mouthwatering scents drew me away from the balcony.

We ate in silence, both too hungry to carry on a conversation. Afterward, I walked to the bed and sank onto the covers, both mentally and physically exhausted.

Kael rose from the table and sat beside me as I fingered the gold key around my neck.

Could I give someone control of my soul, even if it meant saving the world?

"What are you going to do?" Kael asked.

I let out a surprised laugh. "You mean you aren't going to try to talk me out of giving away the key?"

"It's your soul and your decision. You may be my mate, but I am not the lord of you." His fingers rose to brush against my cheek. "I don't want to see you come to harm, nor do I want you to have to give away such a great and powerful part of yourself, but I know you will make the right choice."

I dropped my fingers from the necklace with a sharp sigh. "I don't know what to do. Vehrin is on his way. There will be a fight tomorrow." I glanced out the open doorway to the night. To all of the beautiful gardens, the buildings, the people. The tapestry had shown them in ruins. "More pain. More loss."

"Not for you," Kael said. He cupped my chin and turned my face to his. "Not for us."

I curled into him, snuggling against his broad chest, and listened to his steady heartbeat. "I like the sound of us."

A soft breeze filled the room with the scent of pine and pink blossoms. It may have been the reality that tomorrow would be the day we could stop running, one way or another, or maybe it was the strange, peaceful lull of the dragon city, but I was starting to feel truly at ease for the first time since I'd discovered the relic in the Amazon jungle.

"Kiss me," I said.

Kael's lips twisted into a crooked smile. "Is that a command?"

I wasn't in the mood for games, so I grabbed his face and pressed my lips to his. I kissed him with a fervor that had my magic buzzing within me, and Kael responded with an enthusiastic growl that sent delightful shivers down my spine.

I broke apart from him for only a moment so I could shift to straddle him. His hot mouth kissed my neck and elicited a moan from me as he left a blazing trail back to my lips.

Kael's hands trailed up my ribcage and dragged my shirt along with it. He pulled it over my head and tossed it to the side before rolling me to my back. My mate hovered over me, his golden-brown eyes drinking me in slowly, even as need raged behind his gaze.

I smiled, and even though my heart was jackhammering at the breathtaking sight of my mate, I managed to speak. "I love you, Kael."

"I love you, too." His fingers traced the edge of my jaw. "More than anything."

His words broke through any restraint he'd had left, and as he lowered himself back to me, I had a fleeting thought that this moment was so damn cliché. How many stories through countless lifetimes told of two people with the possibility of being torn apart by upcoming war, who spent one first, and one last, night together?

But this was too perfect, too achingly magnificent to pass up. My mate's heat, his quick breaths, his scent blanketed me, and as we claimed each other, I couldn't help but think Jade may end up with my soul…but Kael would always have my heart.

* * *

KAEL HAD long since fallen asleep, but my mind was a whirlwind. I smiled at his sleeping form, amazed at how perfect we were together. It wouldn't last if Vehrin wasn't defeated.

Or if I couldn't find a way to end my curse.

I climbed from the bed and wrapped a shimmery silk robe around myself, then stepped outside onto the balcony. The city slept below, the quiet rest before war. By tomorrow, things would be different. Vehrin would be here.

I needed the fourth key, but could I really trust Jade with my soul? Even if I had the fourth key, how was I going to defeat the dark mage? He was powerful, even more than myself since he had embraced the dark strength of the curse.

I chewed on my lip and glanced at the sand garden. My palms tingled, and I stepped over to it. Something curled within me, urging me to move. Curious, I grabbed the little rake and made a small line in the sand. There was a flicker of warmth within me, like a tiny bolt of lightning beneath my skin. I made another line, and the edges of my mind blurred as I was pulled farther into the sand garden.

I moved the rake through the sand, giving my thoughts over to the strange force guiding me. For several minutes, I curved and swiveled, stepping delicately over the drawn lines.

Finally, I broke from the trance. Sweat trickled down my

back even in the cool mountain air. Silver moonlight spilled onto the marked sand, revealing images of a key on one side, and the twisting figure of a dragon on the other, with wavy lines connected the images.

My pulse quickened, and I thought of the fourth key.

It could bind souls.

In that moment, I knew I had my answer.

CHAPTER 23

PALE MORNING LIGHT spilled into the room, the glow warming the smooth, wood planks of the floor. My gaze was drawn to the sand garden from where I stood in the middle of the room. I'd smoothed the marks over with my feet. The revelation I'd uncovered made my gut clench. I felt despicable, and I hadn't even done anything...yet.

Perhaps I would ask Jade for the key one more time, no strings attached, and if she didn't agree, then I'd have no choice.

After all, Vehrin would be here soon.

Kael wrapped his arms around me from behind and pressed a kiss between my neck and shoulder. I sighed into his touch and wished with everything in me this day was over and things were all right.

"You're an incredible person," Kael said. He turned me around and pulled me into a hug.

I rested my face against his bare chest. Impossibly, our ties seemed stronger now than they had been since we'd become mated. His awe, passion, and love for me curled around our mating bond. I squeezed him and didn't want to move an inch.

"When this is all over, I'm taking you home and never letting you go again," he said, stealing the thought from my mind.

When this is over. First, we had to face Vehrin.

I pulled back. "So many things are riding on the outcome of this one little day. *One day*, out of the whole existence of the world, and all that we know could be taken from us."

Kael's eyebrows drew together. "Livvie…"

"I'm scared. I'm afraid of losing everything. Afraid of losing you." I crossed my arms. "Afraid of losing myself."

"We'll be fine." Kael grabbed my hand, and his fingers threaded through mine. "We have each other, and nothing, not a curse or a lunatic mage or anything else, can stop us."

I smiled, but my throat burned at his words. "Thank you for choosing me."

"Don't," Kael growled. "Don't do that, don't say goodbye." His grip tightened on my hand. "We'll get through this."

Maybe my mate was right. We *could* do this; I just had to stop being so negative. Yet, I couldn't settle the unease within me.

A sensation brushed over my skin like a shadow-swathed whisper, and my breath froze. I knew that power.

"Vehrin is getting close," I said.

Kael's grip on me tightened, as though unwilling to let me go. He couldn't hold me here forever, though, even if it was what we both wanted.

Sharp cries, screeches, and roars broke through the air. I looked up at Kael, and we both hurried to the balcony. The city below was empty of human form. They had all shifted, leaving nothing but dragons posted everywhere along the cliffs, among the buildings, and in the gardens. Sunlight danced across their scales, and I wondered morbidly how many of those scales would be gray and dull with death by the end of the day.

Several of the shifters ushered smaller dragons into buildings, and my breath hitched. *Children.*

The tapestry ran through my mind once again, and I couldn't shake the image of death and destruction.

My hands tightened into fists as my gaze ran across the beautiful city. I refused to let this place become a ruin.

In the distance, the mountain rumbled. Jade was still at work. Would she bring the whole mountain down if it meant keeping Vehrin's demon army at bay?

Birds broke into the sky as another earthquake ravaged the land, and as they took flight, I wondered where Renathe could be. Had he gathered those willing to fight? What if he'd already faced Vehrin and had been overrun? Bile burned my throat at the thought.

Vehrin was a poison. He desecrated everything he touched, and left nothing but pain, death, and ruin in his wake. I ground my teeth as I turned from the city.

Today, he would go no farther.

Our clothes had been cleaned for us and placed on a table in neatly folded piles. Kael had tried to convince me to soak in the hot spring, but I'd refused. I was too on edge to enjoy it, and besides, what would be the point of enjoying such a luxury when I knew there were those suffering outside the mountain's walls?

Kael pulled his black T-shirt over his head. "When this is over, we're getting in that bath together."

I smiled. He was trying to cheer me up, and the possibility sounded wonderful. "It's a deal," I said.

I started to grab my olive-colored jacket, but left it on the table. Today I would likely be swinging my sword until my muscles burned. I didn't want it to hinder any movement, so I settled on wearing nothing but my pants, broken-in boots, and a charcoal tank top.

"You look too good to be going to war," Kael said. His gaze openly appraised me.

I chuckled. "This is how I look every day," I said. "Besides, you're one to talk." The man really could pull off a pair of jeans, and the way his shirt stretched across his muscles...

Kael closed the distance between us. "Don't forget. Later, me, you, and that hot spring." He jabbed his thumb over his shoulder at the steam curling up from the water.

I smiled. It was a nice thought, but first we had a war to win. "Come on. I need to talk to Jade."

Kael reached an arm out to block me from leaving. "Have you made a decision?"

I curled my fingers around the golden key tied to my soul and felt the weight of the touch wrapping around my body. "I have, and I hope you don't hate me for it."

"I would never hate you."

Raising up on my toes, I gave him a kiss. "It's time to go, my warrior."

Kael's eyes sparked at my words, and I ducked under his arm. There was a guard posted a little way down, and when I told him I wanted to see Jade, he led us to the main hall we'd been in the day before.

The witch was there, along with Hagen, Lina, and several others. Jade wore an emerald green dress and had on sandals today. She also wore a piece over her chest that looked to be some kind of thin breastplate and had a katana strapped to her side. Determination hardened the edges of her face.

The others were in battle gear as well, wearing the same stiff tunics and armed to the teeth with blades to use if they needed before shifting. I felt woefully underdressed for battle, but I wouldn't have been comfortable clothed in anything else.

Jade spotted us and left her generals. I glanced over at the table with the incense.

"Did you see anything new?" I asked.

"No, though I wished I had." Jade's gaze flicked to the tapestry on the wall. I didn't need to look at it; the fabric had been burned in my mind since the day before.

A chill raised goosebumps on my bare arms that had nothing to do with the cool breeze whistling in through the cracked doorway. "Vehrin will be here soon," I told her. "I can feel it."

As the dragon shifters joined us, Kael spoke. "What are your plans?"

Hagen motioned us over to a map resting on a nearby table. It showed the entire city, plus the mountains beyond. "The mage will likely come from this direction." He pointed to the bridge we'd crossed the previous day. "It's the most direct route. Jade has reinforced the glamor on the city, but I don't think it will fool him for long."

"We're posted all along the edges of the city, with our strongest here." Lina leaned forward to indicate cliffs on either side of the one-and-only way into the city. "We will strike hard and fast when they arrive."

I admired her fierceness but hoped, for all of their sakes, it would work.

I turned to Jade. "Vehrin will come for the remaining keys. It's crucial that we stop him. He needs the keys to open that box, and he'll do whatever it takes to get them."

"Don't forget, Vehrin's key can override your own," Kael said.

"I know. He can't take away the power that's mine," I said, "but he can lessen it by blocking the power of the keys. I can't get too close to him unless we retrieve the relic currently in his possession."

The witch nodded. "I'll work with my best fighters to get the key *and* the box from him." Her gaze dropped to my necklaces. "Have you made a decision?"

"I have."

Before I could elaborate, a loud gong sounded from the city below. Another clanged, and then another, until the air practically vibrated with the warning call. Our group hurried to the doors and pushed them open. The dragons posted outside the gate were uneasy, restless. Their bodies practically trembled with restraint, and when I looked down, I could see why.

The demons hadn't made it through the tunnel...but only because they hadn't needed to. They spilled over the mountain, their eager shrieks piercing the air. Some had wings, their bodies twisted forms of birds and beasts. Others had climbed up and over the mountain with long, spindly limbs. There were thousands of them, pouring into the city like massive ants, ready to devour every living thing in their path.

Somewhere in the horde was Vehrin.

Time slowed even as my heartbeats quickened. I'd come so far, from nothing more than a simple archaeologist just looking for my next adventure to being the cursed reincarnation of an ancient sorceress getting ready to have a showdown with an evil mage.

There was only one way I would be powerful enough to take him down, and I had written it in the sand under the moonlight.

I had no choice but to embrace the darkness within me and hope I could pull myself from it when all was said and done.

"Jade, may I have the key?"

She studied me for a moment. "You will give me the key to your soul?"

I nodded, and hoped she couldn't read the tension that sent my heart beating faster.

Jade took it from around her neck and set it in my outstretched hand. "Do not forget our bargain," she said.

I took a deep breath and put the final key around my neck. I glanced down to see the demons stretching closer. The first of them had already made it into the city.

Kael watched me, his gaze cautious as I reached out a

hand. The new relic chilled like ice against my chest. I needed more power, and I had to be cruel enough to take it.

Darkness unfurled within me as I tapped into the power of the fourth key. It came alive in my mind, and I could sense every soul around me, from those perched on the cliffs, to the dragons down in the city. I picked out the strongest dragons, the quickest, and most lethal. Then, I wrapped myself around their beings and pulled.

Hagen yelled behind me, along with Lina and the other dragons in the room. I turned as they clutched at their chests, stumbled for a second, and then straightened. Throughout the mountain, many of the dragons roared, then quieted.

Every single one of them dropped like a weight in my mind.

"What did you do?" Hagen asked, his strange eyes wide as he stared.

Jade looked between the two of us. Understanding flickered to life in her amber gaze, then quickly fanned hotter with anger.

If the survival of our world hadn't been hanging in the balance, I would have been ashamed, but the threat was too real, and my moral compass wasn't pointing north at the moment.

"I stole the souls of the dragons," I said. "Bound them to me so I could use their power."

Hagen started to argue, and I wished he would be quiet for a moment so I could speak to Jade. His mouth clicked shut, and inwardly, I cringed. I hadn't thought it would be *that* effective.

"I will gladly return their souls, and the fourth key, to you after the battle, but I get to keep my own soul."

Jade glared at me with such ferocity, Kael edged closer with a growl in his throat.

"That wasn't the deal."

I matched her cold gaze with my own. "You were never in

a position to make a deal with something that was already mine. These are *my* keys, and down there is *my* enemy."

Screeching cries hooked our attention from each other and down the cliffs.

In the city, the winged dragons had started to take flight. I could feel their hate burning through the souls in the key as they set flame to the intruders. The ones on the cliff needed to help, and as soon as it went through my mind, dragons left their rocky perches.

Vehrin may have brought his horde of demons, but I'd just bound together an army of my own.

Now I just had to hope mine was stronger than his.

CHAPTER 24

The demons' bloodthirsty shrieks melded with the roars of the dragons as the opposing sides collided. I took a breath and released the mental hold on the shifters, giving them free rein to fight their own battles.

Kael brushed a hand up my arm. "Did you really take their souls?" he asked quietly.

I tilted my face up to his, and a flash of guilt flickered through me at the slight accusation in his gaze. "Yes. I mean, I bound their souls to the key. I *borrowed* their souls; I didn't take them." I was babbling excuses. This was war, it had been necessary, but I still feared my mate would see me as a monster. An apology tumbled from my lips. "I'm sorry. I didn't want to, but there was no other way, Kael. If we don't win today, we will lose forever."

He looked out at the dragons. "Are you controlling them?"

"No. I'm letting them do their own thing. They will fight in the way that best suits them."

Kael swept a quick gaze to Jade. She was speaking urgently to Hagen, no doubt readying him for the mission to steal the key from Vehrin. "If you have their strength, how will they fight?"

"It isn't their physical strength I took. It's more like a spiritual energy." Inside me, the energy of a hundred dragons swirled and melded with my own magic. It was strong and fierce, like the raging flames of a dragon's fire. The sensation made me restless. If I didn't release some of the energy, I was certain it would burn me up from the inside. "I need to go. I need to *do* something."

Lina pointed down to the city. "Look!"

Fae had started to fly over the mountain. There had to be at least fifty of them. My heart jumped.

Renathe! He'd done it! He'd brought reinforcements!

But my hopes shattered as the fae started attacking the dragons.

I stepped closer to the edge of the cliff. "What are they doing?"

Kael grabbed my shoulder. Thunder cracked through the mountains, and I watched in horror as several dragons were struck down from the sky by lightning.

I searched for Ren, but there was no sign of his ice-blue wings among the fae. These were no allies of my friend. These fae were loyal to *Vehrin*.

Hagen stepped forward and pointed. "The tunnel!"

The tunnel Hagen had led us through the day before had been breached, and all manner of shifters were pouring through. Wolves. Bears. Large cats. They went for the serpentine dragons without wings, or leaped up to catch small ones from the sky, like the little dragon who had flown from Hong Kong. My stomach clenched as I wondered if she were down there.

Flashes of light burst among the chaos in the city, and a chill ran over me as the sensation of different magic hummed through the air.

Witches.

Jade was seething where she stood, her hands clenched

into fists at the sight of her own kind taking down the dragons she loved.

"It is time to go," she said. "Now."

"How?" Kael asked. "It will take a while for us to climb down."

I peered down from where we stood on the summit. He was right. It would take at least twenty minutes to traverse down all those steps.

Jade quirked an eyebrow. "We have dragons with us, remember?" There was still anger at my betrayal flashing in her gaze, but with death knocking at the door, perhaps holding a grudge was not something she would worry about at the moment.

I was the first to catch her meaning. I glanced at Hagen, Lina, and the other dragon shifters. "You want us to ride them down?" I couldn't help but feel a sudden thrill at the thought.

What woman *wouldn't* want to ride a dragon into battle?

"Don't get used to it," Lina said. She walked over to me. "I'm not a pony, especially to a betrayer such as yourself, but I'll do what needs to be done."

I'd thought she hated me from the moment she set eyes on me, but as she stared at me, I found an ally, if a reluctant one. We both wanted to save this city, and her people, from destruction.

Kael and I had been through so much, had so many people against us, from the lion shifters to the gryphons. Now we had finally found those willing to fight by our side.

I gave Lina a smile. "Let's do this."

It was quickly decided Kael would ride with Hagen and Jade chose a dragon named Onyx. When he shifted, his scales were as black as his name. Plans were quickly finalized.

"Your mate and I will go after Vehrin," Jade said. She adjusted the katana at her hip as she climbed onto the back of the black dragon. "We'll separate him from his followers so we can steal the key."

I nodded, though it made me uneasy to be going to battle without Kael by my side. "We'll take down some of the heavy hitters." I gestured between Lina and myself. "Hopefully it will give everyone a better chance."

As Hagen and Lina shifted, Kael pulled me into a tight embrace. "Stay safe," he murmured into my hair. He eased me back and leveled me with a hard gaze. "And stay away from Vehrin until we have the key. It won't do any good to have dragon souls if he overpowers the keys so you can't use them."

Cries and screams of pain and fury continued to rise from below. The shadows in me soaked it in. I peered at Kael's golden eyes.

"Don't let me get lost," I whispered.

He took my face in his hands. "I'll always find you."

The kiss he graced me with was over too quickly, and my heart squeezed as I watched him walk toward a great red dragon. One of the scales on his arm was gray.

Hagen.

A quiet growling sound hummed behind me, and I turned to find Lina crouched low to the ground. She was a beautiful blue with glimmers of silver.

"I've never ridden a dragon," I said.

Lina huffed as if to say "obviously."

I climbed on her back just behind her forelegs but in front of her great silvery wings.

I peered over at Kael as the dragons halted at the edge of the cliff. He looked a little ill. I was grinning like a fool in anticipation.

The dragons launched from the cliffs, and the sudden rush stole the scream from my lungs. It took a moment for me to breathe again, and when I did, I focused on finding Vehrin. We circled with the others, and I concentrated, reaching out mentally until I found an enigmatic force not far from the entrance of the tunnel.

"He's somewhere over there," I shouted, pointing.

Jade nodded, and Kael waved as they turned toward my enemy. It took everything in me not to follow.

"All right," I said. "Let's go."

Lina dove down toward the city, and I gripped tighter with my legs. The place was a teeming mass of slashing claws, bursts of fire and magic, and so many screeches and screams. I did my best to block out the din and focus on where we were needed.

When I spotted a trio of fae taking down a pair of dragons who were guarding a small building, my nostrils flared and my teeth clenched. I remembered seeing the structure that morning as I watched the dragons prepare for battle.

There were children inside.

Lina found the fae at the same moment. Her wings flapped harder as we soared in their direction. Magic sparked at my hands as the fae eyed us diving toward them. I had no doubt they knew who was in that building, and I was going to make them pay for their intentions.

A fierce and sudden wind caught us, and we tilted violently to the side. I gasped and tightened my hold on Lina. I'd forgotten the fae could control the elements.

Lina smashed violently into the face of a cliff. The impact reverberated through my limbs, and I screamed as my shoulder slammed into the unforgiving rock, though Lina had taken the brunt of the force. The dragon fell several feet before she recovered with an indignant roar. The heat of her fury singed beneath my skin, and I used her wrath.

I conjured up a great amount of magic and threw a blast of vibrant purple flame into the trio of fae. We landed on the ground, and I swung from Lina's back. I stopped at her shoulder with a fierce smile on my face while the fae burned.

They screamed as their skin sizzled from their bones, and I drank in their pain. I held up my hand, lessening the power of the flames, making them die slower. So much agony. The darkness in me reveled. So much *power*.

I fought through the shadows in my mind and shoved back the darkness. I threw my arm forward and released a blast of magic that obliterated the fae to ash. I inhaled deeply, and instantly regretted it as the scent of burned flesh filled my nostrils.

Keep a hold of yourself.

Lina let out an ear-splitting shriek of pain. I turned and saw her stumble to the ground as ebony currents of electricity danced over her blue scales. A witch held her hand toward my new ally, and she grinned, watching the dragon's claws scrape against the ground. The sight soured my stomach with guilt, considering I'd just done similar to the fae.

I took a step toward the woman, and my body seized. I screamed and twitched as the sharp current bit into me.

Fight! I told myself. *Fight!*

With my body still writhing from the crackling current, I pushed my magic outward from myself. It met the witch's power, and I pushed harder until I felt a snap in the air. The woman stumbled a few steps in retreat.

My lips peeled back as my breath whistled through my clenched teeth. The witch started to raise her hand, either in defense or to conjure another attack.

"You chose the wrong side," I spat.

I thrust my palm forward, and this time, the darkness inside of me didn't have a chance to revel in her pain. The witch was dead in seconds.

A massive groan vibrated through Lina as she picked herself up from the ground.

I hurried over to her. "Are you okay?"

Lina's head whipped to the side, and her snake-like eye grew round. She cried out and started to fly, but stumbled. The witch's attack had taken a toll. Her sides heaved as she pulled in quick, frenzied breaths and stared across the city.

Something was wrong.

"Is it Hagen?"

Lina dipped her head.

Oh, God. Kael!

Had they been struck down?

I tried frantically to sense him through our bond, but I had so much emotion and magic coursing through me, I couldn't concentrate. If the others had been taken down, then Vehrin still had the upper hand.

I had to find Kael, consequences be damned.

"Stay here," I told Lina. I jerked my head toward the building, where a few scared dragon faces peeked up through a window. "Protect the children. I'll go help the others."

I didn't wait for her to agree before my boots were pounding across the ground.

Smoke filled the air, making it impossible to see where I should be going. I caught sight of a shadow ahead and hurriedly ducked behind a stone statue. I held my breath and tried to calm my racing heart as a large wolf trotted by. Thankfully, he was too focused on seeking out dragons to notice me.

There was a small bridge nearby, arching over a pool of disheveled lotus blossoms. The wooden planks beat hollowly as I ran across. I was nearly over it when a fae stepped in front of my path. I lurched to a stop. Her skin was the sea green color of a sunlit ocean, and her silver hair danced as if caught in a current. She raised her hands, and the pool beneath the bridge rose.

Before I could summon my own magic, she thrust her arms forward. Streams of water punched into me and sent me flying backward. I hit the ground, and the water continued to crash over me. I kicked and sputtered, and just before I was certain I would drown, the water stopped.

I sat up, coughing and blinking water from my eyes. The

fae stepped closer, mirth dancing in her large, shark-like eyes. Her gaze dropped to the keys on my chest.

"He will pay well for you, little one," she hissed.

Another jet of water rushed toward me, but before it reached my face, it stopped. The water creaked as it froze to ice that stretched all the way to the pond. I remained on the ground and stared at the sparkling ice in confusion.

Had she done that? But when I looked at the fae woman, she was sneering at someone behind me.

I turned and my heart burst. "Ren!"

My friend flew down beside me, and behind him, more of his brethren joined the fray.

He gave me a quick glance before he shoved a fist forward into the ice he'd formed. It shattered into a thousand fragments, but instead of hitting the ground, they soared at the water-manipulating fae. She only had time to open her mouth as shards of ice pierced through her. She hit the ground with a thud.

As I started to climb to my feet, Ren quickly moved forward to help me.

"I'm pleased to see you're still breathing," he said.

I let out a short laugh and brushed wet hair away from my face. "Barely." I glanced up as more of his friends flew over us to battle with the evil fae. "How do they know who to attack?"

Ren held up his arm to show me a bracelet around his wrist. There was a snowflake charm hanging from it. "Everyone is wearing one of these."

"Maybe you should give up the club and go into the jewelry making business," I suggested. I shook my head. "I've got to find Kael. He was supposed to be getting the key from Vehrin."

"I'll come with you," Ren said.

I shook my head. "No. You and the others work on taking down the fae who chose the wrong side. There are shifters, too, and witches. We can't win this fight against all of them, demons, and Vehrin."

Ren hesitated, then nodded. "All right, but be careful." He wrapped his arms around me in a sudden and surprising hug.

"Ow."

He instantly released me, and I rubbed my sore shoulder. Without asking, he felt around on it.

"Hm. It's not dislocated. I don't think it's broken either." His gaze ran over the rest of me. I probably looked like a mess. "What happened?"

"I was riding a dragon and slammed into a cliff, immediately followed by fighting off a witch trying to electrocute me to death. Then, as you saw, I was being drowned where we stand."

A large grin spread across Ren's face, and his teal eyes danced with amusement. "There's never a dull moment for you, is there?"

I had to smile back. "What's life without a little adventure?"

The sudden screech of a dragon overhead snapped me back to reality. "I have to go."

"Go." Ren jerked his head. "And try to stay alive."

I waved a hand as I made my way back across the bridge. The fae started to battle behind me and dragon roars pierced the sky as I ran toward what I knew was certain destruction.

Either for Vehrin, or myself.

CHAPTER 25

I RAN my arm across my face in an attempt to wipe away some of the sweat stinging my eyes. The air above shimmered with the heat of dragonfire, and I found myself thankful yet again that I'd opted to leave my jacket behind. I was half-tempted to remove the tank clinging to my body, as well.

Hopping up onto a bench, I craned my neck and squinted. I'd lost sight of the tunnel entrance again, which was the last place I'd seen Vehrin. His power inundated the entire city, and it was growing difficult for me to sense where exactly he was located.

A tingle scattered up the back of my neck, and I ducked just in time to avoid an orb of emerald light. It struck a statue not far from me, and the chiseled stone crumbled to gray dust. I pivoted, but before I could strike the witch down, a dragon descended.

His massive, webbed wings spread wide to slow his drop, and as his hind legs hit the ground, he opened his jaws. The witch didn't have a chance as he clamped down. Her scream was quickly squelched behind the sound of large teeth piercing her skin and crunching her bones.

Flame flickered from between the dragon's jaws. Then he

dropped the dead witch, broken and sizzling, and fixed me with a level stare before taking to the air again.

Note to self: never piss off a dragon.

I started off again and kept my eye out for Vehrin. "Where are you?" I muttered.

Battle surrounded me. I tried not to think about the way my boots sometimes squished wetly in fresh blood, or the sudden rain of ash that would fall from the smoke-heavy sky.

I did my best to keep clear of confrontation, though occasionally someone would catch me off guard, just as the witch had done. After a moment of hesitation, I let my magic kiss above my skin. The worst it would do would be to draw Vehrin's attention, right? If I could just get him close enough for me to attack him, but not close enough for him to block the power of my keys, I'd be fine.

But how close was that, exactly?

I tried to sense Kael's location, too, but my system was too manic to latch onto our mating bond.

After making my way around a small house, I paused to catch my breath. I braced my hands on my knees and promised myself just a minute of rest. I should have known stopping would only invite trouble.

A strange clicking noise sounded from the smoke to my right, but I didn't expect the monstrosity that emerged. The demon had to be seven feet tall with wicked, bared yellow teeth, curved horns on the sides of his mouth, skin the color of sour mud, and a smell that was worse.

I wrinkled my nose. "What sewer did you climb out of?"

The demon took a deep breath, and as he did, he clicked again, like some twisted insect. If only his limbs were thin as a bug's. Instead, they were wrapped in thick, hard muscle. I noticed with disgust and a thrill of fear that much of his skin was stained with fresh blood.

Large, pale yellow eyes locked on me, and he charged.

I threw my hand up in a flash and sent a bolt of energy

straight at him. Despite his hulking frame, he was impossibly fast. He sidestepped just in time to miss most of my attack. Instead, my magic hissed along his ribs. He swung out his arm as his momentum carried him past me.

His thick arm collided with me. I yelped, hit the ground, and lost my grip on my magic in the shock of impact.

A dark buzz, like a swarm of bees, sounded from the creature. I flipped over and climbed to my feet. As I stared at his wide mouth, I realized the demon was laughing.

Anger prickled through me. I didn't have time to mess around with this guy. With hardly a thought, my sword came to my hand.

"Is that the best you can do?" I taunted.

The demon ran toward me, and I rushed forward to meet him. Magic sparked at my fingers and licked up the blade of my sword. I swung it out in a horizontal arc as the monstrosity barreled toward me. The blade ran across his abdomen with all the success of a butter knife slicing leather.

Only my tripping feet kept him from caving in my chest with his meaty fist as I tilted sideways. I landed on my already sore shoulder and barely managed to keep from not falling on my own sword.

I quickly recovered as he turned back toward me. There was hardly a line across his skin where I'd struck. Whatever he was made of must have been hard, like the exoskeleton of an insect. If I could only get to the gooey center…

I tossed another energy-fueled attack at him, and this time it him with enough force to pitch him backward. He hit the ground, and for a heartbeat, he was so still I thought he was dead.

Until he climbed back to his feet.

The demon's yellow eyes bulged as he opened his mouth wide in a clicking roar. The horns on the side of his mouth opened and shut.

No, not horns. *Mandibles.*

It was time to squish this pest. I sent forth a burning stream of magic…straight into the demon's mouth.

The creature stumbled backward with a look of surprise then hit the ground. Smoke curled up from his mouth as his strange horn-like mandibles clicked together one last time.

Kael's voice suddenly bloomed into my mind. He'd shifted, and his voice flitted through my consciousness. *Are you all right?*

I'm fine. A wave of relief washed over me that he was alive. *Just put a cockroach to rest. Where are you?*

I didn't catch his answer as something slammed into my back. I hit the ground with a grunt. My breath whooshed out of me. I blinked several times before I could finally fill my lungs again.

"And here I'd heard you were nearly as powerful as the great mage himself."

I rolled over to find a fae standing a few feet away. As every member of her kind happened to be, she was gorgeous. Her figure was lithe and slim like a whip, and her bronze hair shone in a multitude of braids. The woman stood with her hip cocked, examining her fingernails.

"Of course," she continued, "we all know how rumors can get carried away." She finally turned to me with bright eyes. "Nice jewelry. I know someone who would very much like to have it."

My mind still spun from the hit to the ground, and my magic barely flickered over my fingers. As the fae stalked toward me, I fumbled for my sword that lay more than an arm's length away.

As she burst toward me, I rolled. My fingers closed around the hilt of my sword, but I wasn't fast enough. I cried out as her hands gripped my shoulders and shoved me down.

"What are you going to do now?" her voice hissed in my ear.

My nostrils flared as I took a deep breath and slammed my

head back into her face. She gasped, and I twisted to face her. Not wasting a second, I folded my legs back then thrust my feet up into her chest. She stumbled away as a figure emerged from the smoke behind her.

Jade's katana was silent as a shadow as it sliced through the air and right through the fae woman's neck. I grimaced as the lithe woman's head hit the ground, quickly followed by her body.

"Where's Lina?" Jade asked as she rushed toward me. I didn't see any sign of Onyx, the dragon she'd been riding, or of Hagen.

I climbed to my feet and went to retrieve my sword. I let it twine back into a bracelet for the time being. "She's protecting the children." I looked behind her, then returned my gaze to her face. "Where are the others?"

"Kael is on his way. Hagen is fighting a group of fae trying to bring the mountains down on our heads. Onyx fell." The glimmer of sadness in her gaze told me he would not be rising again. "Vehrin withheld our attacks with ease. It was impossible to get close enough to him to get the key."

Though I had hoped our plan would work, I wasn't surprised it hadn't. The only person he would allow to get near was me...which was exactly what he wanted.

"I have to confront Vehrin."

Jade jerked a nod. "Your mate said you would. He's on his way here to stop you."

Of course he would try to stop me. He likely had an idea how this would all play out. I feared the same.

"Do you still hold the dragons' souls?" The witch didn't look angry, but I heard the steely accusation in her voice.

"Yes, I do." I hadn't tapped into the power they were providing yet. I had to save as much as I could for Vehrin.

Jade didn't respond immediately. She took a deep breath, then pointed with her katana. "Last I saw Vehrin, he was this way."

We hadn't gone two steps when a demon with curved horns and a vicious scorpion-like tail emerged from the smoke. His hooved feet clopped on the stone path stretching before us. Magic wrapped around me, and I thrust my palm forward.

I didn't have a chance to see if my attack hit my target. A surprised yell left my lips as I was hoisted from the ground. I twisted to find a troll-like demon sneering at me. His hot breath smelled like fish guts left outside on a hot summer day. I gagged as I squirmed to break his hold.

Then, a familiar roar feathered over my soul like the caressing touch of a lover.

Kael.

I grinned fiercely at the demon right before my mate leaped up to latch his jaws on the side of the demon's neck. The gruesome beast dropped me and tried to reach Kael with his thick arms, but the jaguar was too fast. His sharp claws tore into his throat. The demon gurgled, and Kael jumped back to the ground as the creature stumbled into a nearby sand garden. He hit the ground with a thud.

The demon's blood soaked into the sand, filling the wavy pattern that somehow still remained from the previous person to use the garden. For some reason, the gryphon elder's final words came to my mind.

We must all descend back into the marked earth.

There was something important about it, but I couldn't for the life of me put my finger on why.

Kael padded over to me. *You can't confront Vehrin. Not yet.*

I climbed up from the ground and tried in vain to brush off the ash and grime. "Well, hello to you, too. Besides, who says that's where I was going?"

He gave me a level stare. Only he could make a jaguar look scolding.

I threw my hands in the air. "Fine. But I don't have a choice, Kael. I have to do this now, before things get worse." I suddenly remembered Jade and the other demon. I pivoted to find her scowling down at the beast as she shook blood from her blade. His scorpion tail still twitched.

Kael snarled. Even pissed at me, he was beautiful. *Going after him now would mean giving up over half your strength. You can't stand against him while he still holds the other key. If you think I'm going to let—*

A wicked force practically speared me in the chest.

"Look out!" I gathered my magic and pitched it forward.

The wall I'd created flashed as shadows cracked into it. My defense dissipated easily and I stumbled back. I tried again, but my magic barely flickered.

The dark mage strode forward.

Darkness hung from him, the black wisps catching the wind like tattered cloth on a skeleton. He smiled, and his chest rose as he took in a deep breath. The shadows intensified. He was consuming the pain and suffering around him to feed his curse.

"We meet again," he said. "For the last time, I suspect." He held out his hand. Strangely, his skin looked blotted with ink.

The curse. Couldn't he see how it was overtaking him?

"Give me the keys, Olivia. There is nowhere else to run. Nowhere to hide."

He was close enough for me to sense the box on his person, the one he wished to unleash upon the world. Vileness billowed from it, and the evil within called for me to release it.

My own curse scratched for freedom within me. It would be so easy to open the box…

I curled my fists. "Go to hell."

Vehrin's answering grin made my blood run cold. "How about I bring hell to us?"

I threw my hands forward, but the attack wasn't nearly as strong as it should have been. Vehrin waved a hand, and it burst apart before it reached him.

His key was blocking the power from my own relics.

The mage held his arms wide. Smoke from nearby fires curled toward him to join the shadows rolling from his hands. To my horror, beads of blood from the deceased lifted and coiled to join the smoky blackness. Bile burned my throat as I beheld Vehrin's creations.

Black dragons circled around him, their figures made of smoke and shadow. Ruby flecks dotted their forms. I could sense the pain that echoed through their twisted bodies, a pain that wanted more loss to satisfy their own suffering. The horrific dragons took to the air...and straight toward the dragon shifters.

I had no choice but to watch as the mage's dark magic took them down. Fire didn't burn conjured dragons. Gnashing teeth and tearing claws only passed through them.

One of the shifters crashed to the ground, and as it took its dying breath, something flickered within me. Another screamed out in pain, it's roar fading into nothing. Another warm flicker. Energy buzzed inside of me, an energy that wasn't my own.

My eyes grew round. *The dragons.* As they died, I grew stronger. Could it be because their souls bound to the key were no longer connected to a physical body?

It was morbid to think that I was growing stronger as the dragons fell, and a great sense of self-loathing draped over me. Binding their souls was keeping the fallen dragons from going on to rest. I hated it but I would use it to stop Vehrin.

Magic engulfed my arms, and I locked eyes with my enemy.

What are you doing? Kael asked.

I ignored him and started forward.

A wrath-fueled scream of rage came from Jade as she dashed past. I tried to stop her, but my words fell on deaf ears. The dragons she loved were falling from the sky, and no one was going to stop her charge for revenge.

The ground suddenly shook beneath my feet. The tremors grew with every step Jade took. There was a loud crack, a crevice tore through the earth in her wake.

Jump! Kael spoke to my mind, leaping to the side as the ground ripped open toward us.

I took one step, and the ground gave way beneath my boot, sending me tumbling down into the waiting maw of the earth.

CHAPTER 26

I SQUEEZED my eyes shut against the debris falling onto my face. The scrape and groan of stone finally stilled until the only sound I heard was my pulse hammering in my ears.

I was still alive, despite the earth attempting to swallow me.

A sharp breath hissed in through my clenched teeth as I raised myself up on my arms. My bones ached, and my ribs screamed. I carefully pressed a hand to my side. I had to have at least two cracked ribs. Gingerly, I tested out my limbs, but nothing seemed broken.

Smoke and dust blanketed the air above me, so thick it was impossible to see how far down I had fallen.

Though I couldn't see, the sound of battle still raged above me. I feared for Jade's life. The witch wouldn't stand a chance against Vehrin on her own.

Kael? Are you up there?

A spike of worry reached me. *Are you hurt?*

I'm fine. I need to find a way out. I rose carefully to my feet. Walls of dirt and rock surrounded me. If I could just find a place sturdy enough to climb on…

I paused as something caught my eye. Squinting, I made

my way closer and found an opening. It looked to be some sort of doorway. The outside was faced with ancient stone, and when I ran my fingers over it, I could feel runes carved into the surface. Beyond the doorway was nothing but darkness. There was no way to tell where it led. Could it be some sort of storeroom?

Stay put. I'll make my way to you and get you out of there.

I didn't answer Kael. I stepped curiously into the doorway and summoned my magic. It was faint, even with the strengthened souls of the slain dragons tied to me. Vehrin's key was still overriding my powers, but I had enough to light my way. Several feet in, the space opened up.

This was no storeroom.

It was a tomb.

A sarcophagus stood in the room, the stone smooth and untouched with age. Atop it sat a carved dragon, its tail draped around the lid and the detailed head laying across its feet. It looked like it was sleeping, a peaceful rest after an immense struggle. A warmth filled me, and I knew, without a doubt, I was standing before the remains of the very first dragon.

The ceiling cracked above me, but I made my way closer to the stone coffin. Runes ran along the edge of the lid, a language even more ancient than my knowledge could place. My heart beat faster as I took in the rest of the room.

Images of dragons were depicted on every wall. They rose up from the earth, their limbs breaking free of roots and their bodies uncoiling from the dirt.

I'd been right. Dragons truly were born of the earth.

Every pore tingled at the thought, and I knew I'd stumbled upon something important. The pieces were poised to click together. My past and my curse, the gryphon elder's dying words, the earth and the dragons. It all meant something. But what?

A boom echoed above me, and the entire tomb moaned.

Dust drifted from the ceiling, and cracks splintered up through the walls.

A sense of urgency rippled through Kael. *Olivia! Where are you?* I turned to leave, and a large chunk of rock fell free of the ceiling. Only quick footwork saved me from being crushed. I let out a yell as I hit the sarcophagus, the impact rattling through my aching ribs.

The massive stone had blocked more than half the doorway. I glanced around for another way out, but found nothing. Kael was shouting in my head. The only way out would be to wiggle through the doorway.

I clenched my teeth and dashed forward as more of the ceiling broke free to smash into the floor.

"In here!" I yelled.

I clambered up the chunk of ceiling and cursed when my foot slipped, my knee cracking hard against the stone. The collapsing of the tomb filled my ears, and dust clouded around me. My muscles burned and my ribcage screamed as I hauled myself up through the narrow opening.

The magic around my fist failed me just as I squeezed through, and the light faded.

Warm breath huffed over my face as something sniffed and nudged at me.

Kael.

I wrapped my arms around his neck and buried my face in his soft fur. "You're here."

I told you I was coming. What were you doing in there?

Behind me, the doorway had collapsed under stone and soil. "I think…finding answers."

My mind buzzed as I tried to make the pieces fit together. The answer was so close, but I couldn't see it.

"We have to get back up. Vehrin is still up there, and we won't be able to defend ourselves stuck down here," I said. I got to my feet and pressed a hand to my side.

Kael bumped my hip lightly with his head. *You're hurt.*

"I'll be fine, Kael. Help me find a way out of here."

My mate hesitated, then dipped his head in a nod and started off. He led me to a steep incline of earth, bits of rock and roots tangling the way. I followed him as he climbed and put the aching of my body to the back of my mind.

I was afraid of what I would find when we reached the surface, and my heart fell when I saw those fears realized.

Jade lay not far from where the earth had collapsed. Her body was still, and I wasn't close enough to see if she still breathed. Overhead, Vehrin's dragons continued to attack the shifters. Most were trying to avoid the warped forms of smoke and shadow the mage had created. I wanted to cry out every time I felt a soul break free of their earthly body as a dragon shifter fell from the sky.

Kael pressed against me, and he vibrated against my leg as a menacing snarl ripped through him.

Vehrin stood across from us. The third key around his neck glowed softly as it buffered my power.

"We have to get that key, and the box, or we aren't going to win."

Kael didn't argue or hesitate as I started forward. We had to get that key, and we would fight together, as we had always done.

We charged. I used the souls of the fallen dragons to muster up as much power as I could under the influence of the mage's key. No one stopped us as we neared Vehrin, no demons or traitors, no magic-wreathed dragons. It was just us and him, a battle the centuries had been waiting for with bated breath.

I threw my hands forward with a yell, and bright energy erupted from my palms. It soared toward our enemy, and as my magic surged forward, so did my mate.

The attack crashed into Vehrin's left side, and as his body twisted with the impact, Kael leaped up. His massive paws widened as he reached for the key with deadly claws.

My breath hitched, then Vehrin whirled and caught Kael with a hard blow of magic right before his claws reached the relic. Kael hit the ground, and before he could recover, Vehrin struck him again with a blast of power.

Pain crackled through our bond, and my voice broke as I screamed his name.

Vehrin didn't stop. He sneered at my mate. "Your former self was the downfall of such a mighty sorceress," he said. "She gave her heart to you, but her soul will always be cloaked in darkness. She cannot escape it." The mage's gaze swept to me as he finally ended the attack on Kael. "Her only hope is to give in to the curse."

Shadows rippled around Vehrin, and darkness whispered across his skin. Kael climbed to his feet and twitched once more as the remnants of magic pierced over him. The sight incensed me, and I charged forward again with another attack.

Vehrin tossed up a flat, inky shield of power, and my magic evaporated on impact. My legs shook as I pulled in shallow breaths. Kael came to stand beside me, but even his presence couldn't stop the hopelessness from sinking into my bones.

Demons shrieked around us as they hunted down victims. Fae clashed against fae with the clanging of metal and beating of wings. Foreign magic snapped through the air like static from the witches.

We were going to lose.

"It's time to give in to the curse, Olivia." Vehrin held his hand out with a pleading expression. For a brief moment, I saw the man he used to be, inquisitive and earnest, before curiosity, greed, and selfishness warped him into the mage before me. "It's time to stop fighting and just accept that some things are not meant to be changed."

Exhaustion weighed down every inch of me. My mind was

heavy, and my energy drained. I had no more strength left to fight Vehrin.

Give in? Oh, how I was tempted. It would be so easy to give in to the curse.

I hung my head and stared at the earth beneath my boots. *Give in to the curse.* My heart skipped as I studied the trampled grass. I needed more power. *Give in to the curse.* The curse, which I'd been given because I'd stolen power...from the earth.

My breath quickened as I realized what I had to do. I glanced up at Vehrin. He eyed me eagerly, waiting for me to give in—*expecting* me to give in—to come crawling to him. I needed time.

I searched the skies. Where was my fae friend?

"Renathe!" I screamed at the top of my lungs. It would be a miracle if he heard me over the din of war.

A cold breeze suddenly brushed over me, and in the next moment, Ren landed in front of us.

"You rang?" My friend grinned, though his heart didn't seem into it. Blood marred his clothes, both his own and the greenish ichor of demons.

I glanced over his shoulder. Vehrin's eyebrows were pinching together as he realized I wouldn't be groveling today.

"Shield us," I said.

Vehrin started to raise his hand.

"Quick!"

Ren didn't ask questions. He spread out his arms, and a thick wall of ice burst from the ground. His creation enclosed us in a dome and the sounds of battle fell away. He bared his teeth as Vehrin's attacks slammed against the ice.

"Whatever you have planned, you'd best hurry," he said.

I knelt to the ground and closed my eyes, bringing up the memory of the day I gained my curse. A vision of patterns in the ground, and an incantation, came to me.

What are you doing? Kael asked, his golden cat eyes watching me carefully.

I summoned my sword from my wrist and turned to him. My throat burned. I pressed the sword to his forearm, then let it braid back into the bracelet. It entwined just above his paw. Through our bond, I gave him the knowledge and magic he needed to summon the blade.

"When this is over, run this through my heart."

Kael jumped back with a surprised huff. Then, he snarled. *Never.*

My nostrils flared. I couldn't break now. Couldn't show my fear. Couldn't show my loss. "It's the only way. *This* is the only way. Otherwise, the entire world, every living being, every man, woman, and child, will perish. Kael, I will not let that happen." I swallowed. "Not even for us."

My mate watched me, his ribs heaving in and out with quick breaths. *I promised I wouldn't lose you*, he said. *And I'm going to keep that promise.* He glanced down at the bracelet, no doubt contemplating tearing it off.

"Olivia!"

I glanced up to find Ren's arms shaking with the effort to hold the shield against Vehrin's power.

It was now or never.

I looked at Kael one last time, and prayed he would do the right thing when the time came.

Without another word between us, I reached my hand down to the dirt.

Then, I began to trace markings into the earth.

CHAPTER 27

SOMETIMES, evil could only be defeated with a greater darkness.

That's what I told myself as my finger scratched a pattern in the cold dirt beneath me and ancient words tumbled from my lips.

I ignored the crack of the ice-formed shield around me and ignored the anxious pacing of my mate. There was nothing but me and the earth.

A hum of energy reverberated beneath the soil, and I splayed my fingers across the complicated lines and swirls I'd drawn. The earth's magic resisted as I pulled, drawing the energy up into my palms.

I had to do this; I had to damn myself to save the world.

The magic did not come to me easily. My muscles tightened as pain seized them, and I ground my teeth to the point of nearly cracking them. I drew in quick breaths through my nostrils and pulled harder. I squeezed my eyes shut as a strangled cry escaped me.

Kael came closer, but when he tried to nudge me, a zap of energy shot through me. He jumped back with a startled snarl. *Olivia, stop. You can't do this.*

I kept going. I drew in the ancient magic of the world, and the power of my curse fed on the new sustenance. It felt vile to steal from the earth, but I couldn't stop. Not now. The thought of destruction and Vehrin's downfall filled my mind. I needed more power.

Wanted more power.

With a snapping sensation, I finally broke free from the earth.

My chest heaved with ragged breaths as I stared down at the marred dirt. Power roiled in me, so much I wouldn't be able to contain it for long without being shredded to pieces from within. I stood as Renathe's shield cracked apart and shards of ice rained down upon us.

I spread my fingers and let every ounce of magic in my veins rise to the surface, both my own, and that born of darkness. Wisps of shadow melded with the fuchsia light of my energy. It swirled around me, licking down my arms and hanging from me like a windblown cloak. At my back, Kael growled his displeasure.

Ren stepped in front of me as I ambled forward. I didn't turn to him as I spoke.

"Move." My voice was strange—ancient and distant. Cold, and utterly unyielding.

Across from me, a slow grin spread across Vehrin's face. "You have pulled more magic from the earth. Now, you are twice cursed."

I swept past Ren. My boots crunched on the cracked stone steps of a garden. I held up one of my hands. Inky blotches grew across my fingers.

"Twice cursed, and twice as powerful."

I didn't run toward the mage as magic coiled around me. I took my time, savoring the way his smile faded and delighting in his steps of retreat as he backed away. His cruel gaze had faded, and his eyes widened with uncertainty.

"Why do you run, Vehrin?" I asked. I could sense his key

trying to work against my own. It was futile. My magic was beyond even that of the relics. The power was past any kind of suppression…and so was I.

The mage didn't answer me. He merely wheeled around and took off. The corners of my lips lifted, and the darkness inside me trembled eagerly at the new game.

As he fled, I pursued at a steady pace. I shoved my palm forward, and a swirl of light and dark twisted outward. Vehrin looked back just in time to deflect the attack. It didn't matter. I would catch up eventually, and I would take back what was mine. Then, I would drink in his screams.

Magic billowed around me as I hurled another volley of attacks, and though they missed Vehrin, the darkness inside of me savored the destruction it wreaked around me. I drew in the screams of pain from the fae who still quarreled, from the witches, and from the demons. Stone cracked around me as my magic swept across buildings and the earth trembled beneath every step.

I let the darkness beckon me forward as shadows caressed my soul. So much power. Power I would use to crush Vehrin into oblivion.

One of Vehrin's magic-wrought dragons soared overhead, wreathed in smoke and freckled with fallen shifter blood. Their souls lamented within me and further fueled the hate I had toward the mage, hate my cursed magic soaked in.

Ahead of me, Vehrin disappeared behind a house nestled up against the towering cliffs.

"Oh, no you don't," I snarled.

I flicked my fingers, and the energy sped from my hand and smashed through the house. It burst apart in bits of wood and stone. Chunks of rock shook free from the cliffs and rolled to the ground. The dust settled to reveal Vehrin holding up a shield on the other side.

I thought he would stand and fight this time, but he ran

again. Frustration and anger fueled my steps as I started after him.

"Olivia, wait!" Ren called.

I ignored him and worked my legs faster. It was time to stop playing. I flung magic ahead of me. It crumbled a stone statue to dust as it soared past Vehrin. The mage disappeared behind another building.

Please. Don't. Kael's voice was so soft and pleading, I nearly turned around. Then, I had to step over the body of a small, blue dragon. She looked very much like Mara, the young woman who was a scout.

Black wrath filled my vision. I could not afford softness now. I could not afford restraint. There was nothing but the need for pain and screams as Vehrin squirmed in my grasp.

I lashed out with the intertwined magic of light and dark, and buildings, statues, and gardens blew apart in my wake. Vehrin was hiding, and I had to get to him.

Dust billowed with the smoke in the air, and I squinted, my eyes burning.

Where did he go?

I let out a sharp yell as something hit my already injured side. I stumbled, then wheeled toward the direction of the attack. Without a second thought, I threw forward a blast of energy.

Screams ripped the air, and for a moment, my heart rejoiced. Then, a witch stumbled into view. She cried and tore at herself as my magic ravaged the skin and muscle from her bones. I felt no sympathy as she hit the ground, her half-burned body still twitching.

"Where are you?" I muttered. There was no sign of Vehrin anywhere. I couldn't let him slip through my fingers. I would raze this city to the ground before I'd let him get away.

In my search for the mage, I lashed out again and again. Magic shredded the ground and left trenches of open soil like fresh wounds on the earth. Chunks of rock fell from the cliffs to smash into houses and storerooms. A statue toppled into a pond as I passed, the magic billowing from me sending the lotus blossoms burning into the wind.

People screamed and yelled around me. Not demons, or fae, or witches. People. Around the buildings, running through the gardens, hiding behind statues.

My mind flickered. Something was wrong…

Then, I caught sight of Vehrin's cloak through the swirl of smoke, dust, and shadow. I started forward again as my magic crackled around my clenched fists.

I stopped short as Ren landed in front of me. His eyebrows were drawn together, and his ethereal features were hard.

"Stop this, Olivia." He started forward, and I could feel a cold wisp of wind tugging at my hair, making the air smell frigid and sharp, like a deep breath on a winter's day. "There has to be another way."

I narrowed my gaze at him. He would dare try and use his magic on me? I slashed my hand through the air. My magic caught Renathe hard, and he was brushed roughly to the side and out of my path. His wings flapped as he tried desperately to find balance. He landed on a bench, and it flipped over.

My heart tried to skip with fear that I'd hurt him, but all I felt was annoyance at the interruption.

Ren hooked an arm over the bench and lifted himself up.

"You have to stop her!" he yelled, gazing past me.

I turned, wondering who would dare try…and found Kael.

He'd shifted from his jaguar form, had managed to somehow find a pair of pants, and was holding a sword.

And he was pointing my sword at *me*.

Sparks hissed and popped around my body as I bared my teeth. *Betrayal*, my darkened soul sang. *Traitor. Deceiver.*

Magic thrummed through me, ready to be released.

Dead man.

"Livvie."

I paused. His golden eyes held mine, and for a moment, it kept the darkness at bay. My fingers loosened from the tight fists, and my hands shook. Dark magic tugged at me, urged me to strike down the man keeping me from my enemy.

His screams would be delicious, the curse seemed to say. *His pain would bring much power, enough to take down Vehrin.*

I squeezed my eyes shut and pulled in a shuddering breath. My heartbeats raced in my chest as I tightened my grip on the cursed magic fighting to be unleashed.

"Kael." The sound of my mate's name rolling off my tongue was like a lifeline. I grabbed a hold of it as I attempted to pull myself from the dark. I had to break free of the rampant darkness inside of me.

A laugh broke through my internal battle, and my eyes flew open.

Vehrin stood several feet away. The key still hung on his chest, and I could sense the box in his pocket. A confident smirk lifted one of his cheeks. Hadn't he been fleeing? Why was he here now?

"It has taken a while, but you have finally let the curse become what it was always meant to be," he said. "It felt good, did it not? That much power coursing through your veins, every ounce of magic ready at your fingertips. It is not something many are fortunate enough to experience. You have finally lived up to your true potential, Olivia."

Vehrin swept an arm out, and when I turned to look, my heart cracked.

What had once been a city of serenity and beauty, was now a city of rubble and death. Bodies lay amid the broken buildings. Loose stones littered the torn ground, and splintered wood floated among the ruined lotus ponds. Bridges had collapsed, and statues reduced to grit and dust.

A stillness draped over the city. Demons, witches, fae, and

shifters alike had been forced to stop their battles under the havoc I'd wreaked.

"Livvie…" Kael's voice was a quiet plea, but I couldn't face him.

All I saw was the tapestry that hung in the palace on the summit of the mountain. I saw the half that was lush, green, and alive. Then, I saw the other half, the one of destruction, death, and chaos. It was the half of empty promises, of lost hope, failure, betrayal, and pain.

My throat burned as my gaze swept across the ruin I'd helped create. Jade had been right. There was something dark and devious in my veins, and I hadn't been able to run from the fate she'd seen.

I stared out at the destruction, and blood, and death.

I had done this.

I had given in to the shadows of my curse, and I had ripped through this city with no regard for anyone else.

The dark began to creep back over my soul.

I was, indeed, a monster.

CHAPTER 28

"Livvie, look at me." Kael's voice fought through the ringing in my ears, through the shadows wrapping around my being and pulling me under. "Look at me."

Shame filled me as I slowly lifted my gaze. I expected condemnation, hate, or fear, but what I found in his eyes was...love. It warmed down our bond and wrapped around my soul, shadow-stained and all.

Kael lowered the sword to his side. "Come back to me. This isn't you. You aren't capable of doing these things."

My chin trembled, and I swallowed. "But I am."

I started to scan the wreckage that had been *my* doing, but Kael quickly stepped forward.

"Look at me," he repeated. He took my hand, and the sword twined back into a bracelet around my wrist. He caged my face in his strong hands. "Nothing else matters right now but you and me. You are more than this. You are more than a curse, more than a reincarnation. You are my mate, and I know your soul better than anyone."

From the moment I'd seen the ruin I'd left in my wake, I'd reined the cursed magic back in, but it fought to claw its way back out, and I wasn't sure how much longer I could contain it. It was going to tear me apart, and I feared it would tear my mate apart, too. The pressure continued to build, threatened to rip through my every pore.

I tried to reach for the bracelet before we ran out of time, but Kael grasped my wrist.

"After Vehrin is gone, you have to stop me," I said. "The power...I can't hold it in."

"I won't do it." Kael grabbed my arms and squeezed them, anchoring me to this world, to him. "Don't ask me again."

Renathe walked over, and guilt flashed through me. I'd attacked him, but his gaze held no animosity. His features were hard, but he gave me a smile and gestured to Vehrin. The mage had wisps of magic caressing his fingers, readying for an attack.

"A quick suggestion?" he said. "If you can't hold back your power, then focus that weapon on the enemy, aim true, and fire. Fire everything you have."

I hesitated, afraid if I released the cursed magic a second time, there would be no coming back to myself. I'd barely made it back this last time.

Kael squeezed my hand. "I'll be with you. I won't let the darkness take you away again."

The three of us turned to Vehrin. Energy crackled through the air. Before he could release his attack, I let my magic flow. I threw my hands forward and sent a torrent of power. The twisting mass of light and shadow crashed into the dark mage.

Dirt erupted from the ground, and the earth shook. The impact echoed off the cliffs before the ruined city of dragons fell silent.

My body shook with adrenaline as the dust and smoke dissipated in the final swirls of my attack.

Vehrin was powerful, but he had to have been knocked out by that much magic. There was no way he...

The mage's cloak stirred slightly in a dying breeze, then fell still. He lowered his hands, and amusement sparked in his eyes.

I was too shocked to speak. How had he not been incapacitated by my attack? He shouldn't be conscious, let alone *standing*. I sucked in a shaky breath as I fought against the light-headedness brought on by my attack.

Vehrin stood strong and powerful, and I realized something chilling: All this time, he'd been holding back.

His hurried retreat through the city had been merely a ruse to urge my darkness to come forward, to let the curse feed on my anger, to try and get me to come join him.

The mage held his hands out to the side. "Do you honestly believe I have not done the same as you?" He curled his fingers, and bits of dirt floated up in the air to rest in his palm. "I have pulled magic from the earth *dozens* of times. You will never defeat me."

Dozens of times? I'd been cursed thanks to his deviousness, and that had only been the first time. The second time, I'd nearly lost myself. How wasn't he being crushed beneath so much darkness?

Vehrin suddenly raised his voice to address those he'd brought to fight with him. "Now is our time! Kill the rest, including her companions. It is time to make a new beginning!"

The demons, fae, and witches loyal to Vehrin rushed forward in droves. My whole body tingled as my spent energy started to replenish. I gritted my teeth as Renathe impaled several demons with a wall of icicles, and Kael shifted back to his massive jaguar.

I would not give up without a fight.

I rushed forward, and my boots had only tapped the ground four times when the earth shook violently beneath my feet. Ahead of me, Vehrin stumbled as the earthquake growled around us.

Confused, I paused and did my best to keep my balance. An earthquake? My eyes widened. That would mean…

A dragon swooped down from the smoke-filled sky, with Jade astride her. She was riding Lina. The dragon shifter had been wounded. Several of her beautiful scales had turned gray and were smeared with blood. I thought of the children she'd been protecting, and prayed they were unharmed.

With a deafening roar, Lina dove at Vehrin. The mage scowled and started to raise his hands for an attack. I punched my fist forward and managed to hit him with a large enough ball of energy that made him jerk. His attack missed, and Lina crashed into him, her great wings flapping.

Her vicious roars turned into frantic screeching. I gasped as the dragon went flying backward in my direction. I quickly retreated, and Lina landed a few feet in front of me with a crash of crunching bones.

Lina didn't stir, and I felt another dragon's soul light up within the key. She was dead. I swallowed as I ran my gaze over her, certain I was mistaken. I waited for her chest to heave, for her wings to twitch, or her claws…

I squinted. Her claws were curled around something. I hurried forward and dropped to my knees, then pulled her large hands from around a key.

Lina had managed to grab Vehrin's key.

My heart raced as I quickly added the relic to the chain that held the key bound to my soul. Vehrin roared, surely realizing it was missing.

This was it. I had all four keys.

I stood. No longer blocked by the third relic, my true power swelled. The magic felt wonderful, now that I wasn't relying solely on power tainted with darkness or tied to dragons' souls.

Jade disentangled herself from her fallen friend. "Olivia, go!" she yelled.

I nodded, steeled myself, and ran straight toward the dark mage. It was time to end this once and for all.

Vehrin raised his hands as I neared, but I was ready. His attack struck against my own with a sharp crack and blinding light. With quick footwork, I dashed to the side in an attempt to hit him while he recovered. He was too quick and blocked my attack. I ground my teeth and fought for an opening.

The energy crackling around the pair of us was so intense, it kept away anyone in the vicinity. I had no idea how the others were doing and resisted the urge to check on Kael. He would be all right, and I had a mage to defeat.

Vehrin's strikes were relentless, one right after another, until I was forced to move solely to defense. It was tiring, and it took everything in me to keep my muscles moving through the burn of exhaustion.

A cry left my lips as a strike of his magic snapped across my face like a whip. Kael's furious roar filled my head, but he wouldn't be able to reach me to help. I wiped at the blood dripping down my cheek. My energy was waning despite the power of the keys and the dragons' souls. If I sent another attack now, the loss could render me unconscious. All Vehrin had to do was get a hold of me, and he'd have the keys he needed to open the box.

I summoned my sword and squared up to face him. If I could hold him off long enough for my energy to replenish, I may still have a chance.

"Enough with the magic tricks," I said. "Or do you know of no other way to fight?"

Vehrin smiled. "You always were better in tune to your more visceral side. Of course, you did learn from the best." He conjured up a staff wrought with shadow and twirled it as he strode forward.

Once again, the pair of us clashed. I sliced my blade through the air, and he brought up his staff to block my vicious attack. The impact shook my bones, and my teeth clacked together. I twisted my arms, and my sword arced toward his neck. He was quick, and his staff swept my legs out from under me.

I hit the ground and rolled just in time to avoid him striking me in the head. I got to my feet and brought up my sword, narrowly missing his abdomen.

Vehrin took a couple of steps back with an amused smirk. He was toying with me. He wouldn't let me wear him out, or give me a chance to gain the energy I needed.

I wasn't going to win. Not this way.

I had no choice but to unleash the darkness within me once again.

I let the walls fall that held back the vile magic, and it rushed through my veins, merging with the power of all four keys and the souls of the dragons. Black lightning crackled around me and snapped across my skin. I screamed as a rush of power filled my ears. The sword fell from my fingers, and I thrust my hands toward Vehrin before the magic tore me to shreds.

The dark current wrapped around the mage, and he jerked under the attack. His arms flailed, and his knees shook as my cursed magic ran through him.

I pushed harder, and when his arms flung out to the side, something fell from his pocket.

My heart jumped. *The box!*

The magic swept away from me and I dashed forward. My fingers closed around the box, the wickedness within soaking into my fingers. I brought it to my chest. Vehrin roared and hit me with an attack so ferocious, it sent me flying through the air.

I landed hard against the face of the mountain. Sharp rock tore at me with every roll, then finally hit the cold ground.

Each breath was agony as I lay there, my fingers still clenched around the vile box. Vehrin would not be far, but when I tried to raise myself up on my arms, they trembled so hard, I couldn't do it. The cursed magic inside ravaged me, drinking from my pain and fear. It was going to consume me, and there was nothing I could do now to stop it.

My eyes stung as I tried to hold back the pain of the curse. I curled my free hand against the ground, my fingers digging into the earth in an attempt to anchor myself to it, even as the darkness devoured me.

The earth. It's where it had all started. If Vehrin and I hadn't taken the power from the earth, this never would have happened.

"I'm sorry," I croaked. My tears mingled with the blood on my cheeks and dripped to the soil beneath me. "I'm so sorry for what I did. No one needs this much power. I don't want it."

I pulled in a deep breath. Vehrin was advancing. I could sense his magic as my own called to him. Kael screamed my name in my mind, and it shattered my heart that I would never be able to answer him.

I lay on the ground and studied the box, my cheek pressed against the dirt. There was a keyhole on each side. I reached up and closed my hand around the keys, and a vein of warmth slipped through the dark power raging inside me.

A terrible idea came to my mind as everything I'd been struggling to understand clicked together.

"Take it from me. Take everything I have and everything I am. I'll give it all to you…and more." I spoke to the Earth as if she could hear me. I hoped so.

I fumbled at the keys around my neck and took them from their chains as fast as I could. I put the golden key in the side of the box with green vines twisting around it, and turned. A sensation of heavy rain and a scent of citrus flowed over me. Then, I put in the second key into the keyhole framed with trees, and could have sworn I was laying in a place of wild forests and rich soil.

Vehrin was closing in. My body seized as the dark magic cursing me scattered over my bones. I twisted in the third key, and I could feel the hot sun and whispering grass against my skin. My hands shook so hard I could barely get the fourth key into the box.

A shadow fell over me, and I knew Vehrin was standing at my back. He nudged me over with his foot, and I felt a flash of satisfaction as shock froze his features.

We must all descend back into the marked earth, the gryphon elder's words murmured in my thoughts.

Back into the earth. I could almost feel her reaching up, ready to grab us both and pull us into retribution.

I unleashed the dragon's souls, and they whispered around me. They were as ancient as the Earth herself, born from her very soil. We had stolen from the earth, and with the earth, we would be bound for our sins.

I didn't have any final words for Vehrin as he reached down to snatch the box from my hands. What do you say to someone when you're going to share the same fate?

I opened the box, and shadows wrapped around Vehrin and myself. They soaked into my soul, a sensation more malevolent and wicked than anything I'd ever known. I thrashed against the cruel power of the box as it drank from me, savored in my pain, my fear, my loss. I screamed, but Vehrin screamed louder.

The dark mage tore at himself as the inky splotches spread across his skin, consuming him. His eyes bulged and turned red, the vessels bursting from the pressure of the dark power.

Every pain imaginable wracked me while the wickedness fed on my curse, on my magic, and on my very being. The ghostly cries of dragons swirled around us to sing with my screams.

I regretted their sacrifice, and that of so many others. I regretted sacrificing myself to this damnation, and what it would do to my mate when I was gone. More than anything, I regretted taking a power that had never been mine.

My body jerked and writhed uncontrollably. Black started to fill my vision, and the air turned cold inside my lungs.

When the darkness finally pulled me under, I gave in without a fight.

CHAPTER 29

THE SMELL of citrus and fresh rain swept over me, and I couldn't help but think I didn't deserve to have his scent with me in the afterlife.

It was so strong as I drew in a deep breath, I could have sworn the brushing of warm fingers against my face accompanied my mate's scent. I was too afraid to open my eyes, certain as soon as I did, this dying dream would fail, and I would find myself in a hell without Kael.

Oh, how I wished I could have said goodbye, seen his smile, felt his touch, even for a moment. Now, he would be gone from me forever.

"Livvie."

I moaned as his ghost uttered my name. Would his voice haunt me, as well? The sensation of his fingers continued to brush my cheek. I reached up to swipe the feeling away, not wanting to be reminded of what I had lost, when my fingers found something solid.

I traced my fingers across the warm skin of a hand, and when it squeezed my own, I slowly opened my eyes.

Kael's face hovered above me, his eyebrows creased with worry, but a growing smile on his face.

There were so many things I wanted to say, and so many questions erupting in my mind. Instead, I said, "Hi."

My mate chuckled. He reached up to brush his fingers across my forehead, sweeping hair back from my face. "Hi."

"I'm not dead?" I asked. I wanted to be certain and was hesitant to give in to the hope that I had somehow survived.

"You look pretty alive to me," Kael said.

I swallowed, then blinked. Something was missing. My lips parted as I sucked in a small gasp.

Kael's smile fell. "What is it?"

There was no longer darkness corrupting my soul. I felt clean and new in its absence. Tears pricked my eyes. "It's gone. The curse. The curse is gone!"

I held my hand in front of my face and drew on my magic. It tickled around my fingers with a fuchsia glow, and I smiled in relief. I still had my magic, but it was wholly my own. I was no longer tainted by darkness.

Kael pulled me from the ground and to his chest in a crushing hug. I didn't even mind that he was making my ribs groan painfully. He seemed to sense it, though, and instantly loosened his hold.

"Sorry," he said. "I'm just so relieved you're with me."

The reality that I was here with him, that I hadn't been killed, was setting in. Events started to catch up with me.

The box and the keys...

But if I was alive, then what had happened to Vehrin?

It was at that moment I realized I was clutching the box in my other hand. The keys were still in the keyholes, but the lid was firmly closed.

My heart jumped as I ran my fingers carefully along the edge. I could feel Vehrin trapped inside, suffering, screaming, and writhing against the blackness that would constantly feed on his soul.

The box also held another sensation, strong and beautiful, like a silver light wrapped around the box. The dragons' souls.

"How did you do it?" Kael asked.

I crossed my arms, feeling as if the mountain had tumbled down on me. The remnants of pain from the dark power that had ravaged me still flickered within, and a heavy exhaustion weighed down my shoulders.

"Vehrin and I sinned against the earth, had taken power which was not our own, and so it was earth that would have to bind us," I explained. "I used the dragons' souls to do the binding, because dragons were born of the earth."

"All of their souls?"

I shook my head slowly. "I don't think so. Just the ones who didn't make it." I wondered at what kind of existence I'd thrust upon them. Had I stolen their chance at a happy, peaceful afterlife because I'd bound them to hold the dark mage?

Kael laid his hand on my knee. "What about *your* soul, Livvie?"

I dropped my gaze to the golden key, but sensed no tie to it. I gave my mate a small smile. "It's yours for the taking."

Leaning forward, Kael pressed his warm lips to mine. It was a brief kiss, too brief, but once again, reality brought me to the present as the wind shifted and carried the scent of smoke.

"I have to admit," Kael said, "when you started to unlock that box, I thought you had given into the curse. The whole reason we wanted to get the keys and the box was so that Vehrin wouldn't unlocked it."

"Yes, but when I was in the tomb, I learned something. What's inside the box wasn't evil. Just powerful. Vehrin would have used that power to unleash destruction, yes, but I was using the power to bind the evil to the earth. I just... I just assumed that would mean damning my own soul, too."

My mate's shoulders fell, and he pressed his forehead against mine, his hands lifting to hold my face to his. "What you did was foolish. Why would you even try something like that? You almost made me lose you forever."

My throat burned at the thought of what we both would have suffered, but I couldn't bring myself to regret my decision. "It was the only way to save the world, Kael."

I peered out at the dragon city and the destruction that lay around us. The fighting had ceased, but in its wake was a heavy silence that was somehow worse than the clash and clamor of battle.

"Most of the demons fled when Vehrin was defeated," Kael said. "Renathe and his companions are dealing with the other fae, and there were only a couple of witches still alive. Jade had them taken to the palace to await punishment."

"All of that happened while I was laying here?" I asked. I worked my mind, trying to come up with some sense of time, but couldn't. "How long have I been out?"

Kael's grip tightened on my knee. "Nearly three hours, I think. Every time I tried to wake you, you would scream." His face paled slightly. "You had so much agony ripping through you."

He pulled away with a snarl and turned as Ren landed beside us with a frown.

"Are you all right?" he asked, studying me. "Every time I tried to come over, your guard cat nearly took my head off."

Kael grumbled under his breath, but let Ren step closer.

"I'm fine," I said. My ribs throbbed painfully as I twisted to face him. "Mostly."

Ren smiled. "Glad to hear it, little warrior." He jabbed his thumb up toward the palace. "The witch would like to speak to you. Want a lift?"

The thought of traversing all the steps to get up to the palace made me cringe, but there was no way I was separating myself from Kael now.

I got to my feet, quickly followed by Kael, and took his hand. "I think we'll walk."

"You two are so in love, it's disgusting," Ren said, but he smiled. "I have to take care of the traitors." Judging by the vicious spark in his eye, he was eager to return to the ones who had followed Vehrin.

I stepped forward to give Ren a hug. "Thank you, for everything." I eased back. "I'll see you again soon."

"Of course, you will." A huge grin lifted Ren's cheeks. "You still owe me a date."

I rolled my eyes and waited on Kael to snarl something threatening, but he didn't. Instead, he reached out and shook Ren's hand, thanking him for his help.

Wow. "Are you sure I'm not dead?" I mused.

Kael scoffed as he stepped back to my side, but he had a smile on his face. I never thought I'd see the day he would get along with Ren.

Ren chuckled, gave me a wink, and flew off.

I watched him soar over the wreckage. "What is he going to do with the traitorous fae?"

"They have their own laws. My guess is they will not be kind to them," Kael said. "I almost feel sorry for them. Almost."

I didn't want to think about pain and suffering, no matter if they deserved it. "Let's get going."

As we started to walk through the city, I almost wished I'd taken Ren up on his offer to fly me there. The scent of smoke, blood, and death clung to my nostrils. Everywhere I looked was destruction, pain, and loss. It had been such a beautiful place, a serene city that offered refuge to a dying people. Now it was nearly rubble. The only solace I found was the place was mostly empty.

"They've been collecting their dead," Kael said when I mentioned as much. "And tending to the wounded."

Guilt tried to strangle me. Much of the damage had been my own doing.

"It wasn't your fault," Kael murmured.

Perhaps not entirely, but I would always carry the remorse with me, just as I did with the lion shifters I'd killed. I needed to hold onto it, so I would remember them and fight to never let myself cause so much pain again.

We were silent for most of our trek. Once we reached the path that would lead us to the palace, I'd had to concentrate. The way was difficult. Much of the path had been damaged, with collapsed stairs and missing bridges. My body protested with every step, and if Kael hadn't been gripping my hand like he was afraid I'd float away, I likely would have given up. I nearly cried in relief when we reached the summit.

A pair of dragons still guarded the entrance to the palace. One had a ripped wing, and the other bore his weight heavily on his right side. Even wounded, I knew they could kill us in an instant. Thankfully, the dragons let us pass with barely a glance.

I tightened my grip on the box as we stepped into the palace. Jade was there, uttering soft words to Hagen. A pang tightened my heart. Lina had died so she could get the key to me. I wanted to say something to him, to tell him how grateful I was for his mate's sacrifice, but I couldn't bring up any words that would soothe that sort of pain.

As we approached, Hagen stepped back from the witch. If he held any animosity toward me, he didn't show it. I had to look away from the devastation on his face and focus my attention on Jade.

The witch eyed me. "I want what I bargained for," she said.

I sighed. "My soul is my own, and you won't be getting any of the keys."

Jade closed the distance between us angrily, but I held up my hand before she could even speak.

"I have something far more valuable you can have." I held up the box. "Vehrin is trapped inside, and is bound with the souls of the fallen dragons."

"What?" Hagen's voice croaked. He peered at the box. "Lina's...Lina's soul is bound to hold the mage? For how long?"

"The box can never be opened," Jade said.

Hagen was quiet for a moment. "Eternity?"

There was so much unspoken in that one word. Yes, for eternity. Lina's soul, and those of the other dragons, would never find rest. Instead, they would be charged with keeping the mage from breaking free.

And it was my doing.

"I'm sorry," I said. "I'm so very sorry, Hagen. It was the only way."

Jade reached a hand toward the box, but stopped before touching it. "How did you accomplish this?"

I explained as best I could the events that had led to Vehrin's final downfall. It was difficult to recall the exact details. Things had happened so quickly, and I was exhausted, but I told the witch as much as I could.

When I finished, I chewed on my lip in thought. "I don't know why I wasn't trapped with Vehrin. I should have been."

Kael growled a disagreement beside me.

Jade studied the box, and me. "Perhaps because Vehrin had been the one to truly cause the curse in the first place. You had been cursed merely for being with him. You never wanted power for evil doings, and maybe the Earth herself left an opening for you to redeem yourself. You delivered Vehrin, and the Earth forgave you." There was no smile on Jade's face as she spoke, but a kind of approval shone in her eyes. "You were the key to Vehrin's demise all along. No one else could have done it. Despite your curse, you overcame the darkness to ensure his downfall."

Could she be right? I'd been forgiven of my thievery because I'd delivered the true enemy to the earth?

The witch sighed, a heavy sound that spoke of the same

bone-weariness I felt. "It's not what I wanted, but I will take the box and keep it safe."

I took the keys out carefully, not wanting to turn them in their locks. The chains still dangled from the keys, and I put them back around my neck.

Hagen reached out and took the box. "My mate's soul is bound to this. It will never leave this mountain."

I nodded, knowing there would be no safer place for it.

"What will you do with the keys?" Jade asked.

"I'm not certain, but they must be hidden." The smell of smoke still permeated the palace from the destruction below. "I'm sorry for all of the damage and ruin I have caused. I will never forgive myself for it."

Jade looked out through the open doorway. "It is only stone and wood. Things can be rebuilt, trees replanted. What is important now is for us to heal from within, to grieve, and not forget those who have fallen."

I lifted my hand to the keys at my chest and thought of all that had been lost. Countless lives had been taken, and ancient cities had fallen.

We could never allow such destruction to take hold again.

CHAPTER 30

"ARE you sure this is a good idea?" Kael pulled into the driveway beside the small Victorian house I grew up in.

"No, it's probably a terrible idea."

I stared out of the window of the rental car and drank in the sight of my home. Everything, from the wide front porch to my mother's overgrown rose bushes, looked like open arms welcoming me home.

It had been so long since I'd sat on that porch or paced the maple floors in the study or searched for a tool in the old shed out back, that parking in front of the garage behind the house was indescribable. I couldn't get out of the car fast enough.

We'd stayed a couple of weeks in the dragon city while my body healed of the beating it had received, though we'd mostly kept to ourselves. Once we'd left, we caught up on all the news from around the world as we'd traveled back to the States. The unusual weather patterns had dissipated, though many places were still recovering from the spike in crime, physical damage, and overall ruin.

Kael had barely turned off the ignition by the time I was already at the back door. I bent down and pried a rock from the half-frozen ground and found my spare house key, then hurried inside.

Of all my keys, that had to be my favorite one.

I'd been afraid life would be too mundane, too quiet after traversing the world for magical relics and a cursed mage.

Now that I was home, I didn't find it mundane at all. I wanted nothing more than to curl up on the couch with a good book, a cozy blanket, and just *breathe*.

Unfortunately, there were important matters to attend to before I could even think about relaxing.

Mist rose in front of my face as I stepped through the kitchen and into the living room, where I dropped my bags on the couch before going to crank the heat up. When I returned to the kitchen, I found Kael rifling through the cabinets.

I propped my hands on my hips. "Really?"

Kael shrugged a shoulder. "I'm hungry, and since we're mated, what's yours is mine."

I scoffed, but my lips quirked in amusement. "Fine. Don't complain to me when you eat something expired and spend the next few days in the bathroom."

"Would you take care of me if I were sick?" Kael asked. He eyed a can of refried beans before shoving it back onto the shelf.

I scooted a chair out at the table and slid in. "No, I'd leave you to suffer."

He grinned over at me. "Liar."

He found a jar of peanut butter and an unopened jar of raspberry jam. I don't know why he expected the bread to be anything other than the hard and nearly blackened lump it was, but he sighed regretfully. He settled for grabbing a spoon and eating peanut butter straight from the jar.

I fell silent and played with the four keys hanging from my neck. What if this didn't work?

Kael sat beside me and gave me a nudge. "Hey. Don't worry. After today, everything will be back to normal."

I laughed as I leaned back in my chair. "Hopefully not everything. We don't want life to get too boring."

At a sudden knock on the front door, I left Kael and his jar of peanut butter at the table. I opened the door and smiled.

Cordelia stood in the doorway. I hadn't seen the witch in ages. She'd been one of the first ones to help me and Kael get started on our journey and had pointed us in the right direction for finding the second key. She owned a tea shop downtown, and even after I'd returned home before being shuffled off to PITO, I'd enjoyed going to the little shop for chats.

The woman smiled, her cheeks red with cold and her brass-colored hair hanging over her shoulder in a thick braid.

"It's been too long," I said, gesturing her inside. She brought a warm scent that had my mouth watering.

"I brought scones," she said and gave me a one-armed hug.

I started toward the kitchen when there was another knock. "Just in there," I told Cordelia, and pointed toward Kael.

When I opened the door for a second time, I found Renathe standing there. A brilliant smile lit up his face.

"Olivia, darling, did you miss me already?" He bent down and gave me a kiss on the cheek.

"I was practically beside myself," I said, earning a laugh from my friend.

We made our way to the kitchen, and when Ren spotted Cordelia, his grin deepened. "Why, Cordelia, I wasn't expecting to see you here. I'll have to come visit your shop soon."

Cordelia made an irritated noise, and I wondered at the history between them. Ren had been the one who had told us of Cordelia's shop in the first place. Perhaps it would be better if I didn't pry. I had enough on my plate as it was without adding some fae and witch drama to the mix.

I sat back down in my seat, and the four of us engaged in polite small talk. Neither Ren nor Cordelia asked why I'd called them there, and I didn't tell them. Not yet.

Kael was just ruining one of the witch's delicious scones by smearing it with peanut butter when there was a sharp knock on the door. I started to stand, but Kael grabbed my arm.

"I'll get it," he said.

Kael stalked through the living room, his whole demeanor having gone from relaxed to on edge. He opened the door.

"Kael Rivera," a hard voice said from the other side.

My mate stepped back to let the man in.

It was the chief of the lion shifter pride. He wore a suit, an unusual contradiction to the lion's mane I'd seen him wearing in Africa. He was still a man of granite and intimidation, perhaps more so since Vehrin's attack on his people. The house fell silent as he strode inside. Kael leaned out of the door, his head swiveling left and right, before he came back in.

"You're alone?" Kael was going to burn the chief onto my living room floor with the unwavering glare he gave him. We were trusting the chief enough to bring him here, but didn't know of his feelings toward us. My mate wasn't fond of the uncertainty.

The lion shifter gave a short nod. "Yes. As promised. Now, to what do I owe the honor of being included in—" He gestured at the kitchen table, his gaze narrowing at the sight of Ren and Cordelia. "—this."

"Please, sit," I offered. I had to work to keep my voice neutral and remind myself this meeting was of my own doing. Guilt still threatened to choke me as the chief settled his stare on me, the one who had slain his mate. The hard steady gaze was a weight on my shoulders, reminding me of everything I'd taken from him.

No. Vehrin was the one at fault. I'd done what I had to do to survive, to end the destruction. If I hadn't, the dark mage would have succeeded.

I would continue to tell myself those words and hope that one day I would believe them.

I reached behind my neck and unclasped the chains threaded through the keys, then placed the relics on the table.

"This is why I called all of you here. These relics must be kept hidden. They can never be found again, or else we risk the chance of Vehrin being freed once more." I didn't let on there was also a guard of dragon souls binding him, but after what I'd been through, I didn't want to take any chance he could be unleashed on this world again.

The chief clasped his hands and rested his forearms on the table as he leaned forward. "And where is the mage?"

"Locked away for good," I answered. Aside from Kael and myself, Renathe was the only other being who knew the whereabouts of Vehrin. It wasn't that I didn't trust Cordelia, but the less who knew, the better.

It wasn't good enough for the lion shifter.

"I deserve to know where the mage is being held." His voice was steady, authoritative, and he pinned me with a stern gaze.

Despite my remorse at killing his mate, I glared right back at him. "No, you don't. You may not willingly divulge his location, but there are ways for those powerful enough to take the information from you." The chief himself had been tricked by Vehrin into believing me and Kael were villains. I would not risk such knowledge being unearthed. "If you will be patient, there *is* something I can trust you with, provided you have agreed to our bargain?"

"Maybe I will keep your bargain," the chief said. "Or maybe I will let PITO have your mate."

My nostrils flared. He would dare to threaten Kael? In my own home? A soothing sensation whispered down my mating bond, and I took a steadying breath.

"We're here to make amends," I said. "PITO has agreed to drop all charges on Kael, and stop hunting him, but we can't trust them. We want you to assure his protection. If PITA believes Kael is under the protection of your pride, that is our best chance of them upholding their promise. In exchange, I will give you one of the keys to hide with a group of shifters of your choosing, as a sign of good faith."

The chief fell silent, and he pursed his lips. I'd had my qualms about asking the lion shifter for such a favor, but Kael had insisted he would take such a charge seriously. They had held the third key safe in their grasp for years. The leader of the lion pride knew the importance of keeping it hidden.

I turned to Ren and Cordelia. "I ask that you each take one of the keys, as well, to hide among your own kind. I don't want to know the whereabouts of any of the relics, and you cannot tell anyone. Ever."

"Fae and witches cannot be trusted," the chief grumbled. I wanted to argue and tell him such prejudices were not welcome at my table.

It was Kael, however, who spoke. "That kind of division is what kept many from coming to us in our time of greatest need. Thousands were lost in those mountains when Vehrin arrived with demons, witches, fae, and shifters of his own. How can we defeat such darkness again, when even our enemies know how to stand together? Shifters quarrel amongst themselves and witches prefer seclusion. Only the fae came to help, and not many of them. If this happens again, we need to be united."

Our group fell silent, though I was beaming with pride on the inside at Kael's speech. Slowly, the chief nodded.

"Very well," he said. "I pledge my pride's protection over Kael, and will make this crystal clear to PITO as well. And of course I'll hide the key. None will even know of its existence."

I slide the dark key Vehrin had taken from the lion shifter tribe back to its former protector. He studied it for a moment before giving me a nod and putting it into his pocket.

Next, I gave Cordelia the bone-colored key I had found in

the ruins in Scotland. It seemed appropriate that she should have the one the Scottish witches had helped us find.

When Ren held out his hand expectantly, I gave him the jade key of the dragon city. There was no one else I would trust with a relic capable of binding souls. He'd been the only one who had stood by us through it all.

The three didn't linger. They stood and prepared to leave, no doubt already deciding where to hide the keys. The lion chief left with a curt goodbye and a promise to Kael PITO would leave him alone. Ren gave me one of his winks and invited me to the club soon for drinks. He said I could even bring Kael along if my mate would behave.

Before she left, Cordelia nodded at the golden key remaining on the table. "What about that one?"

I picked it up and traced my thumb over the length of the relic. I'd thought about keeping it. After having my soul once bound to the relic, I was hesitant to give it up. However, I knew hiding it was the right thing to do.

"I have just the place for this one."

* * *

I STOOD ATOP THE RUINS, my back slick with sweat from the jungle heat. If I concentrated hard enough, I could almost see the sun-kissed buildings, tiled murals, and flower-scented shrine the crumbling place had once been.

A groan sounded behind me, and Kael pulled himself up over the edge. "I thought you wanted a beach and margaritas?"

"Beaches are overrated."

He laid back against the light-warmed stone, looking every inch a cat basking in all its lazy glory, even in his human form.

I smirked. "Did you do that often back when you were assigned to guard this place?"

He didn't answer, but closed his eyes and smiled.

I got down and straddled him. His golden eyes sparked when he opened them again. Above his head were scratches in the stone, marks he'd left there when we'd first met.

"You almost killed me here, once," I noted.

Kael leaned up and circled his arms around my waist. "And now I'm going to kiss you here. Crazy world, isn't it?"

"The craziest."

I drank in his scent and touch as he claimed my mouth. The warm breeze pulled at my sweat-damp hair, and I couldn't help but feel I'd never find a more perfect moment.

Kael made a growling noise deep in his throat that made me fist my hands in his shirt. His need pulsed through our bond.

I broke our embrace with a laugh. "We have to put this back first," I said. I tugged on the golden key around my neck and climbed to my feet.

Kael moaned his disagreement but stood beside me. "Are you sure hiding it here is the best idea? It didn't work out so well last time."

Magic sparked at my fingers, and I grinned. "I don't plan on making it so easy to infiltrate again."

"It was easy the last time?" Kael said, grinning and raising his eyebrows.

"Well, I lived to tell about it, didn't I?"

I swept another gaze out at the rainforest, at a jungle so deep, most had never traversed here...and never would.

"You almost look at home here," Kael said.

I gave him a smile. "You're my home."

He reached up and grabbed my chin. "I like the sound of that."

Before he could pull me in for another kiss, I wheeled away. "Come on. Down here." I sat and swung my legs over the hole I'd fallen in so many months before. I eyed Kael as he hesitated. "Don't tell me you're still afraid of a little bit of tomb-exploring."

Kael squatted down beside me. "I'd follow you anywhere, mate."

I grinned. "Good."

Then, I dropped down into the hole.

After a few choice words, Kael dropped down beside me. "Now what?"

I pointed down the long stretch of catacombs. "First one to the end gets to choose the next activity," I said with a bright smile.

The eager and daring growl Kael gave me was so delicious, I decided I'd let him win.

We made our way down halls we had once roamed together, and perhaps in another lifetime we would again, but for now, we had each other, and a new adventure on the horizon.

The End

ABOUT THE AUTHORS

ABOUT MIRANDA BROCK

Get a **FREE** Book from Miranda Brock!

From an early age Miranda Brock has always loved fantasy and adventure everything. Since she doesn't live in a world of enchanting powers, mythical beasts, and things unbelievable she has decided to write about them. (Although, if you happen to see a dragon flying around, do tell her.) Born in southern Illinois, where she still resides with her husband and two children, she grew up running through the woods, playing in creeks, and riding horses.

ABOUT REBECCA HAMILTON

Get a **FREE** Book from Rebecca Hamilton

New York Times bestselling author Rebecca Hamilton writes urban fantasy and paranormal romance for Harlequin, Baste Lübbe, and Evershade. A book addict, registered bone marrow donor, and indian food enthusiast, she often takes to fictional worlds to see what perilous situations her characters will find themselves in next. Represented by Rossano Trentin of TZLA, Rebecca has been published internationally, in three languages: English, German, and Hungarian.